The Last Director of Shoreditch

It's Shoreditch, London, in the late 1950s, and Frank Pollock is fixer-in-chief for the Posties, a feared band of locals descended from paupers thrown out of the notorious Old Nichol slum at the turn of the last century. Ruthlessly led by their director, they fought back to commandeer wharves and warehouses with illegal glee across the East End. Those who get in Frank's way risk disappearing in a puff of smoke. He is helped out by Elsie, who heads a team of international shoplifters by day, and pines for a husband by night.

Fast forward to the Shoreditch of today and semi-retired Nick Carter has been asked by his former colleague Julie to spy on Tom, her young, dapper husband. Trailing Tom among the elite siliconeastas from east London's tech start-ups, and the bars rammed with mass millennials – not all with beards – Nick discovers that Julie's other half is from the hidden world of Posties, with their ritual tattoos and suspect property deeds. Nick is forced to face up to some home truths just as the days of the Posties may be numbered.

In The Last Director of Shoreditch, the past and present are no further apart than two coats of varnish on a Chippendale cabinet.

Huw Jones is a journalist living in Shoreditch.

THE **LAST** **DIRECTOR** OF **SHOREDITCH**

HUW JONES

ISBN: 978-0-9935108-0-9
First Print Edition

Published by Huw Jones.
Cover Design by Kit Foster.
Formatting by BB eBooks.

I Dad, ac er cof am Mam

Acknowledgments

This novel could not have been completed without the advice and feedback from friends and publishing professionals. The practical guidance on creative writing from Heidi James at the Bishopsgate Institute provided a jump start onto the page. I am also grateful to Tom Bromley from The Literary Consultancy for his constructive comments, and to Ben Galley of Shelf Help for advice on self-publishing. Kate Tracy and Rob Matthews were immensely helpful at the proofing stage. Also thanks to Kit Foster Design for the cover, and to BB eBooks for the formatting. Feedback from Suji Barnett and Jenny Sheridan gave encouragement to stay the course. The streets, history, and people of Shoreditch provided inspiration in spades, and for those who want to read more about this corner of London, they can turn to *The Child of the Jago* by Arthur Morrison; *The Shoreditch Tales* by Carolyn Clark and Linda Wilkinson; *Gone Shopping: The Story of Shirley Pitts – Queen of Thieves* by Lorraine Gamman. Above all I want to thank my partner, Patrick Conlon, for his patience and support.

THE **LAST DIRECTOR** OF SHOREDITCH

I

1

THE THIN MIST CLINGING TO the canal's smooth surface barely parted as the barge puttered along on a freezing January night with Charlie Pooter, hand on tiller, scouting the sparkling towpath for passers-by.

Not that this cargo would raise eyebrows round here, he thought.

No, just a few planks of cherry wood that were no doubt destined for a local cabinetmaker whose name Pooter had not even been told. And there was also the bag of bones, unwashed ones at that, given the stink wafting up from the hold. It all pointed to a chippie in line for a nice bit of cash on the side for knocking together something fancy.

He'd heard they pay handsomely for quality handiwork. If you don't brag, that is.

To Charlie's relief, all was quiet along the waterway, its silence and stillness drilling into him like the cold. Just as well there was only a half mile left until he reached the wharf where, according to their strict instructions, he must berth, offload the goods and scarper before dawn broke. Shame it was so late otherwise he would pop in to see a cousin of his who lived in this neck of the woods. He wanted to thank her in person for passing on this job, but he should have sent word beforehand that he might call. It was getting late, so best leave it for another time.

In the deep winter chill, the industrial landscape on both sides of the canal was coated with frost that caught the occasional shafts of moonlight from the partly clouded sky. The damp had long seeped under his donkey jacket, his cap too small to stop his ears from stinging. Should have put on a balaclava. He'd already smoked his last Woodbine to keep himself warm.

At least he knew the route well enough to pick out landmarks by their silhouettes as they loomed up one by one on each side of the waterway: over there, the remains of a storage depot that had been bombed by Hitler in the Blitz well over a decade ago. Funny how even the War could slip into the past so quickly. All it took was a little optimism that better times lay ahead, that life could only get easier, Charlie thought, gripping the tiller harder. It certainly was a relief not having to worry about where the next meal came from, that like the War, rationing really was over. He was equally grateful there would be no more locks to navigate before mooring, though he still needed to keep a watchful eye for flotsam that could snarl up the propeller. It was not a night to be up to your waist in freezing water, as there would be nobody around to help. Well, nobody you'd want to ask.

'To think that all this stuff could just as easily be delivered by horse and cart, or van,' he muttered, his breath condensing. But no, it must all go by canal, they insisted. All in keeping with the tradition of transporting timber by water, a respectful nod to how this canal helped the furniture trade flourish here in the capital. Or so their lackey had tried half-heartedly to convince him over a pint the other night. Can't be sure what the real truth is with these people, so best not to ask too many questions. Still, the backhander was not to be sniffed at. To think that just a few chilly hours at the tiller would pay for a new leather jacket.

No, not a bad night's work at all.

Regretting once more that he hadn't bought the jacket already to keep out the cold, he began steering the barge in a long arc towards the other side of the canal, away from the towpath, and cut the engine, allowing the vessel to glide silently with just enough momentum to reach a large brick building that rose from the water.

Hope Wharf.

He could just make out the faded, peeling letters, painted in white on the arch over the middle of three large windows that were covered by dilapidated wooden shutters. A small crane jutted from the wall but was not rigged with ropes, pulleys or wires. He tied the barge's aft to a metal ring on the wall and then walked along the edge of the deck towards the fore, where he could see light seeping through cracks in the shutter of the far window. Okey dokey, all going to plan. He was looking forward to warming himself up inside the wharf for a few minutes after handing over the barge and its cargo.

He heard a sharp metal-on-metal scraping noise and the shutters of the middle window opened with such force that they banged against the outside wall, creating an echo that bounced down the canal. Having expected the far window to open, Charlie almost lost his footing, but recovered his poise after seeing a head poke out of the dark void, its eyes briefly catching the moonlight. The head looked up and down the barge, across to the towpath and back at him.

'What time do you call this? Think yer transporting the crown jewels or something?' the man asked in a low voice that barely reached Pooter despite the stillness of the night. The man hopped onto the wide concrete window ledge and stepped onto the bow of the barge, barely two yards from where Charlie was standing.

His frame was bulky enough to make the vessel bob up and down.

Charlie smiled when he noticed the bloke was wearing a kilt, even though he could have sworn the accent was pure East End. Was it Burns Night already? The man's bare shins and heavy leather boots also drew the eye.

'Evening. Bit misty tonight, so thought it best not to hurry. Who are you then, mate? Just want to check I'm in the right place.' Charlie tried to sound as casual as he could.

There was no reply apart from a muffled grunt and condensed breath.

'Right then. I'll unload the stuff and get going. Might even visit a cousin of mine who lives round here. Perhaps you know her,' Charlie said, in another attempt at small talk that also fell flat as the man showed no interest and simply shrugged his shoulders, causing his kilt to ride up slightly and draw Charlie's gaze to a bulge near the groin.

'Get on with it then. It'll be daylight at this rate,' the man said, catching the glance.

Charlie jumped into the open hold and threw a large piece of tarpaulin to one side to uncover the planks and the bag of bones, which he grabbed first. He used the short ladder screwed into the side of the hold to climb back onto the narrow deck, and walked sideways to the open window of the wharf, the bones rattling against each other with each step he took.

The man had already stepped off the barge and retreated into the building, standing just inside the window. Charlie followed, first onto the ledge and then walked sideways for a few feet before descending a row of shallow wooden steps into the main room of the wharf. He put the bag in the middle of the stone floor, a spot the man silently pointed to. Around them were a couple of sawing machines, a large workbench and other furniture-making equipment, all neatly lined up against two walls. Through an archway cut into a third wall, Charlie could see a side room with a large, shiny metal vat. It took him a few seconds to realize what was puzzling him: the workshop was spotless, with no offcuts of wood or drifts of sawdust. Nor were there pools of machine grease or streaks of dried varnish. Even more curious, near the vat there was a high-backed armchair upholstered in a dark cloth and next to it, on the floor, an old-fashioned gramophone, its lid up and trumpet pointing silently to the ceiling, waiting no doubt for one of a stack of records nearby to be placed on its turntable.

Charlie went back to the barge to fetch the planks.

On his return he pretended to give his full attention to keeping the planks bunched together, so he could look down at the man's kilt while walking past. It wasn't made from tartan but a thin, maroon cloth that swelled around his unusually large crotch.

'You looking at something, mate?' the man asked, cocking his head to one side.

'Not sure what you mean. It's been a long night. Bloody

freezing as well, and I don't want to be getting splinters from these planks here,' Charlie said chattily as he placed the wood on the floor next to the bones, whose smell was already hanging heavy in the room despite the open window.

'Well, that's done. OK if I leave the barge here?' Charlie asked. 'That's what I've been told to do. And if that's alright with you I'll be off. Is that the way out to the street?' he added, nodding towards a door opposite the canal.

The response was another low grunt, which he took to mean the man was happy with the arrangements. But in his eagerness to get away, he didn't see the hand clutching a brick slam down on his head, nor did he feel the many subsequent blows to make sure the job was done.

'Told those bloody amateurs there wouldn't be enough bones. They never listen,' the man said out loud, a little breathless. He straightened his blood-spattered kilt and walked over to the window to check the canal and towpath. All was quiet, the barge securely tied, the acrid engine fumes already dispersed into the night air. He closed and bolted the shutters and went into the side room to give the gramophone a vigorous wind-up before putting a record on the turntable. After lowering the needle gently, he began humming along to the first Vera Lynn song, stopping after a minute to light a cigarette, before kneeling down to inspect the deliveries.

2

NICK CARTER WAS FINISHING A skinny latté and waiting for the caffeine to kick in, having had an early start as there was much to do after last night's unexpected confrontation.

He was sitting at his favourite table in Jimmy's Cafe, the one by the window that looked out onto a high street where people streamed by on their way to work. They were mostly young, slim and dressed in a carefully casual sort of way, with beards featuring heavily this season: they were the siliconeastas, the thinking people's hipsters. They were on their way to a virtual Internet coalface mined at cutting edge start-ups in scrubbed Victorian warehouses. Their herding past Nick each morning left him feeling like a limp fish out of water in his own neighbourhood. He sighed, causing his paunch to chafe against the edge of the orange plastic table. Well, at least he still had a head of hair halfway through his fifth decade.

'Another latté, please, Mavis,' he called out to the cafe owner. 'Make it semi-skimmed this time, thanks.'

He mused how this corner of the capital had been home for nearly a quarter of a century. It was a slice of Manhattan-style urban living that had allowed him to walk to work and not rely on screwed-up buses or delay-prone, jam-packed tubes. He'd moved here after leaving university, buying the top floor of a former furniture factory with his first bonus. The high ceilings and huge windows of what he now described to his friends as a 'real McCoy loft' was his prized eyrie above the narrow streets whose brothels had long been pushed aside by Vietnamese restaurants, and they in turn were now being priced out by designer tea shops, cafes for stroking cats, vaping emporiums, and unique burger joints whose belching extractor fans failed to mask the stench of piss from the pavements.

He used his teaspoon to scoop the froth off the top of his second latté as he thought hard about whether he should forget this favour he'd rashly promised Julie. It's not that he didn't have the time. A new project still hadn't come through from the consultancy. He'd been glad to finish the last one and get the hell back from Frankfurt: he could only take so much of delivering job cuts to order, even for a thumping fee. It felt like piloting a flying abattoir at times – land, do the grim reaper bit, shove the scythe back in the hold and come home.

How could he fob her off?

'I think Tom's screwing around and I need your help, Nick darling, just so that I know for sure,' she had said a week ago at Jago's, one of the area's less rammed bars and a street away from his flat. 'Let's just call it a woman's intuition. I can't put my finger on it at the moment, but fancy checking things out for me? It's not as if you're rushed off your feet, and it could be a giggle being a private eye for a few days. And no, I don't expect your time for free.'

He had never pictured himself as an investigator, but as they had downed nearly a bottle of wine by the time she sprung the request, the thought of being paid to stalk her husband had made him smile. Maybe not Columbo. A new millennium Marlowe, perhaps?

'You only work when you're in the mood, you lazy bastard. So why not help your bestest friend? I've helped you out with Amanda. I don't want to get a real private eye just yet. Besides, it would look pretty desperate stuff if he found out. I just need a few discreet checks,' she'd explained. 'Let's face it, tailing Tom for a few days should be a doddle. We can meet up again in a bit to see what you've found out. I'll pay all expenses, of course. Bet you haven't had a better offer for a long time,' she'd said, swinging the near-empty wine bottle by its neck in the direction of the barman, her usual way of ordering another. After quickly negotiating a free, peak-season week at her and hubby's time-share chalet in Switzerland, he'd agreed.

Now, staring down at his second coffee, it was only days before they would meet up again and he had bugger-all to tell her because Mr Thomas Fry had been up to bugger-all. Well, nothing he would let her know about just yet. He stroked the small Moleskine notebook that lay on the table in front of him, its spine still without a crease but the cover warped by steam and blotched where drops of hot water had dried. Apart from doodles, the times of a film he wanted to see and basic information about Tom, all filling half of the first page, there was nothing to justify an alpine-sized fee.

Last night he'd been convinced something was about to land in his lap. It was not as if Julie's husband was hard to pin down or spot. The man was clearly bright, good-looking and, at only 35, already a successful property developer – an annoying combination that would keep any older wife permanently on edge, he smirked as began drawing pictures of houses and cranes on the notebook's second page, occasionally looking out onto the street where the stream of siliconeastas had turned into an older, dowdier trickle.

Tom left work early yesterday. At 5.29pm. Nick had wanted to be precise in his note-taking to remind himself of the smarter type of TV detective. The man had emerged ebulliently – there was no other word for it – from his office building just as the humid July weather reached breaking point to release a downpour that was more like a tropical storm than an average English summer shower. Tom had looked up at the sky, stuffed an envelope inside his jacket, and opened a large black corporate umbrella with a flourish before walking briskly up the street. Nick meanwhile had stuffed the notebook into a small rucksack and followed him, keeping several paces behind to avoid being spotted. The rain was falling so hard that it bounced off the pavement and into the scuffed black leather brogues Nick liked to wear throughout the year.

Like the previous occasion he'd followed Tom from work, he turned right at the end of the street to head for the railway station, but this time instead of taking the tube home to north London, he'd carried on walking, past the tall, seventeenth-century church on the right, and continued north towards Nick's own neighbourhood. If Julie's husband suspected he was being followed, he didn't let on. If he'd glanced back, Tom would probably have recognised his wife's ex-colleague and now closest drinking partner, drenched in a T-shirt that was sticking to his round belly like cling film to a turkey.

Where the hell was he going, Nick fumed while following in the downpour without an umbrella. A few minutes later they'd reached a busy junction where Tom took a left into another busy main road and sprinted across to the other side, forcing Nick to hold back until there was a gap in the rush-hour traffic. The rain was beginning to ease by then as the storm moved east and he could see Tom in the distance, turning right up a narrow lane and disappearing from view. Using a break in the traffic, Nick ran across the road, his socks squelching with each step. After reaching the turn Tom had taken, he slowly stuck his head round the corner to see a cobbled cul-de-sac lined with industrial buildings clad in scaffolding. He was just in time to hear the bang of what sounded like a heavy metal door shutting a few metres up ahead on the right-hand side under a large neon sign. He leaned against a wall to consider his next move as he shivered, despite the summer warmth returning to the air. It was a toss-up between going home for a beer and a bath, or visiting Jock's Hangout to see what the hell Tom was up to.

'You know this is a gay sauna?' the skinny man in a tight black T-shirt at the till asked while taking Nick's twenty-quid note.

'Oh, right. Cool. Can I have a receipt?' he replied, the assistant nodding slowly.

Grabbing a towel and locker key, Nick went through a doorway into a dim world of steamy heat and the faint smell of perfumed bleach, where he pretended to fiddle with his phone to give Tom enough time to get undressed. A few minutes later in a near-empty changing room he was glad to get out of his dripping clothes, but nervous about what lay ahead, given he would only have a skimpy towel around his waist between himself and uncharted territory. Who the fuck would have thought that Tom was gay? Jesus! Man-eater Julie, of all people, should have sussed that one out by now. A touch of the denials? Or was she too preoccupied with someone else to mind or notice?

Keeping a straight face while telling her about this would not be easy.

With the towel wrapped as tightly as possible round his waist he left the changing room, wishing he was still wearing his boxer shorts as an extra line of defence. He entered a warren of dark corridors, though after his eyes got used to the poor light he could see the place was teeming, making it easier to blend in with an after-work crowd that was clearly eager to get the weekend started. He remembered asking a gay friend what went on in places like this. Naff-all unless you're young with a six-pack, had been the rapid and slightly bitter response. And now he knew why. Nobody was even looking at him, let alone stopping to chat or grope. His paunch and untoned tits would keep all but the desperate or blind at arm's length. One less thing to worry about. He breathed out in relief, forcing himself to tighten the towel. At least the shivering had stopped now that the heat raised his core temperature after that deluge outside. It took a few minutes standing in a corner to get his bearings before he felt confident enough to continue on down the narrow corridors with their darker crannies and inner sanctums, while keeping an eye out for Julie's husband. He had to be here somewhere as the place wasn't that big. A fat old man from left field lunged for Nick's arse, but all it needed was a deft body twist to outfox him. He realised the doddery bloke was only trying to find his way out.

It must have been at least twenty minutes later – it was hard to keep track of time in that surreal, clockless world – when he spotted Tom. There he was, looking so out of place as he stood awkwardly, clutching the same envelope against his thigh while talking to a tall, slim man by the steam-room door. After a few moments the two walked towards a corridor that was lined with cubicles. Case proven, Nick concluded, feeling a tinge of sympathy for Julie. He followed them, his feet sticking to damp patches on the smooth, warm lino. The two men slipped into a cubicle and luckily for Nick the one next to it was empty. He went in and bolted the door as quietly as he could before pressing an ear to the chipboard partition.

Bloody waste of time, he thought after a few minutes of listening hard. There was definitely no sound of carefree sex, though he did hear the envelope being torn open. After that, as pop music blared, he had no clue what was going on or being said. His neck began aching after a while so he sat down on the plastic-covered foam mattress. A few minutes later the door of the neighbouring cubicle was unbolted and the voices of Tom and his companion rose and then faded as they passed by and retraced their steps up the corridor to the steam-room. Nick decided to wait a few moments, and just as he was about to unbolt the door, he heard tapping. He stepped out into the corridor to find two almost bald men in their thirties, both built like nightclub bouncers.

'Looking for someone, mate?' heavyweight one asked, cupping Nick's chin in his warm, moist left hand.

'You don't want to be sticking your nose into other people's business,' heavyweight two chipped in. 'Think it's time you went back to the day job, don't you?' He twisted a thumb clockwise into Nick's right nipple, making him wince.

The two then grabbed Nick by the arms and took him back inside the cubicle and made him sit down on the mattress with a bump, causing his towel to unravel. He slid sideways to get away from them, only stopping when his body banged against the wall. The two men squeezed inside and bolted the door. At first they didn't say a word as he listened to the pop song about a little prayer, thinking he may need a bigger one to get out of this pickle in one piece. Heavyweight two's towel was no match for his girth and it dropped to the floor, and as he bent over to pick it up, Nick noticed a cannon barrel tattooed on his pimply left buttock.

3

TWO DAYS LATER, IN BED, and Nick was musing on how the muffled screech of orange and blue carriages looping above the high street had become a reassuring constant over the years in the vast continuum of the capital, like the tick tock of a well maintained clock. Thinking of which, he checked the alarm on his bedside table: it was well after 10am, late for a weekday. The evening before had been a rewarding one, unlike that confrontation in the sauna.

He often drank at the Cock and Cardinal, one of the oldest pubs in the area, which had once been run by the mother of the mobster Kray twins. The place had been tastefully renovated to attract the siliconeastas who spent their legally earned money on bottled beer from all corners of Belgium. He remembered one time trying to strike up a conversation at the bar with a famous and very dishevelled artist who quickly lost interest after he'd mixed up her work with that of a rival who'd just won a famous prize that so far had eluded her. He liked these encounters with people he'd seen on late-night culture programmes as it made him feel connected, or a superior tosser, as his sister teased him.

Last night he recognised one or two of the customers, real locals who often came for a pint in the early part of the week. They were not what his New York friends called the 'bridge and tunnel crowd' who trekked here at the weekend for an urban fix, before catching the penultimate train back home, somewhere beyond zone two.

He'd arranged to meet up with Trevor, who was so local he could walk to the house where he was born in less time than it took to pull a pint. The man had done well, setting up a plumbing business that was making a mint from gentrification, giving him time to be a local councillor too. Nick thought back to how their friendship, or perhaps acquaintance is nearer the truth, was cemented one evening when they met and chatted at the bar. After Trevor realized he was talking with a bond trader, he'd asked what he should do with a chunk of brewery shares inherited from an uncle. 'Sell in May and go away' was the time-honoured trading-floor response. Trevor followed the advice to the letter and sold the lot for a nice profit that week, narrowly missing a prolonged market rout.

Which is why Trevor was now his best fount of local knowledge, if not quite his best mate, and the man had been on good form last night.

'You know, it's amazing how developers are crawling out of the woodwork everywhere these days. I miss the time when we had the area to ourselves,' he'd said to Trevor while placing two pints of micro-brewed bitter on the distressed oak table in front of them.

'Well, thing is mate, it's all because of yuppies like you who are willing to pay silly money for cubicles,' his friend quipped before taking a long sip.

The bar had become noisier after a bunch of siliconeas-tas arrived and congregated round the list of guest beers on a nearby wall, forcing Nick to edge closer to Trevor to make himself heard, and near enough to count the wiry hairs sprouting from his friend's nostrils.

'I was chatting the other day with my friend Julie. You know her, the one with dark hair who used to work with me. She was here a few months ago, in fact. Great figure and lots of fun. Anyway, looks like her hubby's getting in on some property action round here. I suppose there's still plenty left if you've got deep enough pockets,' he said, keeping the tone chatty in between swigs of Ripper IPA.

'What's his name then?' Trevor asked.

'Sorry, should have said. Thomas Fry. You've probably not come across him in the planning committee. Apparently he's from the East End, according to her, anyway., You wouldn't believe it if you met the guy, though. Looks a bit of a public-schoolboy-in-the-City type, but he's friendly enough and takes care of Julie.'

He noticed Trevor's tone of voice and body language change when Trevor spoke next.

'Frankly, I think you should ask Julie if you want to know more about Tom Fry. Like you say, he's no stranger round here, and believe it or not, he's about as local as I am. And I'm not so sure he's become the public school twat you make him out to be. Appearances can be a deceptive, dear boy, as they say,' Trevor said while waggling his empty glass, oblivious to Nick's twitching at the pally abbreviation of Fry's first name.

With a fresh round of beers in front of them, Nick tried a different tack.

'As I was saying, I'm thinking of investing in another flat round here as work's not too frantic at the moment. Always good to have a project on the burner,' he explained, but was cut short.

'Look, Nick. It may not be obvious to you but Tom's family go back a long way in the East End and he's from the Posties. Believe me, you don't mess with that lot. They close ranks and help each other. My father used to call them the poor man's masons but with zippo respect for kneecaps, if you get my drift,' Trevor explained, glancing round the pub as if to check that nobody apart from Nick could hear him.

By then the pale ale had started kicking in nicely and Nick was already picturing Tom's father and grandfather before him carrying sacks of letters in all weathers along cobbled foggy streets with shoeless urchins skipping behind. What was it he'd read on that huge post office in Manhattan? 'Neither snow nor rain nor heat nor gloom of night stays these couriers from the swift completion of their appointed rounds.' It was almost poetry. Funny how it stayed in the memory, a bit like pop songs from decades ago. Wow. It had never occurred to him that postmen had the same occupational bonding as cops or firemen. Hilarious though, meeting up for a pint to swap stories about escaping from rabid dogs and horny housewives.

'Postie families keep themselves to themselves, though they tell me it all began to fizzle out by the 60s. Guess they had more interesting things on their mind by then. Dad certainly did,' Trevor said, his voice trailing off as he looked at two suntanned women squeeze into the corner bench next to them.

'But why would things change in the 60s?' Nick asked loudly, to drag Trevor's thoughts back to the conversation. 'I mean, they still needed postmen even then, right? OK, I can understand they need fewer these days now that we have emails, tweets and God knows what else on the Web.'

His last comment made Trevor smile at him, as if Nick were a six-year-old.

'Well, mate, you're really not from around here, are you? Posties are nothing to do with the post office, red letter boxes or Royal Mail. It means people who came from the rookery, the Old Nichol, and if you still don't know what I'm talking about then it really is time you retired to Hampstead!'

Nick burped in response to Trevor's sharp tone, making his paunch judder against the table and causing the women's glasses of rosé to wobble. It wasn't quite a classic eureka moment, but it did make him laugh out loud later in the early hours, while sipping a whisky and listening to the radio.

'Ah. I see. So if they're not postmen like my thick brain thought they were, then why the hell do they call themselves Posties?' he asked Trevor, shrugging his shoulders exaggeratedly.

'A maths graduate is asking me what's a Postie? What do you call those things sticking up from the pavement to stop you parking that Porsche of yours illegally? Any ideas?'

'What, a bollard?'

'Bingo, Nick. Top of the class,' Trevor said with a snort and banged his fist on the table, making the women look up again from their conversation. 'Posties marked the entrance to the Old Nichol and the people who came from there will never forget that. And a word of advice, mate. As my gran used to say, Posties think their pee's too posh to stink. I think I've said more than enough about them for one night.

I'd best be off.'

Nick went straight to the bar, deciding that another pale ale was needed to digest what Trevor had said. Two packets of organic sea salt and chilli crisps also improved his mental clarity before heading home to pound the browser for Posties. The people, that is.

4

FRANK WAS EVEN BORED OF listening to Vera Lynn by now, and picked out a Flanagan and Allen record from his small collection that was stacked tidily against the brick wall of the warehouse. The record was a bit scratched but he loved mouthing the lyrics, his favourite song making him think of his mother cooking rabbit for supper in a large aluminium saucepan during the war. Someone pointed out Bud Flanagan to him at Spitalfields fruit and veg market a couple of years ago, and Frank had desperately wanted to introduce himself but couldn't. By then he was losing the confidence to talk with people he didn't know, and he could see from the corner of his eye a bunch of poxy barrow boys smoking and laughing, one of them pointing at Frank's kilt. Those spineless buggers wouldn't have the nerve to take the mickey now, in case he got the Posties after them. Helping the Posties wasn't just about cash in hand and food on the table, it also meant holding his head up high.

He crouched to untie the sack of bones and see what state they were in. The smell had already made him gag a couple of times. He remembered how the last batch of glue he made a few months before hadn't set well after he forgot to wash the bones properly. We won't be making that mistake again in a hurry. Posties like things done proper, and you never know when they'll come calling.

And check up on him the hoity-toity bastards certainly will, he grimaced.

'Run rabbit, run, rabbit, run, run, run…' he sang along, the chirpy rhythm perfect for scraping crud off bones with the bread knife he'd brought from home. An hour later it was time to use the gleaming set of butchers' knives they'd left for him on the workbench. He was nervous about using them, knowing they were sharp enough to slice off a finger if he lost concentration. But he had no choice, given there was the bloke from the barge to fillet as well. He didn't want to be at it for hours on end.

'Bang, Bang, Bang, Bang,' he sang, each word accompanied by a jab of the blade into the naked, cold body that was spread-eagled on the flagstones. A scratch on the record made the needle jump, throwing him off his stride, but he and the happy song were soon back in sync.

'Tickety tock,' he said under his breath. 'Time to get a move on before Elsie calls. Don't want her sticking that pretty head of hers into any of this, or asking awkward questions if she smells something bad.'

Several hours later and the arrival of dawn, he groaned, stood upright and stretched his arms and back before admiring his handiwork: a tidy pile of nicely cleaned bones on the floor. He'd hosed all fleshy traces of the bargeman down the drain and straight into the canal. The reddish mulch would be churned into the dark water by the propellers of passing barges, though he could hear gulls screeching above the water, no doubt sniffing fresh breakfast. The bigger chunks of chopped flesh he'd already crammed into drums, to be incinerated.

He chucked the bones into a barrow and wheeled it through the archway and into the adjoining, room with its low, vaulted brick ceiling. One by one, he carefully let slip the bones into the vat that was three-quarters full of solvents and hydrochloric acid, making sure his fingers didn't touch the liquid as they'd warned he could end up with no fingerprints. All of which had made him wonder why the cops couldn't take toe prints in that case, but before he could think of an answer, there was a knock on the door.

'Bloody 'ell. She's 'ere already.'

He went into the main room and did a quick check to see if he'd left anything incriminating in sight. No, it was all spick and span, if still a bit damp. The front door was bolted, so there was no way she could let herself in before he was ready.

'Morning, love,' he shouted. 'Give us a couple of minutes to get myself nice and presentable, will yer?'

He went back to the side room and rummaged through a large brown leather bag for the clean shirt and kilt he'd packed. Last thing he wanted was for Elsie to see the state he was in, otherwise she'd think he was Jack the Ripper just back from Whitechapel. It would put her right off her morning cuppa and biscuits. He took off his dirty clothes and stuffed them into the bag, frowning at the sight of his bloomers spattered with blood. Ah, not to worry, she wouldn't be seeing them.

5

NICK HAD NEVER DREAMED OF bums or bollards in his life until now, and the combination on the same night had left him unsettled when he woke up and began wondering what it had all meant.

The fragments he remembered were, not surprisingly, the vivid bits: he was sitting in an empty train carriage that was travelling in a gently rocking loop around Shoreditch, not stopping at any station. It was moving slowly enough for him to see up into his own flat as well as down to ground level, all in pin-sharp detail. From the train he counted all the bollards running along both sides of the high street, whose curve in real life would have made this impossible.

'Next stop Postie High Street,' a brusque female voice had said through the Tannoy speaker, while the bollards morphed into heavyset naked men with tattooed arms. Suddenly aware he was dreaming, he'd tried wresting control of events, only to feel himself falling through the air towards a bollard at the entrance of a narrow lane connecting the high street with a large patch of grass and a big white tent, to which an elephant was tethered. In a vain effort to slow down his descent, he used plastic shopping bags in both hands as parachutes, but to no avail. It was just when his bum was about to make high-speed contact with the glistening, cast-iron bollard that he woke up.

His heart was racing, his paunch a sweaty, hairy mush.

He lay in bed for several minutes to think through the dream, trying to decipher its meanings but without success. The mid-morning news bulletin on the radio led with the latest unemployment figures, helping to ground his thoughts back in the real world, and make him smirk: thank God he was no longer chained to a trading floor with only a nanosecond to decide whether to buy or sell the market on news like that.

He picked up his phone and called Jim.

'What's up, slacker?' his friend answered. 'And before you answer, have I told you that blockchain's the future? You heard it here first.'

The guy was in a good mood, though Nick didn't have the foggiest what he was on about. They both lived in the same building, but they rarely saw each other these days. Shame really. The man lived on adrenalin, up at dawn and behind the desk of his latest start-up, trying to reel in more investors. Nick sometimes wondered over his mid-morning coffee what exactly drove Jim, day in, day out, when he no longer needed the moolah after that well-timed float of his dating app. And the guy was still single!

Where was Nick's craving for success? Had it gone for good? He rarely dwelt on troubling, existential questions these days, except just the other week when he was flying back from Frankfurt after his last job for the consultancy. A giggly air hostess had wished everyone a safe onward journey to their final destination, and he'd experienced a unsettling moment of doubt and deep unease. Where was his final destination? Well, before going six feet under, that is? Would he ever know when he got there?

'Jim, mate. All fine, though am a bit rushed off my feet with consultancy work, as usual. You know what it's like, they want it finished yesterday. Anyway, that's not why I'm phoning you about. Bit of a wacky one, really, but do you know of any local historian I could talk to? Someone who knows how round here was like well before the likes of us turned up?'

'Where do I start, Nick?' Jim shouted down the line, with too little sarcasm to mask his curiosity. 'What the hell do you want to know? Isn't it that the whole point of this place is no historical baggage to hamper innovation, just blue-sky thinking all the way to Alpha returns? Well, that's basically what my piss-taking marketing consultant is putting in our prospectus, and he must be right if the fee he's charging is anything to go by.'

His mate had a point, Nick thought.

'In actual fact I'm doing a bit of research for a client. I need grass root themes from local stakeholders for brand-building. You know the type, a pushy suit who wants ideas to call his own and impress the boss.'

Nick was sensing that Jim wasn't going to be much help, but talking out loud had made the next port of call obvious.

'Look, no worries Jim. I'd better let you go. Give us a bell if someone comes to mind. We must meet up for dinner. Why don't you ping me a couple of free slots next month. I'd love to hear how the new company's doing. Maybe I can help out a bit.'

He hauled himself out of bed and nimbly stepped over two aluminium foil containers with the remains of his takeaway curry from last night. Kicking aside a pair of boxer shorts, he headed for the en-suite with a spring in his step as the dream about bollards had all but faded away.

Later, just before noon, after showering and shaving – he never understood why blokes were also meant to shit and complete a morning trinity – he got a text from Julie asking if he was done with the bob-a-job, as she coyly put it. Not quite, akela, he thought, instantly deleting the message with satisfyingly vigorous thumb action. He could shut her up with the truth: that so far at least, hubby wasn't shagging on the side, with either sex. But the guy obviously had a hinterland that was hidden from her. It was the way the bloke went about his life: he seemed to have it all worked out to a tee. Bet he would not only know what to do about Amanda, but would have done it long ago and moved on by now.

Nick buttoned up his shirt as he stared out of the window, thinking of those years when he was Tom's age, a blur of long hours at the office and religious partying, usually on the bank's tab. Nothing strange with that, given the need to give top clients lots of expensive attention. Was that dream of his last night saying he was now drifting through life while Posties like Tom pulled the strings round here? For God's sake, he couldn't be having a mid-life crisis, surely? He was in his prime, anyone could see that.

'Lone ranger looks clean. Need more checks,' he texted Julie an hour later, after tidying up and leaving a pile of washing on the bedroom floor for the cleaner.

He locked the flat, went downstairs and through the lobby into a small, high-walled yard between his building and the street, a space that was used mainly for storing brightly coloured recycling buckets, wheelie bins and chained bikes. Out on the street, he headed for Jimmy's Cafe, counting four piles of vomit on his way, a sight that no longer made him want to retch. Couldn't the pissed twats who'd pissed against the wall over there have done something socially useful and hosed the orangey crud down the drain? Though it must have been a quiet night, with so little fresh puke.

After living here for years, he was inured to this congealed slurry, which had become a daily reminder to write his groundbreaking novel on the three ages of inner city gentrification. It was already mapped out chapter by chapter in his head, kicking off with student squats in boarded-up council flats and discarded syringes sprinkled across mangy grass patches outside. Prostitutes without coats stamp to keep themselves warm on the side streets each night while hoping a lorry stops. The second age, a few years and at least one property boom and Sunday supplement feature later, it would be all about vegetarian cafes and pavements littered with small plastic pouches used for selling class-A kicks to City gents who want to feel edgy. He'd closely observed both phases unfold in real time on his doorstep, all perfect fodder for dinner parties with college mates in leafy north London. The trailblazing novel would end with terminal gentrification whose symptoms range from chain cafes to glass penthouse flats grafted onto nineteenth century industrial blocks and, of course, these pools of hen-night chunder he was now sidestepping. Even dog shit shrinks by the final chapter, the Alsatians and their council tenant owners by now long gone, replaced by petite droppings of pooches belonging to the better paid millennials renting the urban dream in loft-style, bought-to-let flats. Yep, transformation to Notting Hill East would be complete once rocketing property prices sends the last true local to zone six and snuffs out all residual traces of cockney soul. He would definitely hit the keyboard once work was less busy, he thought, as he entered Jimmy's Cafe and sat down by the window.

A few minutes later, and just about to slip into his mid-morning, caffeine-fuelled reverie, it finally twigged where he'd seen the two men sitting in the back of the cafe near the counter. Of course, it was the clothes that threw him. Nope, there was no mistaking who they were. They kept smiling at him, in case he hadn't spotted them. Now which one of them had the bollard tattoo on his arse? Or should that be a postie?

Nick smiled back, as bits of the conversation with Trevor and last night's dream returned. He had an urge to blow a kiss, too, just for the sheer hell of it. Those bald fuckers had penned him in the cubicle for twenty minutes to give Tom and whoever he'd been meeting plenty of time to shower and leave. And when they finally let him go, one of them had given him a smack on the arse and a 'see ya'. Nick had never dressed so fast, and then went straight home for a long bath and a beer, which he should have done in the first place after getting caught in that downpour.

So here they were again, Tweedledum and Tweedledee on steroids. They must know this was his morning hangout, he thought, chewing on his granary toast and marmalade. About ten minutes later, the heavies pushed aside their empty plates, got up and turned to Mavis behind the counter. One of them nodded and she reciprocated with a tight smile, but not a penny changed hands for the meal. Both then headed for the door, smiling again in his direction before stepping out, making a point of not being in a hurry as they headed up the high street.

6

FRANK OPENED THE DOOR OF the warehouse wide enough to check if Elsie was alone. She was, and he beckoned her in, despite still being worried the place wasn't clean enough and that she'd spot or smell something unsavoury.

'Back from yer travels then?' he asked. A gust of chilly wind made his kilt balloon and cause his balls to contract.

But Elsie stayed outside, leaning against the door frame, her arms crossed.

'That's what I came to tell yer. I couldn't go. Thought it best to lie low for a bit, what with the bleeding cops following me day and night,' she said, shivering in a new-looking navy mac, which was no match for the bitter east wind. The goose pimples round her neck made him want to pull her close and warm her up with his arms and chest.

'Eh? For God's sake Elsie, I hope they're not out there now. Last thing I need is trouble. When am I going to get the felt, then?' he asked, twitching at the thought of police following her to the warehouse. Would they want to look inside? Had they already tried peeking through the windows? Not that they'd see much with all that dirt.

'Well, I ain't going up west just for that, but let's say I know the perfect place to get some in ol' gay Paree,' she replied, arching an arm over her head with a girlie flourish. 'Don't worry, Frank. I'll have the felt by next week. Maybe I'll get you some nice material for a new kilt as well, if you like.'

That's Elsie – nice and cheeky, he thought.

Without waiting for a reply, she turned on her heels and walked off over the patch of semi-frozen waste ground that stretched about fifty yards from the front of the warehouse, her fluffy slippers leaving a trail in the early-morning frost. Shame he was that way down below, otherwise he'd have asked her to marry him long ago. He sighed and slammed the door before warming his balls with a quick rub.

7

'I'M THINKING OF GETTING A tattoo. What do you think? Bit too male menopausal?' Nick was shouting in Julie's ear to make himself heard in the noisy bar. 'They're everywhere. Blokes of all ages are getting one these days, right?'

She was in a good mood and had snapped up his offer of an after-work drink, not that she ever seemed in a hurry to get home. At the start, it was just the two of them and a scattering of pensive siliconeastas, but barely a glass of red later and the bar was rammed with oh-my-godding young things: the mass millennials had landed. Not all of them with beards, though. He and Julie ceded ground as gracefully as they could by standing next to the fire escape, their near empty bottle parked on a narrow ledge between them.

He'd had a brainwave in the bath that afternoon after an internet search on the Posties had uncovered naff-all that made sense. The hidden sub-strata of society described by Trevor simply didn't exist in the virtual world. Surely some sociology postgrad would have written a neo-Marxist deconstruction of them by now. Curiously, the one interesting thing he did find was a photo of bollards in the narrow alley that led off Shoreditch high street which, now with hindsight, probably instigated that unsettling dream.

Apparently it had once been the entrance to a nineteenth-century slum that was pulled down by Victorian philanthropists, as Trevor had hinted the other evening when he first heard about Posties.

Staring at bollards online felt like watching street porn, though.

There had to be a better way of digging up the dirt about Posties without having to sift through back issues of local rags. There was no guarantee that would uncover much either. Anyway, he didn't have the time.

'I had a henna tattoo in my wild youth!' she shouted after taking a big swig of the rather pricey pinot noir as if it were blackcurrant juice. He couldn't quite picture her being truly wild at any age; she was too much in control to have misspent her youth.

'Have you ever wanted Tom to have a tattoo? That's a romantic thing to do, right? He strikes me as a cool guy with something tasteful somewhere discreet,' he said, topping up her glass with the remains in the bottle.

'You still haven't told me everything you've got on him so far. Bet you I was right. Never doubt a woman's intuition is what mum used to say, though the old dear took her time to spot dad's away day activities,' she sniggered.

A roar of laughter from the centre of the room made them look up for a second, a reminder of how millennials were now in full command of the bar for the night. Before replying, he decided to squeeze his way through them to buy another bottle. It was in places like this he felt like a mangy lion that had lost its dominance, shoved aside by a new generation. Not that this lot would survive ten minutes without Wi-Fi.

'Thing is, it's hard to say if he's up to anything or not,' Nick said to her on his return as he placed a fresh bottle on the ledge next to the empty one. 'Think you'll need a bit of patience. Early days and all that. Have you thought about what you'd do if he is up to something? I suppose that might even give you cover to test the water yourself,' he said, prodding her in the ribs as he refilled her glass.

She didn't reply but instead looked round the room.

'Anyway, back to the serious stuff,' he continued. 'How about a dragon tattoo on my perky arse, not that there'll be anyone to admire it outside the gym. It's supposed to hurt, right, when they stick those vibrating needles in you?'

'Tom said he got his tattoo during a drunken afternoon when he was a student. Sounds like the usual crap with pissed blokes. Bloody stupid if you ask me,' she said.

'So what's he got?' he asked, trying his best to sound casual as his pulse rose several notches.

'You won't believe it, but he says he got his because he supports Arsenal. I've never seen him attend a single match, or watch one on telly. It's nothing but golf and rugby with him. And rugby union, as he keeps reminding me. Anyway, he's got the team's mascot on his arse, but only the cannon-barrel bit, not the wheels. He said he sobered up halfway through and told the tattooist he'd come back another day to finish it, but never did, of course. A bit half-cock if you ask me,' she laughed.

He sensed she had little interest in this thread of the conversation and she began fidgeting with her phone again while glancing round the bar, as if hoping to suck in its almost tactile, beery energy.

'Thanks for the advice. I'm not sure whether I'll get

one, to be honest. Think I'll give body art a miss for now.'

Talking about Tom's tattoo brought back that afternoon when he and his mother had tagged along with a walking tour of Shoreditch just after the area had been officially declared the new cool thing by the requisite quorum of Sunday newspaper journalists. The guide said that some of the bollards on his street were recycled cannon barrels. Bet he'd never heard of the Posties, though.

8

'YOU MUST BE SO CHUFFED about becoming the new director,' the short, fat, balding, middle-aged man said to his tall, thin, equally old companion.

They were sitting opposite each other in oddly shaped, high-back armchairs upholstered in puce velvet. The place was meant to be a new millennium twist on the traditional gentlemen's club. Women, of course, could join, but instead of dark oak panels and rows of leather-bound books bought by the yard, there was floor-to-ceiling tempered glass that cut traffic noise to a hum while still letting in every stray sunbeam a cloudy London sky could muster. The occasional flood of summer sunshine illuminated each crack and knot of the lovingly restored oak floor that was recycled from a Victorian school gym in the Midlands.

'Not quite sure about it all, to be honest. It's certainly an honour, of course, but don't you think some of the other Posties will be a teensy bit peeved? Strictly speaking it's not my turn, as I've said before,' the tall man replied in a voice that barely registered above a whisper.

'Well, Mr Director, being next in line is of no use when you're on the run in the Costas, or a tax exile in Zug. They'll get over it, my friend. They made their beds, et cetera et cetera.' The fat companion smiled. 'And you are breaking new ground in the diversity stakes, which earns us a lot of Brownie points among the younger members.'

They both chuckled.

'I suppose you're right. To life as the next director then,' the tall man said, his ginger-haired hand raising a glass of whisky towards his friend's gin and tonic until they gently clinked. They sipped and fell into a brief silence, staring at the floor or out the window, anywhere to avoid the gaze of an over-attentive waitress hovering just inside their peripheral vision in the hope of persuading them to order more drinks, or try the daily special: gluten-free vegan canapés. She gave up and went in search of more receptive punters while the fat man checked his phone, using the thick yellowish nail on his right thumb to prod the gadget into life. Not that he used it much in his line of business. Best not to leave too many electronic trails for sticky beaks to read. No, just a few texts back and forth with the wife, all very normal.

'There will have to be the usual inauguration ceremony, of course. We can't let traditions slip,' the tall man said with a roll of the eyes. 'Besides, it's a good excuse to gather the clan, as it were, don't you think?' He was not fond of being the centre of attention, preferring to pull strings from the sidelines, a modus operandi that had served him well. Still, meeting the other Posties en masse would be a good opportunity to deal with gripes that had inevitably percolated through the extended family over the years. And the greedy little buggers were becoming a tad restless over dosh, and in sore need of reminding about their heritage.

'Let's avoid the river and keep it all on terra firma this

time, please. Bertie was a bit naughty when he tried to drown us all in that hired tub. Off his bloody rocker. Probably seen *Kind Hearts and Coronets* once too many,' the fat man said, arching an eyebrow until the thin man nodded in agreement. 'It left a lasting, bitter taste in everyone's mouth, and I just don't mean Old Mother Thames.'

'Indeed, after that soggy episode, the little shit should have been buried at sea, not in Highgate cemetery!'

They resumed sipping in silence to finish their drinks.

'So who do we have to organise our special soirée to mark my appointment as the new director then?' the thin man asked, hauling himself onto his feet. 'I hope it's someone loyal to the cause and our wonderfully inspiring history. Some of our brothers and sisters have become rather restive of late, muttering all sorts of drivel about wanting to call it a day, to wind down this century-old enterprise of ours. It beggars belief, in my humble opinion.'

The fat man, still seated, flapped his hand to calm his companion's concerns. 'Don't you worry. I've got Fry to take care of all that. Just think about your speech, Mr Director. And, oh, perhaps nothing too harsh about Bertie. He's definitely dead, after all.'

9

NICK WAS HUNGOVER, THE MID-MORNING latté in Jimmy's Cafe failing to fully penetrate his addled brain. He rued again the colossal mistake of accepting Julie's offer of a third bottle of wine. He'd hoped to continue picking her brains about Tom, but ended pickling his own. The *in vino veritas* strategy backfired big time as their conversation in the bar degenerated into an inconclusive debate about what she would do if hubby was, to use her own words, going AWOL in someone else's undergrowth. Other than that, he couldn't remember a single thing.

Even more worryingly, he caught himself staring at bollards all the way to Jimmy's.

They really were on every street, like row upon row of silent, cast-iron aliens lining up to remind him how little he knew about what was really going on in the neighbourhood right under his nose. He was fascinated by their different shapes, heights and widths. A bit like the way women view cocks, he supposed, while looking out the window. The siliconeastas had long arrived at work, freeing up pavements for the jobless, the old, the homeless, mothers with prams, and himself.

So, he summed up, at least one of the two heavies and

Tom have bollard tattoos on their bums.

Progress of sorts, then. Great, but not exactly the smoking gun Julie wants to hear. His attempts at free thinking were hitting a brick wall as he tried to make the connections between bollards, Tom and the two heavies. And his mate Trevor had referred to the Posties as some sort of covert East End brotherhood to which Tom belonged. But how? By birth from the sound of it.

'Another coffee, Nick? Looks like you're in need,' Mavis called out while darting among tables to give each one a quick wipe with her yellow sponge cloth.

'Go on then, what the hell,' he replied, giving her a wan smile.

'Skinny latté with extra cocoa on top, love!' she shouted to her grandson, who was leaning on the counter and flicking through one of the free dailies. A few minutes later the speckled refill was in front of him. He hoped it would put his derailed train of thought back on track, just like the train that was looping round the high street.

'You know the area well, don't you, Mavis? You must have been a bit of a goer down the music halls in your day, right?' he asked the sceptical-looking octogenarian before she could shuffle away. 'Look, I'll tell you why I'm asking. I'm doing a bit of research for a client of mine who wants local stakeholder themes,' he continued, almost biting his tongue for not stopping the twatty marketing babble from slipping out.

Mavis rested her rag-clutching fist on the table, sensing it was her duty to hear out a regular customer, even if he made little sense.

'Anyway, some bloke down the pub the other night was talking about the Posties. To be honest I hadn't a clue what he was on about. You ever heard of them? Apparently he meant the same thing as bollards, you know, those cast-iron things that stick up on the street, and not blokes, I mean people, who deliver the mail. But the Posties also mean people from round here, if that makes sense. Anyway, my research assistant couldn't find anything about them online so I guess he was having me on, right?'

He could have sworn the crows' feet round her eyes had just dug in a millimetre deeper; her strawberry-blonde perm had actually twitched. She let out a short sigh and leaned harder on the table, inadvertently squeezing tiny rivulets of dirty water and small bubbles from the sponge cloth.

'What do you see on the other side of the street?' she asked, nodding towards the window without taking her milky eyes off him.

He shrugged as he looked out onto the usual scene of people walking past and heavy traffic.

'See that alley over there, what's in the middle?' Mavis asked.

Here we go again, he thought, as he realized she was referring to bollards.

'The other end of that alley is where the first Posties came from after they were kicked out of the rookery,' Mavis continued. 'Never cross the Posties, my dad used to say. They stick together like glue, he'd say. And nobody with half a noodle in their head goes mouthing on about them in public. You take care love, we need our regulars these days.' She spoke with what was either a zen-like wink or another involuntary twitch. He couldn't tell which, but the effect was equally disconcerting. After a quick wipe of his table she was back behind the counter, loading the dishwasher.

10

'TICKETY TOCK.'

Frank tossed the bargeman's clothes and belongings against the wall, wound up the gramophone, and lowered the needle onto the record. He beamed as Vera Lynn's silky voice began reverberating inside the wharf. Well, Pooter lad, we certainly won't be meeting again, will we, whatever the bleeding weather, he thought, humming to the tune.

An hour's kip and a luncheon-meat sandwich after Elsie's brief visit had done him a world of good, and he was ready to get back to work. The handwritten instructions were clear, and those postie minders had read them out to him several times as if he was thick and couldn't understand things the first time. Just because that last batch of glue was no good didn't mean he was an idiot. The patronizing bastards had a knack for setting his teeth on edge, but no point picking a fight he'd never win.

He ran a finger down the list of instructions. Right: fat, gristle and cartilage had all been stripped from the bones. Let's tick that one off. He'd also washed the bones in solvents, making sure to wear the heavy rubber gloves and apron they'd given him, though it didn't prevent splashes from burning tiny holes in his kilt. Hopefully Elsie will bring him material for a new one, after all. Draining the solvents had been a bit tricky, but he'd managed to jump out of the way in time when opening the tap and allowing the filthy liquid to course down the drain and into the canal.

Yes, not a bad night's work, all in all, and now it was time to boil the buggers, from what he read on the instruction sheet. Time-wise he knew he was well ahead, but he wanted to make sure the glue would be up to scratch. If it turned out to be a duff batch then he could make some more, though finding fresh bones round here at short notice would not be that easy. He attached a hosepipe to a tap on the wall and lowered its nozzle to the bottom of the vat, his left foot tapping to the music as he kept an eye on the rising water level. No more than two-thirds full, the instructions said in bold letters on brown cardboard that he'd propped up against a paint tin on the workbench. He turned off the tap when the water reached the right height, and packed away the hosepipe. Down on his haunches, he turned on the gas valve and struck a match to light the burner under the vat.

Crossing out lines of completed instructions with a green crayon made him whistle with satisfaction, though he was making sure he could still read the words in case he needed to make another batch. Yes, he'd thought of everything. He read the next instruction under his breath: put clean bones in vat of boiling water, turn down heat to simmer gently. Looking down at the bones in the dishes on the floor, it was hard to tell which ones were from horses and which ones were from the bargeman. Well, it's all glue in the end. He shrugged.

At least the cleaned bones smelt a lot better than the

sack they came in the previous evening. Getting rid of that mound of gristle had made them easier to handle. He looked at his fingernails; they still harboured bits of reddish crud that had so far been impervious to carbolic soap and vigorous scrubbing. At least his fingers didn't smell, though he ought to stop biting his nails for a while.

After tipping the first load of bones into the vat, he bent down to turn up the volume on the gramophone as high as it would go, just as Vera launched into one of his favourite songs. He picked up a few more bones from the dishes and let them slide gently into the simmering water. Columns of bubbles rose to the surface to pop with rhythmic plops.

He lifted the dish with the remaining bones shoulder-high and tipped them into the vat, feeling a sense of glee as they sank in the clear water to nestle on top of the others. Splashes of hot water landed on his bare forearms, neck and face when the last bone rattled across the dish and smacked the surface. With his raw materials now in the vat, the water level rose to just a few inches below the rim, leaving him pleased at how perfectly judged it was. The wafts of steam smelt like an acrid version of the mutton stews his mother used to cook that made the kitchen windows mist up so he could draw pictures of houses and animals on the glass with a finger. He stopped himself from using the same finger to taste the simmering water, and instead went into the main room to grab a long pole with a hook to open the ceiling vent and let the steam rise into the freezing air.

Making himself comfortable in the armchair, he stretched out his legs and had a smoke before turning down the music and dozed while the water and bones bubbled gently.

11

SPURRED ON BY MAVIS'S CRYPTIC references to the rookery, Nick finished his latté, paid and walked to the other side of the high street to examine the bollards she'd pointed out. The alley was flanked by a dancing bar, outside of which two women with big hair and heels were texting, sucking hard on cigarettes and trying to draw two middle-aged City gents into their conversation. That had to be the definition of multi-tasking, he thought.

There were two more bollards – or should he now be calling them posties, though not the Posties as they were obviously not people – at the other end of the passage, where it opened out into a cobbled residential road lined on one side by an elegant estate built from orange brick, and nondescript industrial buildings on the other. The estate must have been scrubbed clean recently, given how its soot-free walls stood in stark contrast to the dirtier frontage opposite. His eye was drawn to a corner of the estate that was round like a medieval tower, rising several floors to a turret roof in grey slate. A bearded man wearing a beanie cap was leaning out of the top window, vaping while speaking on the phone.

Nick often walked down this cobbled street, each occa-

sion bringing back memories of that one-night stand with a
mature student who lived in a flat overlooking a raised,
circular public garden with, of all things, a bandstand on
top. The estate must have been one of the first private
mansion blocks in the East End, almost certainly for the
middle classes working in the City. He'd often wondered
why it featured on walking tours. Probably designed by
some cult architect from the last century.

He walked on to enter a backstreet that joined a busy
main road, which he crossed, and then he headed south
along a shop- and bar-lined street to reach the local history
bookshop he'd found online while finishing his coffee. It was
halfway down, just where the curry houses and their army
of touts were being elbowed out by fashion shops, cafes that
served flour-free cakes, and pricey bric-à-brac dens. The
green shoots of terminal gentrification were everywhere to
his trained eye, like Japanese knotweed that would eventually strangle all remaining East End authenticity. He sighed
while walking past a clothing chain camouflaged to look like
an independent store. Yet more depressing fodder for his
novel, as if he needed any.

Inside the bookshop he leafed through reproductions of
local maps from the 1890s, noticing that one of them had a
blank square in the centre. It was as if the cartographer
wanted to shield prim Victorian eyes from a sordid enclave.
He knew the area well enough to realize that the blank
square was where they built the orange brick estate he'd just
passed, though neither the bandstand nor the side streets
that radiated from it were detailed or named.

'Isn't it hard to believe how places can change?' said the
shop assistant, a woman in her 30s wearing a long floral

dress and white plastic sandals. He was the only customer, perhaps her first of the day, maybe the week by the feel of things. 'Strange to think how quiet it was round here even five years ago. Looking for something in particular?' she asked.

'I know exactly what you mean. To think that when I bought my place here in the 80s, it was so peaceful on weekends. Now it's more manic than Camden Market. Gawd, those were the days,' he said, determined not to be outdone in the local stakes even if she probably knew more about the boring, historical bits than he did. 'Anyway, I wonder if you can help me. I'm doing some research for a client, a household name, but I can't say more than that. They want local stakeholder content for brand-building,' he said, immediately sensing latent hostility from the way she crossed her arms. He looked back down at the map and examined the streets bordering the blank square. Intriguingly, they were coloured in black, while streets a little further away were in red or orange.

The legend at the bottom of the map said black indicated lowest class, vicious, semi-criminal.

'How the hell can anyone be semi-criminal? Isn't that like being a bit pregnant?' he said, though given that the assistant was obviously not going to share his joke, he continued with barely a pause: 'Any idea why this square in the middle was left blank? Someone was saying the other day there were loads of dairies round here. I suppose the cows had to graze somewhere.'

The woman jerked her head to one side to rethread her long, brownish hair through an undyed wool scrunchie before replying, 'Thought you've lived here for years. Looks like you need some local history lessons.' Nodding down at the map, she continued, 'That square you're looking at used to be the rookery, the Old Nichol.' Seeing no sign of light in his eyes, she ploughed on, 'The rookery was the slum they tore down at the end of the nineteenth century. Surely you must know that? They replaced it with the lovely orange brick buildings that are there now. It's the country's first council estate, that is, before the flats were flogged off under Thatcher,' she explained slowly.

He'd been none the wiser.

Let's face it, there must have been loads of slums torn down in the East End by Industrial Revolution-era capitalists cum philanthropists, eager to launder their cash from the colonies into something more conscionable than a humongous country pile – and burnish their own social standing to boot. Hadn't Mavis, or Trevor, said something about the Old Nichol, or – what did the shop assistant say just now, an old rookery? Well, he certainly hadn't noticed an abundance of crows round the bandstand.

'Er, that's really interesting. By the way, do you know anything about, um, the Posties, as in locals from round here? My client wants a logo connected to the area and there's supposed to be some link between bollards and slums. Did bollards have a special significance for people back then?' he asked, trying not to snigger.

She went over to a set of shelves and picked out a slim volume, which she handed to him.

'I think you could do with reading this. It's a novel, by the way, though it's largely based on real life. Bit like a documentary, if you follow. Anyway, the first chapter should be self-explanatory but I can recap for you. Posties, as in bollards and not people, marked the entrance to the Old Nichol, a pretty lawless place in the book. Even the police didn't go there unless they had to. Some historians think that's where Jack the Ripper would hide for a few hours after murdering women,' she continued with the tone of voice of a nursery-school teacher.

He was about to try pumping her for more information when he felt a vibration against his thigh. 'Tom's going extracurricular again. Overnight. Proof this time? Call me!!!!' Julie's text screamed.

'Bugger, it's that client I mentioned just now. There's never a moment's peace, is there? They all want everything yesterday,' he told the assistant, making her breathe in sharply.

'I'll take the map and the book, I mean, novel,' he said, handing the woman a twenty-pound note. 'Forget the change. I'll claim it anyway. Please accept it as a little thank-you for the help you've been.'

Out on the street he stuffed the copy of *A Child of the Jago* inside his jacket. Not his usual bedtime reading, but it would make a change until client briefs turned up. The phone vibrated again. She's getting a little too pushy, he thought. But it wasn't her, only the local bakery tweeting that a batch of fougasse had just come out of the oven. Must remember to unfollow them, he thought as he headed for home, the map tightly rolled up under his arm like a regimental baton.

12

ELSIE WAS WALKING UP SHOREDITCH High Street, taking care not to tread on the piles of steaming, sweet manure left behind by a horse pulling a cart that was now turning into the side street up ahead. How mam would have scooped up the lot and packed it round her roses. She smiled. Muck is a darn sight more useful than men, she'd often heard her mother say when they were on the allotment next to the railway tracks, where Elsie would slyly eat the peas when out of sight. She never pinned down what her mother meant, and now it was too late to ask.

After seeing Frank down the warehouse that morning she'd gone home to get dressed properly. Didn't want to be walking round the shops in slippers, or people would think she was a hard-up slapper on her way to Daddy Burtt's for dinner. Well, that was a place she definitely didn't want to be seen dead in. No Christian mission mush would be going down her neck.

She was in the mood to do something nice for Frank, someone she'd long had a soft spot for, located somewhere between pity and burning curiosity. After passing St Leonard's church on her right, she crossed over the road at the big junction and turned left down a street that ran past the town hall and the Electricity Showrooms, where that nice cheeky man with spots had taken only ten minutes to sell her a cooker and arrange to fix the wiring in her house. The little charmer. Bit young, though.

It took her breath away how it was all changing round here, what with these new shops selling stuff you wanted to buy. About bloody time, after putting up with the mess from the Blitz.

Yes, how time flies, but what did she have to show for it all?

She wondered why Frank needed the green felt. Must be another special job for the Posties. It doesn't sound like it's for a snooker table, she thought. He must be working full-time for that lot these days.

A select few did special jobs for the Posties, and, trying to be among them, she knew the golden rule was never ask what it was for. She checked her reflection in a shop window. Looking good, darling. The smell of that god-awful prison food during her last stint in Holloway had left her feeling like a scarecrow, but now that she'd put the pounds back on, she had a curvy waist men liked to put an arm round in the pub. Still, no resting on her laurels, given that most women of her age were long married and with at least one nipper under the arm. There had to be a decent bloke out there to cook for with that new stove of hers. Well, not every night, or life would be boring. As for the felt that Frank wanted, she could easily get her hands on a few yards of that, but what did he mean by 'quality stuff'? Felt was felt, for God's sake. 'It's not a favour, love. You'll get paid good money like you always do,' he told her before she could even open her mouth.

The pavements were crowded with Saturday-morning shoppers jostling to avoid stepping into icy puddles and muck on the potholed streets. Ahead of her she saw a scruffy youth make a grab at a box of apples outside the grocery store, but he failed to nab any or escape before the shop assistant had given his arse a thumping kick. The box toppled as the boy ran off, making Elsie stop outside the shop and use her feet to prevent the apples rolling into the road. She knelt down to scoop them back into the box as the assistant came over. 'These lads got no manners these days, have they?' she told him. 'I blame the parents. That's what I say,' she huffed before going on her way.

She carried on past the pet shop, admiring a pair of bright yellow canaries in a cage. As she'd mentioned to Frank, she would kill two birds with one stone during the team's upcoming trip to Paris: orders were already coming in thick and fast. She was looking forward to visiting France for a change; they'd done Geneva twice already in the past year. There would be plenty of top-quality felt in Paris for his lordship. She would sort it all out with the girls down the Cock and Cardinal that night over a gin or two.

Discreetly, she checked if the two apples were still secure inside her knickers. Good. She could feel them bobbing up and down as she walked along. A nice slice of apple pie would lift her spirits. All she needed now was to get her hands on some lard.

13

ON HIS WAY HOME FROM the Brick Lane bookshop, Nick decided it was time, based on research that by now almost filled the first page of his notebook, to act decisively and pre-empt Tom, to put himself back in control, as the hunter rather than headless prey.

It was simple and so obvious, really.

He would wait for Tom inside Jock's Hangout, a tactic that would also outfox the two brick-shithouse minders. The plan was crystallising in his head as he walked with the map rolled up under his arm, putting him in such a better mood that he laughed out loud at graffiti on a disused factory shrouded in scaffolding. 'Flats for cunts' someone had daubed in large, spidery red letters on the developer's board that advertised luxury flats. Shame it would be painted over, he thought, savouring its raw, political anger before moving on with a smile. No selfie this time, though. He'd occasion-ally email or tweet a photos of street art to Julie, Trevor or anyone else he thought would find them interesting. This time he wasn't going to bother, as there was no point giving Julie an excuse to get in touch more frequently than she already was. And he'd obviously tried Trevor's patience the other night by banging on about Tom and the Posties, as if they were a minor rock band from the 1970s. Best to give both a bit of space.

Anyway, he'd already rung Julie after leaving the bookshop.

'Well, looks like things are moving and you're going to get some real live action,' she said in a Brooklyn accent, before reverting to her own voice. 'Tom said he'll be at the office all day and then off to see old family friends tonight for dinner. And he'd probably stay the night in town because he's got a really early breakfast meeting with an important client. Yeah, right. Tomorrow's a Saturday, as if I'm fucking dumb!' She was shouting into the phone above the rising noise of a trading floor that was trying to keep one step ahead of a sliding euro and rising bond prices.

The cacophony brought back memories of his own adrenalin rushes during manic workdays that ended up with high fives and everyone pissed in the pub or, thankfully more rarely, cowed at a post mortem in the boss's glass box where the air turned blue as onlookers gloated at how their own bonus had survived another screw up. He often wondered why she still put up with the stress when she didn't need to earn big bucks any more. He had to hand it to her, though, as few could keep hold of the greasy pole at her age, man or woman, unless they were still raking in plenty of dosh for the bank. The next generation under her would have learnt all the dark arts by now to survive without her. Oh, a bright morning it had been when he told the boss to shove the job up his arse, even if it was only months before he was going to be dumped in a post-bonus cull that everyone and their mother knew was on the cards.

Still, jumping first had kept his nicely-pensioned ego

intact, even if he had no longer had a love interest to share his loft and lolly with.

'Look, why don't you ask him straight out if he's seeing someone? Isn't that what wives do when hubbies keep odd hours?' he asked her while circumnavigating the raised bandstand, or circus as the woman in the bookshop called it. He walked up a set of steps to sit on a bench, the rolled map upright between his legs so he could flick through the novel he'd bought, while listening to Julie rant.

'The last thing I want is to come across as some needy, whiny bitch. He'll sense something's up if I start making unfounded accusations like that. Text me if you find out something, anything. I've put some moolah in your account as a big thank you for all you've done. Believe me, I'm really grateful you're willing to do this for me. Shit. Got to go. I'd better check the options trades in case compliance gets picky. Ciao.'

Looking up to the sky, his eye tracked a squirrel, a skinny, furry Tarzan leaping from branch to branch of a tree above him, before disappearing in thick foliage high up. Bet he doesn't get hassled by mates asking him to spy on someone! Running through the plan in his head again, he remembered that on each of the last two Fridays, Tom had left work about half past five and gone straight to Jock's Hangout. After what happened there the first time, Nick had refused to follow him inside the second time, not that the two heavies waiting by the door would have let him pass anyway. No big deal though, as Julie confirmed that he came home at the usual time.

As for tonight, he may as well give things another go inside the sauna. Let's face it, he was at a bit of a loose end socially. Why had his mates not replied to his round-robin email suggesting drinks? Even tailing Tom was better than staying in on his own on a Friday night, and hopefully those two heavies who'd literally bumped into him in the sauna, won't be around this time. If only he could find out where Tom was staying the night then it could be case closed, which would be no bad thing for his nerves. He had enough stress with work as it is.

Back in the flat, he lay on the sofa and opened the book he'd bought, thinking there must be a clue between its covers as to why Posties were so into stupid tattoos, a thought that made him giggle like a demented schoolgirl. What had Mavis warned him about? Tread carefully. Still, it was hard to believe what he'd heard so far about them. Why should he get his knickers in a twist about some hidden, sub-strata of society that rose from the wrong side of an East End street separating the law-abiding poor from their semi criminal brethren? As both Tom and one of the heavies have bollard tattoos on their arse, he could safely bet his best bottle of pinot noir the other heavy has one too. And maybe Gingernuts in the sauna as well. What's more, the heavies had to be brothers, twins even given how similar they looked, but he doubted they were related to Tom, otherwise Julie would know about them. No, there had to be another connection and it didn't look like a professional or sexual one. Perhaps they were in the same gang at school? All for one and one for all, that sort of thing, another thought that made him snigger. He tossed the book on the floor and went to lie down on his bed, setting the radio to wake him up in a couple of hours' time. Making a groove for his head in the pillow, he drifted into a half-doze, thinking how best to handle another sauna session with Tom and avoid getting trussed up like a towelled turkey by the two heavies again.

14

FRANK READ OUT LOUD THE next line of the instruction sheet: After simmering for four hours, stirring occasionally, allow thickened liquid to cool. Reheat and cool until jelly forms. Shame it wasn't the red jelly his mother used to make for his birthday. He loved to mash it up with evaporated milk and suck spoonfuls backwards and forwards through gaps in his front teeth to make a pink, sweet froth which he'd swallow slowly.

There we go again, he thought, trying to stop his mind drifting from the job at hand. He knew it was down to tiredness from being cooped up in the warehouse for what felt like days, too anxious to step outside for longer than a quick fag before going back to glue-making. Warnings from the Postie minders to get rid of anything suspicious also rang in his ears. He'd made a point of cleaning up as he went along, having hosed down the floors and walls twice by now, feeling a sense of quiet satisfaction at the sight of dirty, pinkish water trickling down the drain.

Who'd have thought that he'd be earning a living like this? If only he could be back behind the counter in Woolworths, flirting with girls and lining one up for the weekend. He'd never forget the precise moment when he realized that daily routine was about to end, that life would be different forever. Worse than discovering his mortality. He was in front of the hallway mirror with his trousers and underwear around his ankles while he examined himself, thinking he was alone in the house.

'What the hell have you got down there, Frank? They're bleeding enormous,' his mother had screamed behind him.

From then on she and dad had referred to his balls as 'them things', as if they were aliens from outer space that had landed on Hoxton Square before latching onto him like permanent limpets.

'I could join the freak show on Coney Island with the bearded lady,' he joked a few months later in the kitchen, only to be met with stony silence as his mother carried on peeling the potatoes, head down to hide her tears. Then, after no signs of shrinkage, it was off to the hospital on Whitechapel High Street where the snotty doctor, who'd fought his war in Africa, diagnosed in less than a minute what was wrong with him: 'elephantitis of the scrotum', the doctor had said, as he nodded to a bunch of slack-jawed nurses and student doctors behind them, without once looking Frank in the eye.

And that was that.

He sometimes wondered what would have happened if he'd been married. Would she have stayed, or scarpered? Maybe he would be a father by now. Would a son of his have outsize balls too, or would they be normal? Well, he could always ask the doctor if a chance to have children came up. Until then, there was no point.

He decided to hose down the place again, this time aiming at the top corners of the main room to flush out wads of dust and dead spiders. The jet could just about reach the skylight and he let the water course down onto a ledge a few feet underneath and which ran right round the room.

Every nook and cranny must be squeaky-clean.

To think it had been more than five years since that visit to the hospital. Soon after, he was wearing kilts because his nads were just about too big for his trousers, though at least his balls had stopped growing now. Many of these cases turn out far worse, the doctor had cheerfully told him last year.

Call that luck?

The warehouse smelt fresher now and he couldn't see any more red stains on the walls, though he'd check again later with the windows open to let in more light. Using a broom, he began to rub washing soda into the flagstones and soon built up a large mound of foam which he whittled away with the hose. With the cleaning largely done, the next task was to retrieve what was left of the bones from the bottom of the vat. Not a bad day's work so far, he thought, looking forward to sleeping in his own bed that night. Time for another mug of extra-strong tea to perk himself up for the next chore. Where did he put that Eccles cake?

15

NICK WAS FEELING CONFIDENT THAT he was prepared for whatever Tom got up to this time round: technology would be on his side, along with a carefully considered disguise.

He was sitting by the window of a cafe opposite Tom's office, the scene feeling a bit déjà-vu as he recognised some of the people who emerged from the revolving glass door. There was that gorgeous Asian woman again in a flirty floral dress, tapping her way into the weekend on patent leather high heels.

Yep, Julie had described Tom's deputy to a bitter tee.

He rocked backwards and forwards on the stool, his elbows leaning on a narrow, cup-strewn counter that ran the length of the window. The game plan was simple: once Tom emerged and was clearly on his way to Jock's Hangout, he would leg it down a parallel side street, check in and lie low in one of the darker side rooms until Tom arrived. Should work a treat – as long as the two heavies weren't hanging round the entrance, that is.

As he shifted on the stool, it was reassuring to feel the high-tech kit inside his underpants rubbing gently against his cock: it was a Mars bar sized digital recorder the man in the gadget shop swore would pick up conversations several metres away with its multi-directional microphone and background noise compensator, features Nick found no mention of in the minuscule print of the multilingual instruction leaflet. Once in the changing room, he would have to make sure nobody was watching him while he undressed, otherwise they would become suspicious if they noticed he was wearing underpants that were home to this second, metallic member. Unfortunately the recorder emitted a low beep when switched on, so he would have to moan briefly as if he were getting the blow job of his life. A bit of out-of-the-box thinking, just like his consultancy told him to feed clients when he ran out of real solutions.

Finding the right disguise to fool the heavies had, admittedly, been trickier. He'd settled on a longish black wig tied in a ponytail to hide his closely cropped, mostly fair hair. During a dress rehearsal in the bathroom, he'd felt like a well-groomed heavy-metal fan. Well, what the hell. Nothing strange in a headbanger looking for sex, surely?

He checked his reflection in the window again. Good, the wig was firmly in place, though it would no doubt start feeling warm once he left the air-conditioned cafe and hit the increasingly humid July heat. His mobile phone vibrated, though it was no surprise who sent the text: Julie checking again if there was anything to report. Her ninth message and email of the day so far. Must be a quiet one at the office.

'Waiting for him to leave. Spk soon. Miss marplexx,' he replied.

It wasn't until 6.17pm when Tom finally spun through the revolving door and onto the street to end his working week, looking his usual immaculate self with not a single pound of surplus flesh to bulk out his expensive summer linen suit in the wrong place. Over his right shoulder he carried a matte-black leather rucksack. No briefcase, mystery brown envelope or overnight bag. Tom walked across the road to the junction where he took a right up the main street towards the station, just like on the last two Fridays. Nick followed, his ponytail bouncing against his back with each step while the recorder moved rhythmically inside his briefs. He kept several metres behind, glancing down to check his trousers every so often. Nothing to worry about, he thought. All looked normal from what he could see round the rim of his paunch.

Tom didn't look back once and the rush-hour crowd filling the pavement gave Nick plenty of cover as they neared the mainline railway station, prompting him to open up a bit more space between them, and get ready to slip into an upcoming side street on the left so that he could sprint to the sauna. Just as he was about to turn off, Tom stopped at a pedestrian crossing, pressed the button and waited for the traffic to come to a standstill, which it did almost immediately, allowing him to cross and continue walking north, a route taking him away from Jock's Hangout.

What the hell's he playing at?

Nick walked straight ahead, in parallel with Tom, and a break in the traffic allowed him to cross over while still keeping a safe distance. Looks like the sauna's off the schedule tonight, he thought with relief. Bet he's got a date for a drink and dinner.

Julie's dapper husband carried on northwards, passing under a railway bridge and up the high street that bisected Nick's home turf. Must be heading for that pole-dancing bar on the right-hand side, he smirked.

'Shit no!' Nick almost screamed a few seconds later as Tom passed the adult bar and took a right down the alley with its bollards, pancakes of dried vomit, and sticky rivulets of urine whose sweet and sour aromas carried in the warm July air. The summer evening and brisk walking were making his heart beat faster and he could feel a film of sweat building up between his wig and scalp. Inside his under-pants, the recorder's ridged plastic fascia was rubbing against his knob, giving him a gentle erection. Worse still, the residential street Tom turned into gave him little cover for his pursuit. Waiters in white aprons were leaning against a wall, vaping and chatting as a thin trickle of pedestrians passed them by. He could see Tom up ahead, near a grubby, gated office building, then watched him stop in front of a block of flats where Tom tapped the entry system with practised familiarity before pushing open the door to step inside, giving Nick just enough time to catch up and hear the quiet click of an electronic lock shutting.

Now what?

He stopped to take in his surroundings: there was that orange brick estate on the other side of the street with its fairy-tale tower. The waiters on their break had stopped chatting to look inquiringly at him, but they soon lost interest and resumed talking as Nick walked several metres up the street. There were no names, numbers or other clues on the building Tom had entered, just a keypad for tapping in a code. He continued walking to the far end of the street, retraced his steps and then peered through the large metal gate near the entry door. Behind the gate a driveway veered leftwards and down into what must be an underground car park. Bulging wheelie bins were parked in a neat row along the driveway like an overloaded cargo train, with a scruffy middle-aged man rummaging through them, one by one, and clutching a plastic bag for his spoils.

'Look mate, I've lost my keys. Do us a favour will you, and let us in,' Nick shouted over to him while waving a folded fiver through the bars.

'Bleedin' heck. How long did that ferret take to grow?' the man said after coming closer. It took Nick a few seconds to twig he was referring to his ponytail.

'Yeah, well. Bit of a rocker, I guess,' Nick said with a forced smile while waving the fiver again, this time more insistently. The beggar snatched the cash, gave a quick twist to a concealed lock and went back to the bins with a spring in his step. Nick pushed open the side gate and walked along the driveway until he found himself at the end of a passage between the flats and the back of a hotel that faced onto the high street. He looked up at the rows of windows of the flats, his spirits beginning to sag at the thought of trying to track down Julie's husband in this maze. He then almost whooped for joy on seeing one of the heavies lean out of a fourth-floor balcony for a few seconds to catch the evening sun before disappearing inside again. He knew it would be mad to hang around the bins as he could see that cameras were tracking his every move. Security would be onto him in no time if he loitered. Even the beggar was leaving, now he could buy his own dinner. To look less suspicious, Nick pretended to look for something in the wheelie bins, slamming down each lid as if he couldn't find what he was after.

Then an idea came to him. Bloody obvious, really, he

thought, as he cantered round the block, his ponytail bouncing wildly.

'Room for one night, please. It's got to be on the upper floor round the back, otherwise I can't sleep because of traffic noise,' he explained to the hotel receptionist. It was hard trying to appear casual as he gave his address, the postcode certainly almost identical to the hotel's, but the receptionist didn't flinch and carried on with other tasks at the same time, barely looking at Nick.

'No problem. We have good room for you. Does sir need help with bags?' the receptionist asked.

Nick shook his head, snatched his credit card and plastic oblong room key, and headed for the lifts, pausing briefly to pick up leaflets on a cat emporium and pop-up nightclubs from a rack. He didn't want them to think he was a complete nutter.

Minutes later, Nick looked out from a fifth-floor window at the back and felt like he was watching television with no sound; he could spot Tom from his confident poise, hairstyle and clothes, sitting in an armchair, side on, by a set of large French windows. Tom was holding what looked like a tumbler in one hand, his other jabbing the air as if to underline the points he was making. It wasn't possible to see who he was talking to, apart from two sets of stretched-out legs.

Both heavies were there.

As if on cue, a heavy suddenly came into full view as he walked over to Tom, making Nick instinctively shrink back even though he was sure they couldn't see him, as he'd been careful not to switch on the lights. The heavy was handing Tom a large sheet of paper, perhaps a map or a plan. Or maybe a spreadsheet. A few minutes passed and then Tom got up, letting the sheet slide to the floor as he stood with his back to the window, pressing his bum against the glass for a few seconds at a time. Perhaps he's listening to music, thought Nick. Or maybe he suffers from back pain. Looks like Pilates 101 from here. Tom sat and carried on sipping his drink, showing little interest in the sheet, which must still be on the floor next to his chair.

But after half an hour of this, the fly-on-the-wall novelty was wearing thin and Nick was bursting for a pee, though afraid of missing something. The risk was worth it, he thought finally, and went to relieve himself, returning to the window to see no change in the dull scene playing out before him. Bored out of his mind by now, he went to the mini-bar to look for beer and nuts, thinking he may as well eat what he could to file expenses like a proper private eye. As he bent down to break the thin plastic seal on the fridge that was under the desk, a loud knock on the door took him by surprise and he banged his head on the underside.

'Just a minute!' he shouted, and then looked through the glass hole in the door to get a fish-eye view of a well-built, bald man in a grey T-shirt. He was holding a thick folder of papers tightly to his chest. Next to him was a middle-aged blonde in a black-and-white pinny, looking from side to side as she clasped a phone. Ah ha. Bet our dizzy maid forgot to clean up properly and the boss wants to apologise and check all is well. No wonder she looks nervous with her job on the line, he smirked.

'Security. We need to check the room, if you don't mind,' the man said as Nick opened the door. Without waiting to be invited in, the man and maid stepped past him.

'Mind if we switch on the light, sir? It's a bit too dark to see properly. All on your own? Having a quiet one before the weekend?' the man continued in a chatty tone as he paced around the room without waiting for Nick to reply. The maid stayed silent by the door, still fingering her phone and giving him a tight smile during their brief eye contact.

After pushing aside the thin cotton curtain to look outside, the man went into the bathroom and turned the mixer tap on and off several times, nodding as if to show that all was fine before ticking a form inside his folder with a flourish. More annoyingly, he came right up to Nick, making him step backwards to maintain a buffer of personal space between them. 'You jumped-up, pen-pushing shit,' Nick thought with a polite smile.

'Hope you're enjoying the evening and our wonderful hotel facilities,' the man said. 'I know it's a shame there's not much of a view on this side, but you get the peace and quiet. Our team in reception would be delighted to help you with anything to make your stay here as comfortable as possible.'

'Well, thanks for that,' Nick replied curtly, making it obvious he wanted to end the conversation and the man gone.

Instead, the man approached him again but this time Nick was prepared and twisted aside to ease himself into the orange armchair next to the desk. The awkward silence between them was broken by a beep and a muffled, tinny voice: 'One, two three. Look mate, it's definitely working. The red light's flashing, see?' He had somehow switched on the recorder nestling in his underpants, replaying at full volume the facetious git in the shop who demonstrated how it worked. Nick's right hand moved to his crotch to turn the recorder off, but the maid's presence deterred him from unzipping his fly or putting a hand down his trousers. Without an alternative course of action he froze, open-mouthed.

'Think we'd better leave you to get on with it, sir,' the man said.

After the two had closed the door quietly behind them, Nick retrieved the recorder and threw it against the wall, sending batteries flying. Wearily, he went to the bathroom to splash cold water on his flushed face, and as he was about to lower his head into the sink he saw in the mirror that his wig was crooked, to reveal sweaty tufts of his own hair.

16

'AND ARE YOU TEMPTED BY any of the specials, Mr Director?' the short, fat, balding man asked his tall ginger-haired friend.

They had switched their phones to mute with near-synchronised precision before placing them inside their bespoke jackets. It was just past noon on a bright, midweek day though the heavy Victorian drapes with their tassels and glass beads dimmed much of the strong July sunlight, allowing table lamps to create a soft glow in the restaurant, as if it were still winter. The French waiter had already talked them through the *menu du jour*, with the short man fancying the sustainably farmed hake and organic purple carrots.

'The lamb shank with julienne of Suffolk veggies caught my eye,' the tall companion replied, glancing across the room to check if there was someone he recognised, especially within earshot. Nothing to worry about, only a sprinkling of patrons so far, and thankfully the two stuffed dalmatians with tiaras and pearls displayed in a large glass case formed an excellent if surreal sound barrier between them and the next table.

It had been a week since they'd met at the nearby club

to discuss postie business and the tall man was on edge, and twirling a wine glass with his thumb and index finger in a rhythmic, backwards-and-forwards motion.

'Not sure if I'm cut out for this director thing. I fear it will uncover nasty skeletons lurking in the cabinet, so to speak. There's always someone who enjoys resurrecting peccadilloes from the past to bring me down a peg or two,' the tall man said. He dunked a piece of sourdough bread in the shallow pool of very peppery olive oil and balsamic vinegar the waiter had decanted onto a plate in the centre of the table. Funny how two such delicious ingredients fail to blend for long, just like Posties packed into the same room, he thought. It was only a matter of time before sides are taken, that splits emerge.

'Come now. Why worry about little things like that?' The fat companion's words cut across the director's thoughts. 'Those sorts of people are just pissy chancers. The trick is to look them in the eye and not blink. Let's face it, everyone has something hidden if you rub their veneer long enough. How's the speech going?'

The tall man briefly held a dripping piece of bread in the air before popping it into his mouth, another sign of how he was thinking hard about something that must be important. After the waiter had taken their order, they resumed, lowering their voices and moving closer into confessional mode over their bread and wine.

The director outlined what he planned to say at his in-vestiture.

'Is that wise, Mr Director?' the plump man inquired after his friend had finished.

'Well, its a lot wiser than those Victorian dunces who

threw our predecessors out on the street. Though, let's face it, that got us off our arses to build this great cash machine of ours,' the tall man replied with a dismissive shake of the hand that just missed his companion's glass of rosé.

The arrival of food led to another pause in the conversation, giving them both a chance to look around the restaurant and check again who else was lunching. It was difficult to see properly in the soft lighting, the large chandeliers hanging low over several tables also obscuring faces.

'Does it need a polish?' the fat man asked finally.

'Bits here and there are admittedly a tad over the top. It could also do with a trim. You know how dreadfully short people's attention span is these days. Otherwise I think it reads fine,' his co-diner replied, looking a lot more relaxed.

'Oh no, not the speech, Mr Director. The cabinet. It probably needs a proper polish by now to look its best for the investiture. Not French polish, of course, this being England!' The fat man giggled.

'Very droll. As we discussed last time, Fry can take care of those practicalities. That young man is keen to learn and no doubt fancies himself as the next director, though I rather think he may be in for a fruitless wait,' the tall man said, using his knife and fork to tackle the lamb shank with rapid, surgical movements.

They chewed in silence, allowing the background piano music to wash over them as they occasionally swiped a finger over the screens of their phones, which were now back on the table, an unspoken code for how the meal was drawing to a close.

'You don't think we need to order a spanking new cabinet, do we? I know some directors have insisted on having one built in the traditional way to mark the occasion. You know, all that guff about transporting planks by canal and using home-made glue. Bertie's hand-me-down will do, won't it?' the thin man asked as they waited for double espressos and the bill to arrive. 'Personally, I think we should stick with what we've got and see what it's like after a bit of elbow grease. Isn't recycling fashionable these days? I'd best be off, and please keep me posted on Fry's arrangements.'

'Of course, Mr Director. No, I insist. I'll take care of this,' the fat man said, grabbing the bill and reaching for his wallet. 'They certainly do fish well here, but the desserts are nothing compared to Granny's apple pie.'

17

'*BONJOUR MADAME, ET BIENVENUE,*' the shop assistant greeted Elsie.

The assistant, who was standing just inside the department store's elegant, wrought-iron main entrance, wore a knee-length, navy dress that fitted like a glove underneath a white, embroidered apron tied round the waist with a neat double bow on her right hip. So elegant, Elsie thought. She entered the shop with its enormous art-nouveau stained-glass dome, glad to get away from the traffic and noise of the boulevard. She was facing a row of gleaming perfume and jewellery stalls, all beautifully laid out in a broad semi-circle. Everything sparkled or gleamed, a bit like how she wanted Christmas to be and a far cry from the faded paper chains she'd hung up in the living room a few weeks ago. She mused that France was doing nicely, despite having been invaded by the Jerries in the war, while poor old Blighty had barely ended rationing.

She'd been relieved to get off the ferry after a rough overnight passage from Dover, and thankfully the train onwards from Calais to Paris had been quiet enough to let the team catch up on sleep. They still had a few hours to kill after arriving at Gare du Nord at dawn. No point coming here too early, otherwise the big shops on Boulevard Haussmann would not have enough customers milling around like they did now. Mustn't stand out, she always warned the girls during these trips. At least she'd managed to stop them from drinking too much on the crossing to stop things getting messy if they lost concentration at the wrong moment. Don't want to look like a bunch of drunken tarts after a night on the tiles, or it could be a French police station for sleeping off the hangover.

Good. Timed to the minute, all five of them had strolled into the vast store using entrances along the boulevard and side streets, careful not to let on they knew each other. The team had talked through the plan for the last time half an hour ago, setting their watches at a smoky cafe four Metro stops away. It would be the same routine they'd used to good effect in Brussels last year. No need to change something that worked, Elsie reasoned. Well, apart from bigger panty pouches this time round and doubling up on knicker elastic as well, of course. There must be no repeat of Dolly's premature evacuation of two tins of caviar at Fortnum's.

'*Bonjour madame. S'il vous plait. Parfum? Chanel pour madame, peut-etre?*' a short, plump male assistant inquired, rising to the tips of his polished shoes to point a slim, uncapped glass vial at Elsie's heavily powdered nose.

'No, mercy,' she replied, waving her hand near his face a little too briskly as she moved to the next display, determined not to be diverted from a carefully timed plan. A few seconds could determine success or failure.

She looked around to check if the team was in place. Good, that was a relief. They couldn't linger too long without buying or moving on otherwise they'd raise suspicion. Elsie squeezed her left breast twice as if she was starting a bagpipe and it was only a few seconds before the screaming began as the first of 25 rats – she'd counted five into each team member's sack behind the pet shop before paying – were scurrying across the polished wooden floor, relieved to breathe fresh air after being cooped up under long skirts for an hour, where they'd tried nipping free from their canvas sacks.

'*La sortie, s'il vous plait!*' an assistant shouted and pointed to the exits, but few customers took notice and simply ran in any direction to avoid stepping on rats that were more interested in sniffing the displays than the customers. Elsie had already stuffed several bottles of perfume and pieces of jewellery down her panties and was back near an exit from where she could see Katie and Peg leaving through other doors, with Maggie already outside. They kept their distance from each other, pretending to be shocked.

Vera was missing.

The ground floor was nearly empty by now as two policemen ran in to see what the fuss was all about. The small plump assistant who'd plied Elsie with perfume was using a broom to check for rats behind the counters. It was then the Elsie saw Vera running up the wide, wooden staircase two steps at a time, chased by an assistant who stopped half-way up to take off her high-heeled shoes. By the time she resumed the chase, too much ground had been lost, with Vera already at the top and taking a bottle from under her skirt to throw at her pursuer, thankfully clipping the side of her head to break her stride.

Vera then ran from view.

'No way they'll be catching you now, darling. This

place is too big for that,' Elsie said under her breath and walked out onto the boulevard, discreetly checking her skirt in case anything was sticking out where it shouldn't be.

Lovely. All nice and ladylike.

The women, except for Vera, headed for the station and took the Metro back to Gare du Nord to hand over their haul to Stan from Plaistow, who was driving a lorryload of steel bars to London on the afternoon ferry.

'I think Vera will be OK. She knows how to handle herself does that one. I pity any bloke who rubs her the wrong way,' Elsie said as they sat down in a cafe two streets behind the railway station. The perfume and jewellery had already been dropped off with Stan, who bridled at having to sign an inventory.

'Bloody hell, was I glad to get rid of those rats. I can think of nicer things to keep me warm down there, I can tell you,' Peg said as she gulped down a large sugary coffee.

'Well, with what we got today, you can treat a barrow boy from Spitalfields market,' Maggie chipped in.

Elsie loved the banter after a job as it helped to deal with gripes, get rid of tension. But they would have to split up now and lie low for the rest of the day before meeting again outside a cafe by the station at nine o'clock to grab a bite and catch the train to Calais.

Elsie was feeling chirpy as the strong coffee kicked in, and now she had several hours to herself in the city, more than enough time to find a nice bit of felt for Frank. If she had the chance she might even nick some material for a kilt, though she wasn't sure what colour he'd like. Well, if he turned up his nose at it she could always flog it down the pub.

* * *

ELSIE BREATHED IN THE PARIS air with a smile as she walked over the stone bridge and looked across the grey Seine. She was relieved that the morning run had gone well, giving her time to herself in this wedding cake of a city before boarding the ferry back to London.

She hadn't told the team she was meeting up with Jeanne, from the Montparnasse ring.

From their first encounter they had hit it off well. It was in a West End court two years ago while waiting to be fined by the same pompous magistrate with thinning hair and crooked teeth. Since then they'd done each other favours, such as the advice Elsie gave on how best to escape from the Regent Street department stores if spotted pilfering. Jeanne had been a fount of knowledge about when the security guards take their coffee breaks in Printemps the last time the girls were in Paris, which meant they could fill their panty pouches in double-quick time. It had even crossed Elsie's mind whether the two rings should team up.

Best not to. Could get messy. And besides, it was only because Jeanne could speak a few words of English that they were able to strike up a friendship in the first place. Keep things sweet and simple, unlike her personal life.

Jeanne had offered to help get a nice bit of felt for Frank by doing all the talking with the assistant while Elsie got on with it in the shop. It would have been quicker to nab the stuff in London but she'd left things too late as Frank wanted the felt straightaway when she got back. No bad thing to keep him happy, but she would make sure the Posties knew it came from her, so they could put more jobs directly her way.

'How you, cherie? You finish, non?' Jeanne asked when Elsie arrived at the Deux Auteurs cafe tucked up a side street just south of the river, a favourite of the rougher locals. She always envied how slim and elegant Jeanne looked; it made her feel dowdy. The French, just like their capital, seemed to have survived the war unscathed, Elsie thought for the umpteenth time that day.

'We got what we wanted and nobody was caught. Bloody relief, I can tell you. Anyway, love, thanks for meeting up to help with the material,' she said, sitting down next to Jeanne, who had already finished a thimble-sized cup of silky dark coffee. Jeanne twitched a couple of fingers in the direction of the waiter to order two more. Even the hand signals were elegant in France, Elsie thought, smiling as she unfolded a small swatch of bottle-green felt to make doubly sure her French friend was crystal-clear about what she wanted.

'*Ciseaux* in *sac*,' Jeanne said, making criss-cross movements with her fingers and patting an oblong black leather handbag on her lap.

'Mercy beaucoups,' Elsie replied, and they both rattled with laughter, briefly turning the heads of two young men propping up the bar. She slipped a small bottle of perfume into Jeanne's hand, one of the more expensive ones taken from the department store that morning. Who knew when she might need help from her French friend again?

'And how is the *ami* with *grosses couilles*?' Jeanne asked, using her hands to outline a large ball near her crotch. She'd forgotten that Jeanne had met Frank down the Cock and Cardinal after they had appeared in court.

'Oh, he's OK. He's more of an acquaintance than a

friend really,' Elsie said, trying to make a distinction she immediately realized was probably too subtle for Jeanne's limited English to grasp. 'He's not the one that wants the material. It's for someone he knows,' she said, tapping her nose to signal that was all she could give away.

They sipped from their tiny cups, with Elsie relishing the taste of real coffee on her tongue. It was delicious after that disgusting chicory bilge she'd been forced to pour down her neck during the war and for months afterwards.

'*Bon*, we go. I know good place and *serveuse* who work there. All *commode*,' Jeanne said with a more work-like tone of voice. She paid for the coffees and stuffed the change inside her handbag which, Elsie noticed with a shocked expression, was mostly filled with a brick.

'*Sécurité, cherie.*' Jeanne winked and snapped the bag shut. They left the cafe and walked to the end of the street where they took a right down the boulevard Saint-Germain, arm-in-arm like two sisters off to mass.

18

FRANK STARED AT THE SACK of bones, bulked up with a couple of bricks to be on the safe side, which sank quickly out of sight to the bottom of the murky canal. A few inquisitive ducks and coots darted towards the circles that rippled outwards, but with no food in sight they lost interest and paddled away.

He was crouched down on the window sill to release the sack without a splash and avoid drawing attention; he continued biting his nails as he watched the patch of water in case the sack floated back up, but all he saw in the twilight were small bubbles breaking the surface. There was nobody on the towpath opposite to witness what he'd done.

'Tickety tock,' he said out loud, pleased at how he'd planned it all carefully, choosing this in-between time of day when the regulars who worked in nearby buildings had gone home – and too early for the night-time comings and goings between barges berthed further up near the storage depots. There wouldn't even be a fish in that freezing cesspit to poke its snout in the sack. The warehouse lights were switched off to prevent him standing out. The gramophone was silent.

With the bones disposed of, he gave a sharp grunt as he

grabbed the window frame for support to haul himself back up, his knees creaking. Breathing in the chilly evening air, he smiled at how the main evidence, your honour, was gone and Hope Wharf was spruced up testimony that all was going well. The Posties won't have room to complain about the job he was doing so far. Even if the cops called round this very moment, all they'd find would be vat of simmering glue. What would be unusual about that here in the beating heart of Britain's furniture industry?

Ah, if only he were a carpenter himself. A respectable enough trade, but no point in him hankering after all that, even though he was still young enough to train. Besides, it was all going to the bleeding dogs. So much for that fresh start after the war. It was all about the rag trade now, and he wouldn't have a hope in hell of getting a job in that line of business. With the Jews moving to north London for a better life, the Indians were filling their shoes and opening sewing shops. It made sense to stick with the Posties – well, until they got rid of him.

Let's see if they ever would.

Satisfied that the bones would be staying on the bottom of the canal, he stepped back inside, closed the shutters and picked up the instructions. The next step was to separate the whites from the yolks of dozens of eggs they'd delivered the day before. He was finding it harder to read the words as prolonged exposure to steam from the vat had made the ink run and cardboard sag. Mix egg whites into glue liquor. He had no idea why or what it would do, thinking it was such a shame he couldn't have a fry-up. Ladling the whites into the simmering, stinky mix reminded him of school-dinner ladies doling out custard. He stirred the glue for several minutes, his tensed arm aching slightly in its awkward position as he avoided touching the hot metal sides. Using a large wooden stick, he scraped every part of the vessel's inside to make sure the whites were mixed in thoroughly. It was like his granny making piccalilli, her chest pressed against a big metal pot into which she spooned turmeric powder that turned the onions yellow and made him sneeze.

In some ways he was glad she was no longer alive to see what he'd become.

The glue was becoming clearer and more syrupy, slowing down his stirring while sparking a growing pride in a job well done. 'Turn off heat when liquor thick as honey. Burn instructions': he read the final line out loud with a flourish. So far so good then, he thought, scrunching up the damp cardboard and dropping it onto the burner, where it crackled into ashes.

'Tickety tock.' He looked round the room as if hoping for a pat on the back.

He went into the main part of the warehouse to stretch his legs and swing his arms to ease the tension from all the stirring. The Posties would come to check the place in a few hours' time, and make sure all was fine.

Not that he expected any snags.

They hadn't tried messing with him yet, though just as well that he had his 'insurance policy', as he liked to think of the snaps he'd taken of the director all dolled up in a blonde wig, black dress and nylons, chatting away with a couple of rent boys at the exact spot where Frank was standing.

Bloody ponce, he thought, looking up to the ledge near the ceiling where he'd crouched in the dark while the pansies partied below, all off their faces on champagne and thankfully unaware of him. Granted, the snaps were a bit grainy as he couldn't use a flash bulb, but the faces were clear enough for anyone round here to recognize. Wonder why they didn't have sex? Maybe the director just wanted company. And it wasn't his Vera Lynn records they played that night but big band music. A bit of swing was perfect for drowning out the camera clicks, though. Doing his Cecil Beaton act was the biggest risk he'd ever taken, but did he really have a choice? Soon nobody would care tuppence about him and his balls, and he had to find a way to bring in money. Working for the Posties was his best bet, because Woolworths wasn't going to hire a shop assistant who wore a kilt.

He'd kept the snaps in his jacket for weeks, wondering what the hell to do with them. Until the afternoon he was down the Cock and Cardinal, that is. He did get lucky sometimes, after all. There he was having a quiet pint, when the landlord, all panicky, ran over and nodded frantically towards the back, saying the father of some south London mobster was dead on the crapper.

'Not pretty, is it?' the landlord said, after Frank had squeezed his head round the toilet door after it had been forced open.

'Stinks to high heaven as well, but don't pull the chain. Leave everything as it is,' Frank had advised, pinching his nose to stop himself gagging.

'What the fuck do we do?' the landlord asked. 'His lot will blame me and burn the place down.'

'Shut it. Let's leave the cops out of this for now. Go and tell the Posties to come over quick,' he told the landlord, who ran out the door like a whippet, grateful to be doing something. It was then that Frank had fished out a couple of negatives and three of the best prints from his jacket pocket, shoving them inside the dead man's coat. He fought back a dry retch as his hand brushed the man's warm but definitely still chest, and then stood guard outside the door, puffing on a fag to mask the smell until the postie minders arrived, looking inquiringly at him.

'You did well, Frank. You did very well,' one of them whispered in his ear after inspecting the body. Frank had already told them about the photos which, from the corner of his eye, he could see were being stuffed by the other minder into a bag. 'I think the director is going to be grateful,' the minder next to Frank said with a long, hard look. 'Very grateful, Frank. And he'll be even more grateful if you keep what you've seen to yourself. We haven't seen those pictures, have we?'

'Of course not. Nobody wants to be upsetting the director,' Frank replied, trying to sound calm while his stomach churned. 'Things aren't so easy for me these days, as everyone round here knows' – glancing down at his groin in case the man missed the hint. 'Regular work from the Posties would put food on the table, and I'd be more than happy to oblige. We all like to help each round here, don't we?'

Funny how that brief chat had saved his bacon, Frank thought as he paced round the warehouse. And here he was earning his way in the world, and nothing was going to stop him. The place was silent apart from bubbles plopping slowly on the glue's viscous surface. He went back to the side room to turn off the burner under the vat and allow the liquid to cool and solidify.

Time for a brew.

While waiting for the kettle to boil, he bent down to wind the gramophone for a burst of Vera before the minders dropped by. Chuckling softly, he thought how this had probably been the oddest job he'd done so far for them. Still, he learned something new from each task they sent his way.

19

NICK WAS GLAD TO SEE his front door again.

He'd chucked the wig in a dustbin on the high street, but the recorder, not irreparably damaged from its collision with the bedroom wall, had been reassembled and tucked away in his pocket, and switched off properly this time. The hotel manager had cheerfully confirmed what Nick already realized: there were no security checks that evening and no maid fitted the description Nick had given. No doubt hoping for repeat business, the manager had whispered about chat rooms on the internet that specialised in maids in frilly aprons, with special deals on weekday afternoons, apparently.

Back inside his flat, all he wanted was a long, hot bath to wash away his sweaty embarrassments and settle in for a quiet night. He turned on the taps and poured in the last sachet from a six-pack of pink bubble bath his aunt had given him for Christmas. No idea what went through that woman's mind. Soon, there was a cushion of satisfyingly dense foam built up on top of the steaming water and he looked forward to sliding underneath, the bubbles hiding his paunch while he contemplated his lot in life before the inevitable, slippery wank.

He stripped, dumped the clothes in the hallway, fetched a bottle of Chablis from the wine cooler in the kitchen and grabbed a clean glass from the dishwasher. On his way back to the bathroom he noticed clumps of dirt and gravel on the parquet. Must have a word with the cleaner before I pay him, he thought, frowning.

With the taps turned off, he slid through the foam into the water, his toes and bum tingling as heat rose through his body. He massaged his balls and let rip a cathartic fart to help build up a mental buffer between himself and the hotel. The cold wine trickling down his parched throat was equally calming. Good. Life was returning to a comforting, even keel. He heard his mobile ringing in the hallway, muffled by the clothes piled on top of it.

Julie could wait.

He topped up his glass and tried hard to muster raw hate towards Tom, but failed as the wine began working its peachy anaesthetic. He went over what had happened in the hotel which left him envious, once again, at how Tom went about the world with such poise and control.

'Know-all fucking twat!' Nick shouted at the top of his voice, flicking a wodge of foam at the black marbled wall.

After pouring himself another glass of wine, he closed his eyes and tried to conjure up an erotic scene but, worryingly, all that his mind's eye could see was Tom rubbing his arse against the French windows, his own special way of telling Nick to go fuck himself. And Julie could take a run and jump, too? Or was he simply over interpreting things, letting his emotions get in the way? Then again…

The loud bang of the front door slamming froze his train of thought, and he sat bolt upright in the bath, heart pounding, the combination of wine and heat making his head swirl. He stayed still, listening hard for footsteps or other giveaway sounds of an intruder, but heard nothing. Jesus. Here he was, a sitting duck for the second time that day, this time butt-naked and with no phone.

He put his glass of wine down on the floor and grabbed the near-empty wine bottle by its neck as he hauled himself out of the bath, trying to keep calm. He remembered a neighbour being stabbed to death by a burglar a few years back. It was only the smell of his corpse that alerted everyone.

'Get out now. I have a weapon!' he shouted, trying hard not to slur as he clasped the bottle like a mallet. 'I said get out now. The police are on the way.'

Silence, apart from the faint sound of a siren that came and went.

He stepped onto the bath mat and yanked open the door to find the hallway empty apart from his clothes, which were still piled up in the same place and emitting a beep – a voicemail waiting to be played.

Walking slowly towards the living room, he left a trail of wet footprints and limp bubbles on the wooden floor. There was nobody in there, and the French windows that looked out onto the balcony were all shut, just as he'd left them. No sign of anyone in the kitchen or spare room either. All was tidy, no drawers pulled out or papers strewn across the floor like those reconstructions on the TV crime show.

That left his own bedroom, whose door was ajar.

'I've called the police. I'm warning you. I have a weapon!' he shouted, this time with a bit more confidence and gruffness in his voice. He kicked open the door and saw straight away that it too was largely tidy and empty of intruders. The French windows were also closed, with no sign of anyone having entered or fled.

Maybe someone was hiding in the wardrobe? He clasped the bottle harder with one hand and yanked one of the doors open with the other. Empty, but the force exerted caused the wardrobe to rock back and forth and eject a leather handbag and a high-heeled shoe onto the floor. Bloody Amanda's stuff.

He willed his breathing to slow down, causing his shoulders and paunch to sag as he realized how much he was shaking; the remaining bubbles slid down his legs and popped on the parquet. He threw the empty wine bottle at the bed, where it smashed to pieces. Stunned, he managed to jump out of the way just in time to avoid flying shards. He saw that under the scrunched up sheets there was something long and obviously hard. Yanking them off sent even more green shards across the room and revealed a freshly painted City of London bollard, its slim, shiny black body and white cap reminding him of that fountain pen he lost on a stag weekend in Amsterdam. But there was no gold nib here, only a blob of crumbly concrete flecked with dried soil. Stuck on the cap was a yellow Post-it note with elegant handwriting in black ink.

II

1

TED WAS A CARPENTER AND proud of it.

It was a job even the Good Lord's Son had turned his hand to between miracle-making and getting on the nerves of Roman emperors. And now, ten years after he'd done his bit for king and country to defeat the Jerries, he knew instinctively he was at the top of his game.

Not even those pea-souper fogs that often shrouded the street he'd made home since the war ended could cloud his appreciation for a skilfully carved joint. Of wood, that is. The Sunday roast was best left to the wife. Carpentry was work, a calling even, that had led him to Shoreditch like a mouse to cheese. He'd heard the place was big in furniture, a real Mecca for the ambitious woodworker, and therefore more than enough to excite this demobbed northerner. And already hitched with a sweetheart from Ealing, the East End was far enough from the in-laws for a quiet life. Well, most of the time anyway.

Truth be told, assembling cheap sofas for the masses was not really his idea of a vocation, but he had to start climbing the career ladder somewhere. Trouble was, as he silently lamented on Sunday nights, there was no sign of moving up to the next rung to put his top-notch chiseling to more rewarding use.

'It'll happen, pet,' his understanding wife Lizzie would tell him.

He almost felt spiritual when he saw planks. Tracing the grain with his index finger would be enough to set his pulse up a notch and make his hands itch for a saw. He'd suggested to the wife going back up north to set up his own workshop in the Dales, but she was probably right, who knows what would become of it, and giving up guaranteed cash in hand every Friday wasn't for the faint-hearted. Besides, she would have to give up that cleaning job with the Smethwicks in Highgate, whose generous Christmas stocking was a godsend each year.

And so it went, year after year, making sofas and their matching chairs while doing the odd bit of bespoke cabinetmaking or mortise and tenon joinery for friends, and friends of friends, to make ends meet, to add a bit of spice to life, to keep alive the hope of better things.

His big break may have arrived.

It wasn't quite in the way he'd expected. Still, never say no, his dad would always counsel. Wise words from a man that didn't make it past fifty. Ted felt this opportunity was nothing short of divine intervention by Yorkshire's famous carpenter, perhaps the most famous carpenter of all – well, apart from the Good Lord himself, of course. Yes, none other than Thomas Chippendale, who had also beaten a path to London all those years ago. Even his workmates were asking that week why he was smiling and whistling on his tea break. Was the wife finally with child, they wondered out loud.

Lady Luck had turned up last Tuesday at half past five

in the afternoon, just as he was knocking off from work and walking out of the factory gate into Hackney Road. She came up to him, all friendly. Not bad-looking either, though a bulky skirt hid her legs. He'd noticed her before a few times but never to exchange a word – not something a respectable married man would do without an introduction.

'Ted, love, I'm Elsie, a friend of Brian from work,' she explained as they continued walking down the street. 'Looks like I might have a nice carpentry job lined up for you if you're interested. All cash on the side of course, but not a word to anyone.'

He perked up instantly as she continued talking.

'Let's just say someone high up is ready to pay good money for a posh cabinet. Only one thing, though – it has to be made with the stuff they give you. They want you to use their wood, glue and lining and all that. Don't ask me why, but saves you having to get the stuff yourself, I suppose.'

She went on, 'Anyway, it's got to look like something from that Chipsdon bloke Brian says you know all about. The director wants something nice and solid that can be handed down over the years if need be, and not like that rubbish in Hoxton market.' She nodded her head northwards in disdain.

He was keen. Very keen, he told her. This was a chance to impress the right people and show off his handiwork, that he was more than a sofas-for-the-masses man, but she wasn't in much of a mood to listen once she'd delivered her message. Back in touch in a week's time, she said, turning to walk in the direction they'd come from, while holding her stomach carefully with her right hand.

'Blimey, hope she's not ill. Don't want to lose the job before I start,' he thought as he watched her go.

It was as if all the stars had finally lined up in the firmament: a customer that wanted Chippendale. That's class. And it would be made by a Yorkshireman too. He could still remember the moment he first saw Chippendale's book of cabinet drawings, its original date of publication still seared in his memory: 1754. Who'd have thought that almost exactly two hundred years later, he'd be using those copperplate engravings to turn planks into perfection, and earn himself a bit of cash to please the missus.

On his way home he decided not to plump for one of Chippendale's more exotic Chinese, Gothic or French cabinets. Didn't feel right. He would make one of the classics. This was England after all, and we won the war. Sounds like this director chap was partial to a bit of tradition, wanting to use old-fashioned glue, just like the Yorkshire master himself would have all those years ago. The thought of making a Chippendale cabinet cheered him up so much that he almost forgot to buy that tin of corned beef for his supper. With the wife working late, he could study his book of engravings undisturbed. Deep down he felt she'd never really shown much interest in his career, but the extra cash should stretch to a day trip to Margate. That would put him in her good books.

Later that evening, after his supper, he placed one of the kitchen chairs next to the bookshelf that ran along the back wall of the living room. Standing on the chair he could reach the top shelf where he kept his special volume wrapped in brown paper.

Sitting at the living-room table he'd made himself, he

turned to the first page which, for him, summed up what working with wood was all about. The cabinetmaker of all cabinetmakers had wisely written that his designs were 'calculated to improve and refine the present taste, and suited to the fancy and circumstances of persons in all degrees of life'. He liked that last bit most of all. Sounded a bit commie, but coming from Yorkshire, Chippendale was truly a carpenter for all men and not just the hoity-toity. Ted was so happy when Elsie had told him outside the factory that they wanted the cabinet in the style of Chippendale. No idea who this director was, of course, but he obviously had a civilised mind.

And to think he would be making the cabinet here in Shoreditch, England's capital of furniture. The coincidence was downright uncanny.

He got up to pull the curtains and switch on the standard lamp to examine the engravings and their detail more easily. With a steaming mug of tea at his elbow, he began leafing through *The Gentleman and Cabinet-Maker's Director.* Glancing at the clock, he knew it would be a while yet before the wife would be home; plenty of time to find the perfect cabinet. He was chomping at the bit to get started.

2

NICK WOULD SLEEP ON THE sofa that night.

He'd left the bollard undisturbed on his bed like a body waiting for the forensics. Shards from the smashed wine bottle were still scattered across the floor, like a car-crash scene, with one of Amanda's handbags, and high-heeled shoe resting on its side, making it all the more realistic. All that was missing was blood.

A symphony by one of his favourite composers was at near-full volume, a long piece of pulsating orchestral and electronic chords whose clean, precise and repetitive rhythms were balm to his unsettled inner self.

The bollard on the bed had filled his thoughts for hours with bile and anger. Nick read again the Post-it note he was about to scrunch up and chuck against the wall: 'Does the taxman know about Geneva? Leave the Posties alone or the Director will be angry. Sleep tight x,' it read.

Had they really been able to hack into his Swiss bank account? He doubted it. No, they must have found out about the money in some other way. A bank statement from a rubbish bag perhaps? Should shred them like sensible people do. And who the hell was the director?

He kicked an empty takeaway curry container that was

on the floor, making it fly awkwardly to the other side of the room, sending gobs of congealed ghee in its slipstream. He went over to the armchair by the French windows. From here he liked to stare into the middle distance of sky and the many new towers that had sprouted across the city. He looked down on the railway track that threaded its way through Shoreditch, the trains having long stopped running for the night. The music drowned out the hum of traffic and, apart from the bollard on his bed, the only intrusion was the occasional flash of blue light bouncing off windows of nearby buildings when an ambulance or police car sped down the high street.

Nick felt most alive at this hour, especially after coming home from dinner or drinks, hoping to glimpse a skinny fox sniffing round the wheelie bins or, far more rarely, catch a graffiti artist finishing off a work before slipping into the darkness to nurse dreams of becoming the next Banksy or, at the very least, become the backdrop to a fashion shoot or pop video. Bless. Few merited a detour for selfie-obsessed tourists on guided walks these days.

True, as the Post-it note said, there was still a pile of dosh in his Geneva account, parked after his depressingly lonely stint at a private bank with its unrestricted view of the famous water jet. He'd lasted three long, dull years by which time even the obscenely high pay packet and bonuses had failed to dull the acute social sterility. What the fuck was the note going on about? Her Majesty's Revenue and Customs knew all about the cash. Even his accountant had given up asking if he wanted a tax-efficient wrapper for it. Well, the only wrapper he wanted was for his dick in bed, and fat chance of needing one these days given that his social life revolved round getting pissed with Julie.

Of course.

Tom must have found out about his stash of Swissies from Julie. He realized how much the girl knew about him, just as he probably knew more about her than Tom did. It was all bluff, of course. The crafty little shit was trying to put the wind up him, which in a way he had by entering the flat, violating his fort.

Nick swiped his phone to check for emails; still nothing from the consultancy. Could be another week or two, he thought. He never tired of not having to put up with a twatty boss ever again. His wage-slave friends would wonder how he still kept his sense of self at his age and not end up an afternoon lush watching repeats of Judge Judy. Well, he'd give that existential conundrum some deep thought over his next mid-morning coffee at Jimmy's, had been the stock reply. So their own sense of worth had more hinterland than a monthly payslip? Some mistake, surely.

His eyes locked onto a postcard left on a pile of takeaway menus. It had been there for weeks and was from his sister in Manchester, inviting him up again. A nice old-fashioned touch in an age of emails and texts, he thought, but there would be no trips up north just yet. They always ended up being an inquisition into what she called his commitment-free life. No. He'd deal with family another time. The shoe and handbag on the bedroom floor was also a reminder of how he really must ditch Amanda properly, first and foremost. And then he could move on. Maybe he'd rediscover his mojo and get back to the time when not every idle thought turned into long, silent rants. And what should he do about this stupid charade with Julie and Tom that he'd been sucked into? Time to quit and leave them to it? But he owed her one. She'd been a lifeline to him these past few months by helping him get over Amanda.

He sank into the armchair to let the music wash over him as he surveyed the urban landscape. What's the next step after the embarrassment in the hotel and the bollard on his bed? Don't all great detectives go back to square one when they're stuck? That meant trying to find out more about Gingernuts from the sauna who chatted with Tom in the cubicle. The bloke must be a regular there given how familiar he was with the place, no doubt mixing pleasure with a bit of business. But why drag Tom there? Why not discuss things over dinner? A bit of old-fashioned power play, perhaps. Trouble was, there was no hope in hell of tailing Tom in that place without the two heavies butting in, literally. No, it was time to reel in a whopping, long overdue favour. Like at the consultancy, it was all about outsourcing grunt work to a third party. Smiling, he moved to the sofa, turned down the music and wriggled under a blanket. The lights were kept on low as he knew that in the dark, even the faintest click or creak would set his heart racing after his brush with that trespassing postie turd.

3

ELSIE WAS IN FINE FETTLE after her trip to Paris.

The return crossing had been smooth enough for her to spend the early hours of that morning out on deck, smoking the occasional cigarette while staring across the sea as waves buffeted the hull. The team shared stories and ideas in the bar for future trips; they were told more than once by the stewards to pipe down.

Ah, nothing like a bit of zest for life, she thought. Not felt enough like that lately. How travel lifted her spirits, helping her forget about being single. That is, until she reached home to an empty bed and wondered how to dispense her topped up vim.

Stan had left the jewellery and perfume in the basement of the furniture factory on Hackney Road, with some of the haul already delivered to customers. After a short nap, she'd treated herself to a steaming plate of cottage pie at the greasy spoon on the high street. Beats French cafes any day. All three pairs of her working panties had been washed and were now drying on the line out the back. 'Everyone deserves a day off,' she told herself while eating.

A couple of yards of top-quality bottle-green felt lay folded in the bottom of the shopping bag she was now carrying as she left the cafe to walk past the railway station and up towards the canal. It was best to hand it over to Frank at the warehouse, out of sight. Hope the place didn't stink like last time. It had almost made her gag. She needed a proper talk with him as well, and without staring at his balls. It was a bit like her Uncle Albert, with a glass eye. Not gawping was almost impossible after a while, especially after a few drinks. Shame Frank was that way. She could remember the first time he caught her eye, a well built, chirpy lad busy behind the counter at Woolworths. Just look at him now, what a difference. Well, at least he'd been able to sow a few wild seeds.

The canal was quiet and still when she stuck her head round the side of the wharf for a peek, apart from ducks zigzagging towards her in the hope of bread. She couldn't remember if she'd even eaten duck, let alone what it tasted like. Not that she often cooked a roast on Sundays. Being alone, a ciggy and a sugar sarnie was just the ticket.

She studied the warehouse for a few seconds, noticing the poor state it was in, the brickwork puckered and in sore need of repointing. The filthy windows, set behind rusted bars, could also do with repair and painting. It survived the Blitz but at some cost, though not as much as the building next door, which had been bombed to smithereens, the rubble shrouded in weeds. Wrong place, wrong time, just like poor old Uncle William.

She knocked on the door and after a short wait it opened just wide enough for Frank to pop his balding, cropped head round, and beckon her in without a word.

'Well I never. The wanderer returns,' he said after closing the door with a smile whose toothy warmth caught her off-guard. Automatically, she straightened her skirt and patted her hair. She could see he'd been relaxing in his armchair, a mug of tea on the floor next to it. A few 78s were out of their brown-paper sleeves and scattered round the gramophone.

'Hard at it, are we, love?' she asked with a raised eyebrow. 'I must say the place looks clean and tidy. What's that smell? Have you been cooking a stew to keep the frost off your chest?'

She could see how tired he was when he stopped smiling. Poor sod must have been cooped up in this dump for days by now, and still no sign of any work done on the cabinet. He's probably worried the bleeding Posties will start complaining and find someone else to run and fetch for them.

'I hope they appreciate all this hard work you're doing for them,' she said, dipping into her bag to bring out the felt and hand it to him.

'Thanks, Elsie. I'll make sure the Posties cough up, double-quick. Nothing for me from Paree, then?' He spoke only half in jest as he walked over to the large slatted windows on the canal side and opened one to let in wafts of cold winter air. He looked down on the murky water, checking for the fifth or sixth time that day the spot where he'd dumped the bones. Good. Nothing to worry about. He lit the gas ring under the kettle to make fresh tea and invited Elsie to sit down in the armchair.

'I might have something else for you, but it depends whether a regular will buy it. A girl has to put food on her table,' she said coyly, her head cocked to one side as she tried reading the record labels from her upright position in the armchair.

He flashed another warm, toothy smile in her direction before spooning tea leaves into the chipped blue enamel teapot.

'That reminds me, business first. Did you get hold of Ted? The glue's ready for the cabinet, the wood's arrived, and now he's got the felt. Bloody time he got on with it or else they'll be blaming me if it's late,' he said, pouring boiled water onto the leaves, the steam rising high into the chilly air before vanishing.

Sitting next to her on a stool, he leaned over to pour her a mug of tea and picked up his own off the floor to top it up.

'Oh, Ted's keen, believe me, she said. 'I tell yer, I couldn't shut him up once I offered him the job. He kept going on and on about chips and rails, or whatever that carpenter bloke's called. As Brian said, you just want to put a sock in it when he drivels on about cabinets. I made it clear to him that he'll have to keep it quiet, not a dicky-bird to the missus or anyone else. And he's got to make it here, away from nosy parkers.'

As she sipped her tea she glanced sideways to notice how his face was fuzzy with at least two days' stubble. All man, she thought. And he was in a good mood as well. She was close enough to work her right hand up his kilt if she wanted to. She blushed and looked away to sip her tea. That mound between his legs was such a magnet. To occupy her thoughts she began using her index finger to trap bits of limescale that were floating on top of her tea.

'You going to put some music on then?' she asked, surveying the records. The whole bloody lot were so old-fashioned, stuff from the war that her mother would have liked. No chance of Elvis hiding under that lot.

'Do you trust Ted to keep his mouth shut?' he asked. 'The last thing I need is him blabbing about his job on the side.'

'Oh, don't worry, Frank. Ted will be OK,' she said. 'He's keen but harmless, and he won't mess things up for you. I made sure Brian will stop him shooting his mouth off about nice little earners. That's enough about him. How about you? You coming down the Cock tonight to cheer us all up?' She lightly pinched his exposed, hairy left knee.

'Nice to be invited. Thought you'd have found yourself a poncy boyfriend in Paris to entertain you girls.' He looked straight into her eyes with a smile; it was the flirty man from Woolworths again.

'Nah. You can't rely on them foreigners. I like my men from the East End,' she said, sliding her hand a couple of inches up his kilt to lightly tickle his thigh as the smell of his spicy cologne seemed to get stronger.

'We all know that, Elsie,' he said in a hoarse whisper. 'How about you putting Vera on the gramophone while I close the shutters. We don't want to be frightening the ducks now, do we?'

4

'WELL, RUMOUR HAS IT THAT back in the old days they used human bones to make glue for a director's cabinet once in a while. Even as late as the 50s. Complete tosh, of course. I'm reliably informed that such twaddle was simply Chinese whispers among our more senile members.' The short, fat balding man was telling this to his tall thin friend, by turns smiling and shaking his head as he spoke.

They were sitting in dark-brown leather armchairs opposite each other in the club's refurbished creative zone where phones were discouraged to aid 'spontaneous ideation and thought leadership', the anaemic looking receptionist had explained on their way in. There appeared to be little thinking going on, though fortunately there was plenty of blue sky flooding the interior with unbroken sunshine on this quiet, late afternoon. They'd overhead someone chirp that the place was dead because of a big media bash in Soho. Good. They could hear themselves talk.

'I remember Bertie mentioning something about glue while showing me that god-awful cabinet before I became director. "One day all this may be yours, if you're un-lucky",' the tall man said in what he took to be an East End barrow-boy accent. 'The cheeky little shit. Who'd have believed that he of all people ended up telling the truth for once? Well, now I've got to find somewhere to put the bloody thing.'

The fat man smiled in sympathy as he sipped a very peaty whisky, his plump, hairy fingers caressing the cut-glass tumbler to make the ice cubes clink. 'Why can't we have a silver tankard like the Rotary? Or even,' the fat man said, pausing to control his giggling, 'a gilded bollard on a plinth!'

They laughed so loudly that even the barman looked up from his phone.

But truth be told, the new director did actually feel a twinge of guilt when poking fun at the cabinet. People had gone to strange lengths to become its custodian, as his father had often alluded to when he was alive. It was like inheriting a hideous vase from an aunt: you felt a duty to find a spot for it somewhere, even if only out of respect, and a reluctance to tempt fate.

'It's not a bad stick of furniture, though not that original Chippendale passed on from director to director during 20s and 30s of course. That one got burned to a cinder. Shame, really. It would have been worth a bob or two by now.' The tall man spoke wistfully. He mused, as he had done on several occasions over the past few days, on the irony of it all. Honouring their shit-poor forefathers with a stick of furniture that would have never graced the four walls of an Old Nichol tenement. What a load of schmaltz as they say over the pond. The early Posties were never a sentimental bunch wedded to heritage. No, heritage is a preoccupation for the rich. For Posties it was all about revenge. Brick by brick. Well, an Englishman's home is his castle, after all, and they had certainly taken that to heart after what they went through. And who gives a toss about a scratched piece of reproduction furniture? He still twitched while recalling a mobster from south London referring to Posties in a theatrical whisper as the 'pie and mash mafia'. Well, that cheap shot was definitely logged, as they say.

'You know, regarding these directorship handovers, I can't help getting a little misty-eyed. Tell me, how old were you when you had your tattoo?' The small fat companion sensed that his friend needed coaxing gently back to planet earth.

'Oh, around sixteen, like most of us. I felt a bit silly, to be honest. All that baring your arse in the back of a shop. Felt like a cow being branded.'

'Well, you're a little less shy about exposing the *arrière* these days, if I may say so,' the small man teased. 'Anyway, I thought Fry did a lovely job with the investiture ceremony the other evening. It all went rather well and, of course, Mr Director, your speech was splendid. Simply magnificent. I thought your reference to Bertie's scar was the perfect heartwarming anecdote to round it all off.'

'Thank you. And I agree,' the tall man said. 'Fry certainly pulled out all the stops. Those jellied-eel canapés were delicious, though I noticed the younger Posties weren't too impressed. They don't know what's good for them. Speaking of Thomas, I understand he's having a spot of bother with a rather inquisitive non-P. Would you be able to look into that? The sticky beak may need a little special chiseling, as they say?'

'Consider it done, Mr Director. Ah, finally, the barman's on his way. Same again?'

5

TED TURNED THE KEY IN the door of Hope Wharf, his hand shaking with trepidation. He'd wanted to cut and assemble the cabinet on his own bench in the backyard at home, but Elsie insisted that was out of the question. Working from the warehouse was part of the deal – if he wanted to be paid, that is. She wasn't someone Ted felt he should cross.

He'd been standing outside the wharf for a few minutes to pluck up enough courage to let himself in. What unnerved him was the silence that hung over the grubby building. He'd glimpsed the canal as he approached, a sliver of nearly still, narrow, dirty water bordered by a silent towpath. Wisps of mist above the water compounded the sense of isolation that was more in keeping with the moors of Yorkshire than the capital of England.

Ted pushed open the door and turned on the light using a switch on the left-hand wall, as Elsie had hurriedly explained. He placed his heavy bag of tools on the stone floor and surveyed what would be his workplace for the coming week, including a few evenings, no doubt. Everywhere was scrubbed and tidy as it if were someone's home. None of the sawdust, blobs of grease, or offcuts of wood that littered a living workshop.

The workbench was in the exact centre of the main room, directly under a skylight that let in the weak, Monday-morning wintry light. Planks and other sections of wood were neatly stacked at one end of its dust-free, chipped surface, a tightly wrapped bundle of green felt at the other. In the middle were two large hammers and a mallet, all new and fanned out like a trident. In the smaller, adjoining room Ted saw several glue pots lined up on the floor, ready for heating up. There was a pot already resting on the burner and a box of matches beneath it with a matchstick poking out, its red tip ready for striking. An armchair was pushed up against the wall with a gramophone placed next to it on the floor, a stack of 78s neatly piled on its closed lid. The trumpet pointed downwards, as if in mourning.

Such a relief there was no sign of Frank.

Elsie had explained how to get hold of him if there was a hitch. How that man gave him the willies! They'd never exchanged a word in all the years Ted had been living in Shoreditch, but then again most people steered clear of him, and that wasn't because of the man's condition but the company he kept – or rather kept him – as Brian whispered down the pub when Frank was sitting alone a few yards from them, sipping a pint of stout.

Ted returned to the main room where he examined the large slatted windows, with sunlight seeping through cracks in the frame. He raised the latch to open one of the windows and let in air and more light to dispel a vague sense of claustrophobia, helping him to breathe more calmly.

'Right. To work then,' he said out loud, to break the silence and lift his spirits.

He pulled the drawing for the cabinet out of his bag and, after putting the felt, hammers and wood on the floor, unfolded it across the bench to catch the light from above, making him feel like a surgeon about to operate. They wanted the cabinet done by the end of the week and Ted had made it clear to Elsie that he was not happy about that. 'This is Chippendale we're talking about here, love,' he warned her flatly. 'Quality, not quantity. There won't be enough hours in a week to get the job done properly.'

'You'll finish it, Ted,' she snapped back. 'No need to fret. Nobody in the factory will be asking where you are. Just get it finished, and think of the fivers coming your way on Friday.' She walked off before he could think of a reply, let alone dare deliver it. Rather have my goolies trapped in this vice than upset her, he thought, picking up a plank off the floor to make a start.

As he gently rubbed the grain with his thumb, he felt himself connect with something deep, prompting him to hum and banish that sense of unease. Yes, he certainly knew what passed muster when it came to making cabinets. Such a shame the wife would be working late at the Smethwicks on Friday. They must be wanting the place spick and span for another of their fancy dinner parties at the weekend. He wanted her to have a quick peek at the finished work before handing it over to Frank. It would make both of them feel proud.

He'd boned up on Chippendale for the past few evenings, rekindling his spiritual affinity with the great man. The parallels with his own life were downright scary: the master had also been a Yorkshireman who'd come to London to perfect his trade, albeit three hundred years ago.

True, he himself had yet to make a lasting impression on the public with his own joinery, but here was his chance to shine, to impress the right people. Who knows what it may lead to. More orders, hopefully. Perhaps running his own workshop eventually. He took out his pencil, gave it a lick and began marking the wood with bold strokes. At his feet the fretsaw was ready, its shiny new blade taut.

6

HARRY TRIMM WAS ANYTHING BUT, as he could barely see the tips of his red trainers when he looked down at the floor. Most of his hair had disappeared long ago, the remaining active follicles having migrated south to his nostrils and ears; he used battery-powered clippers in front of the bathroom mirror to prune the promiscuous little bastards each week.

As a long-haired young man back in the 1970s, he'd been a popular regular at the San Francisco bar just down from Shoreditch Town Hall. Ah, he could still remember that place as if it were yesterday, squeezing his way through a crowd of sweaty, leather bears down in the basement where a constant drip of warm condensation rained from the low ceiling onto his head. Sadly, the place was closed now, no doubt reflecting progress of sorts, as back-street pubs with their blacked-out windows and kick-proof doors made way for bars with large, clear glass frontages. The metaphor was blindingly obvious, of course, but it was still a sad moment when he discovered that the San Fran had morphed into a co-operative cafe with nothing steamier than a pricey latté.

Still, at 74 years old, his clubbing days were probably over, given that he was usually tucked up in bed by ten with half his teeth in a tumbler. He had his circle of friends, some of whom lived only a few streets away, who helped to ease the loss of Jeff to the big 'A' on August 12, 1985 at the Mildmay Hospital.

He'd had a narrow escape himself, but carpe diem and all that, as they counselled at the time.

And now Nick was buggering up his morning by wanting some off-the-wall favour.

'You do know that stalking is an offence these days? As a retired solicitor, I should know.' Harry cut short Nick's hilarious rant about Julie's marital crisis. They enjoyed an easy banter from being neighbours for well over two decades.

Harry still needed some convincing about this request.

'Anyway, Nick dearest, my sauna days are truly long gone, if they ever began,' he said, patting his stomach. 'All the horny young studs would run a mile if they saw me stumbling towards them. And from the sound of things, I need to check my life insurance policy in case those heavies turn up, as you reassuringly call them.'

Even weirder, on his way into the flat Nick had shouted on the doorstep about borrowing a screwdriver.

'It's just in case the Posties are listening. OK, I don't think they are, but you never know. Look, I'm asking you because you'd be the perfect undercover agent in that place. I mean, nobody will bother you or suspect you're up to something. What do you think? It would be just a couple of Fridays to see if old Gingernuts is talking shop with Tom, or with anyone else for that matter. I reckon Tom will be going there on Friday, though not for nooky I hasten to add, otherwise it'd be case closed,' Nick said.

And then on his way out, he shouted a loud 'thank you' for the screwdriver, which he brandished in the air. The guy was nuts, and really needed something to do.

But after he left, Harry began thinking how it could be a bit of a giggle to be a private eye for a couple of hours. At least he'd be rewarded by a crate of reserve wine for harmless window shopping, and all without having to go very far from his front door. Wonder what those places are like these days? It'd been a while since the sap had risen high enough for him to try them. Sadly, many years, in fact. Nick had promised to slip a photo of Julie's husband under his door so he could recognize him. Harry tried thinking back to when he was in a sauna last and gave up. Instead his mind wandered to a film noir scene, with an unshaved private eye in a sweat-streaked white shirt, standing in front of venetian blinds with a ciggie smouldering between his lips. Ah, the classics had always been the best wank fodder. Shame they no longer worked.

He put on a cream linen jacket, locked the door and headed for the day centre, trying to speed up a bit. She who must be obeyed from meals-on-wheels was always quick to complain when he or any other volunteer turned up late for a shift. The company was fun, but he was glad he didn't have to eat the food. Thinking of which, he wondered if they served drinks in saunas these days, like they did in that comfy cinema down the road. Let's face it, a pint was probably the only thing that would be pulled for him.

7

NICK WAS SIPPING A LARGE milky coffee in Jimmy's cafe, pleased there was no sign of the two heavies this time, only Mavis wiping tables and getting ready for the lunchtime rush. He looked out onto the high street and its intermittent, mid-morning flow of people. A mother was trying to coax a small boy to keep up with her after he stopped to talk with a beggar and his pet dog sitting outside the supermarket. Nick sometimes wondered what sort of father he would make if the opportunity came along, a thought that made him stroke his paunch as if he were going into labour imminently. No point dwelling on things like that for long now that he was well past forty and with no partner in sight. A few days ago, after making himself come on the sofa in the afternoon, it crossed his mind that he could freeze his spunk, in case the right woman turned up, was still young enough to have children, and wanted them. Too many ifs there, he thought. Nope, he wouldn't be sticking a jar of semen into a box of liquid nitrogen: that would be like storing furniture with no end date.

'Another one please, Mavis. Make it a small one this time,' he said as she shuffled past his table. She nodded without a word. Her grandson wasn't around, leaving just her and a woman he'd never seen before to help out. He leaned back in his orange plastic chair, feeling more at ease with himself now Harry was on board, and a critical task delegated. It had been relatively painless, too. Just a quick reminder of how he'd stuck his neck out to persuade a tense residents' meeting to pay the clean-up costs after one of Harry's special friends had lost his rag and painted 'Even buses come faster than old queens in Shoreditch' in three-foot letters on the perimeter wall.

His next task for the day was to get in touch with Julie. She was becoming a little pushy but he had ignored her stream of texts, voicemails and email after finding the bollard in his bed – he'd needed breathing space. The piece of metal was propped up in a corner of the balcony, its base in a glazed flower pot to stop the jagged concrete from scratching his expensive decking.

'Penny for your thoughts, love,' Mavis said, putting the fresh mug of coffee on the table, a split second after wiping the laminated surface with a damp sponge.

'Thanks. Nothing to worry about. Just too much work stuff going on at the moment. Funnily enough, I was thinking about the Posties again after reading this really interesting book the other day about families living in the slum that used to be on the other side of the high street.' He jabbed a finger in the direction of the window. 'It was all about nicking an apple a day to stay alive, that sort of thing. There were none of these food banks back then, I suppose. I hope their descendants have had a better life.'

Mavis picked up his empty mug and looked out of the window in the direction he'd pointed, the entrance to the passageway that was marked by bollards.

'Look, love, I wouldn't waste time feeling sorry for the Posties. Not in a million years, though I wish my Arthur had been one. We wouldn't have been short of a bob or two if he had, I can tell you. And no, we didn't have food banks, but there was the Christian Mission where mam went for a hot meal when she was broke.' There was an edge to Mavis's voice that left him unsure how to play things next.

Thankfully, she filled the silence for him.

'The Woodentops, that's what my Arthur used to call them, though not to their faces of course. Didn't stop him taking their money. Beggars can't be bleeding choosers, as they say. Well, not many of them have stayed round here, though funnily enough we had two in the cafe for breakfast the other day. Won't be naming names, of course. This place ain't good enough for them any more!' Mavis was almost spitting out her words.

'Eh, Woodentops?' he laughed, thinking it must be a brand of varnish.

'Gawd. You're too young to remember them, aren't you? My boys loved them. You see, hubby would call Posties the Woodentops to take the mickey. They're just a bunch of jumped-up carpenters who bent the rules and got lucky, he'd say. Liked to speak his mind, did my Arthur. Well, he was a bit of a handful.' She smiled with a perfect set of stain-free teeth. 'That was in private, of course. As I said, he wasn't picky about taking their money, despite their airs and graces. He said good morning and cooked their fry-up with a smile each time, bless him.' She walked off to give the counter a vigorous rub as her stream of thoughts tipped him into another reverie: he imagined himself fearless but humble, showing Mavis a front-page story about Tom and other Posties being caught literally by the short and curlies. A large photo had the two heavies leaving the sauna with Gingernuts a metre behind, trying to hide his face with a large brown envelope. The perfect shot. Wonder how easy it would be to set up something like that in real life. Had to be a piece of piss, surely, just a matter of dropping a few juicy tidbits into a pliant reporter's ear. All in the public interest, of course. All helping to right a century-long wrong he still hadn't quite put his finger on – but then, who the hell cares if it wiped that superior smile off Tom's face.

A customer brushed against the table, bringing him back to earth. He picked up his coffee and stared at the men and women walking by on the high street, exuding a confident energy that had probably left him for good. Wouldn't it be fun to be their age again, knowing all that he now knew about life? Then again, who was he kidding? After months of pontificating, usually when he was pissed, he couldn't sort out what the hell to do about Amanda. No doubt that Thomas Uphisownarse Fry would have it sorted in a heartbeat.

Seeing his grimace reflected in the window, he toyed with ordering another coffee.

8

IT WAS ALREADY WEDNESDAY, WHICH meant only two more days to complete the cabinet.

Fred's innate perfectionist streak, which until now had unrelentingly fuelled his calling as a carpenter, was fraying. This piece of furniture would not pass muster for England's young Queen Elizabeth. Just as well it was not for her. Why wasn't he the gifted self-publicist like Chippendale at the peak of his powers, milking cash from fashion-conscious aristocrats who lay in the palm of his hand? The king of cabinetmaking would never have put up with a crummy warehouse by a smelly canal. And cherry wood? Nothing less than mahogany for the Lord of the Chisels.

What a relief, not long to go until Friday, when this bloody thing would be finished and he'd be gone; this place was starting to get on his wick. It was the same each day, the mallets and hammers laid out in the exact centre of the workbench, flanked on the left by a set of fanned-out chisels, the screwdrivers displayed in similar fashion on the right side. The tea mug would be squeaky-clean, scrubbed with wire wool. The milk drips and stray sugar crystals he'd left by the kettle the day before would be all gone by morning. At the start of each day there was a fresh stock of shiny brown paper left neatly on an upturned paint tin next to the toilet. Out of sheer curiosity, he checked each time how many sheets they'd left him: it was always ten squares, all carefully pulled apart at the perforations. Even the bar of yellow carbolic soap on a rope was washed and dried, thanks to the fastidious nocturnal char, who must be Frank.

His mood lifted each morning when the thin, wintry morning light began filtering down through the skylight an hour or so into his working day. Opening the windows let in more light and air, the skeleton cabinet casting a faint shadow that almost stretched as far as the threshold of the second room.

Good, only three more days left, he thought as he crouched to open his tool-bag and get to work.

On his way over that morning, using backstreets to avoid bumping into colleagues or nosy neighbours, he'd decided not to bother with any ornate carvings on the cabinet's corners. A plain brass knob would also do for the writing leaf. Anything to save time, he thought as he prepared to glue and tack the back and sides onto the frame. He went into the side room and saw there was a yellow box of matches placed by the burner he would use to melt the glue flakes, as if an invisible hand was chivvying him along. He filled a chipped enamel jug with water and poured the cloudy liquid into one of the metal pots, stirring the flakes with a stick of wood. He turned on the gas, struck a match and the burner burst into a ring of bright yellow flames, sending a wave of heat his way. Turning down the ring until the glue was barely bubbling, he gave the mixture a few brisk stirs and went back to the workbench.

By mid-afternoon the cabinet was taking shape, the glue

doing its job perfectly with the help of clamps. It was good stuff, he had to admit as he cast a critical eye over the drying seals. Would definitely take some of the leftover flakes with him on Friday to save buying glue for the cabinet he'd planned for the in-laws. It was time to butter them up in case he and the wife needed them to look after a nipper at the weekends. Best be optimistic about these things.

The sides of the cabinet were sticking well to the frame, helped by a few strategically hammered tacks that nobody outside his under-appreciated trade would notice. Done with gluing for now, he turned off the burner and went to make tea. A few minutes later, with a mug in one hand and an Eccles cake in the other, he decided to take his first break of the day and eased himself into the armchair. Funny how it was the first time he'd sat in it, preferring the wooden chair he'd placed next to the windows so he could look out over the water and watch the barges pass by with their trails of black engine smoke, and see if he knew anyone walking along the towpath opposite.

As he sipped his tea he felt something lumpy under his left buttock. It didn't disappear when he shifted a little and, irritated, he put the mug down on the floor, crammed the remainder of the cake into his mouth and got up to peer under the cushion.

He saw a squashed, black leather wallet.

Instinct told him to leave it alone, but curiosity got the better of him and he grabbed it. Seated again, he looked inside the wallet but found no money, just a stub from a shoe repair shop in Islington and a tiny key. There was also a folded photo of a smiling young man, his fair hair blown to one side. He turned it overlooked and read the untidy writing: Charlie Pooter, Festival of Britain 1951. Of course, now he remembered where he'd seen that exhibit in the background. It was a few years ago by now, but it had left an impression on him at the time. His mate had dismissed it as a barmy flying saucer on sticks. Spot on, really. He'd walked round it several times with the wife on a Sunday afternoon. It had been a cracking day out, all in all.

The wallet must belong to Frank, but then again, why would he be carrying around a picture of a young man called Charlie Pooter? They didn't sound related. He'd never heard of the Pooters, and didn't recognize him. Maybe it was owned by someone else who sometimes worked here. The wallet looked old, the leather soft and cracked from use, which didn't chime with the picture of the young man. His thoughts were cut short by a key turning in the lock and the door of the warehouse swinging open. The unexpectedness of it all made him accidentally kick over his mug of tea as he jumped onto his feet, the hot brown liquid running everywhere, sending steam rising into the cold air.

'Ted, love, you here? You're not sleeping on the job, are you?' He heard Elsie's voice boom through the building.

He stuffed the picture and wallet into his pocket and stumbled into the main room to greet her, his hands and forehead clammy, as if he'd been caught stealing.

'Well, there you are,' she said, looking past him into the side room. 'Looks like you've had a bit of an accident,' she said, putting down a big bag of groceries on the floor.

'Good to see you, Elsie. Nowt to worry about. It's coming on well, as you can see. I'll be done by Friday.' He spoke with a slight quiver in his voice. She went over to the half-built cabinet, gave it a cursory look, and made a few humming noises.

'Why don't you knock off early for a change? You've been at it non-stop like a blue-arsed fly for days now. I'll hold the fort until Frank gets here. I saw him down the market just now and he was going to pop round to check up on things, make sure you've got everything you need. Hang on for a while if you want to see him yourself.'

His stomach churned at the thought of meeting Frank face to face. Even talking about him with Elsie was not good for the constitution.

'I'll be going then. A bit of time off would be nice. I'll be here bright and early in the morning,' he said, grabbing his tool bag and heading for the open door. A late afternoon pint down the pub was just what his nerves needed after a near-miss with Frank. He headed for the high street at a brisk pace, leaving Elsie bent over, singing softly and rummaging through her shopping bag.

9

HARRY HAD SWALLOWED THE SMALL blue pill with a mouthful of cold water an hour ago while staring at himself in the large bevelled bathroom mirror. Not quite James Bond preparing for a mission. A little too worn round the edges for that, and with only a licence to kill time these days. And it had been a while since he'd been shaken, let alone stirred, which is why he'd decided to try and mix business with, hopefully, a little pleasure if the opportunity rose. It had been a long time since he'd been into one of those saunas. His dignity, if not stamina, had insisted he should call it a day. Besides, it was getting so much harder to find his way round poorly lit places these days. As for reading menus in restaurants, thank God for the torch on his phone otherwise he'd have starved by now.

He was groomed for the occasion, having visited the Turkish barber that morning where his unruly nasal hair had been hacked back and the stubble on his ear lobes singed away by a flaming stick doused in turps.

And now here he was, sitting on a damp wooden bench inside Jock's Hangout with a towel round his waist, waiting for Thomas Fry to turn up. It was getting busier as the after-work crowd streamed in, sending the average age plunging by at least two decades within the space of twenty minutes. Under the brutal neon lights in locker room he'd spotted a young professional discreetly putting his wedding ring into the breast pocket of his pinstriped jacket. Ha! How some things never change. But then again, maybe they had. Perhaps one should no longer assume it's a wife he had waiting back home.

He'd never felt totally at ease in these places himself, born as he was into a generation whose sexuality was long expressed by stealth, well under public radar. The deep-seated fear of a police raid was fused to his DNA since puberty, even though the boys in blue would only be storming this place in someone's erotic dream.

And here they came.

The tall, thin ginger-haired man and Tom Fry were walking towards him, though no sign yet of the two bouncers, or whatever Nick called them.

'Yes, I thought my speech went down rather well. Shame about the riff-raff from south of the river but we had to invite them to avoid any…,' he heard the tall man tell Tom before they slipped out of earshot and headed down a low lit corridor of cubicles whose layout Nick had sketched on the back of a gas bill during their final briefing last night. He got up and followed, the ginger man's height making him easier to track, but the light was very dim by the time they reached the end of the corridor. By running his hand lightly against the wall, he could guide himself along without stumbling until his eyes could adjust more to the poor light. Harry saw them step inside the last cubicle on the left. The door of the neighbouring one was open wide, but inside there was a naked man lying on his front, his bum twitching at the sound of a potential punter approaching. He stood just inside the cubicle and began tickling the bloke's hairy thigh with his right hand to get his attention.

'Piss off, grandad,' the man hissed.

After a bit more tickling, the man got up, snatched his towel off the floor and walked off, leaving Harry worried that it may already be too late to eavesdrop on any conversation next door. He stepped inside the cubicle and bolted the door. What he did next he'd rehearsed several times in his kitchen, following Nick's meticulous instructions. With a wince, he removed the small recording device taped to his inner thigh, switched it on, and unwound the thin black lead with its tiny microphone. Using a blob of pink plasticine he'd kept in the hollow of his belly-button, he fixed the mic inside the narrow gap between the top of the cubicle wall and the ceiling.

Then he sat perfectly still and quiet for the next half hour.

During that time he heard occasional murmurings, but they weren't loud or distinct enough for him to make out what Thomas and his associate were discussing. One thing was pretty obvious though, no sex was involved. Then the voices rose: they must be getting ready to leave. 'Oh, dear boy, I think that's going well beyond the call of duty. Let's go for a beer to cool ourselves down.' It sounded like the ginger man talking but Harry couldn't be sure.

Within seconds they were gone.

Mission accomplished, he smiled, thinking how he was finally free to have some fun once he'd put Nick's electronic baby in the locker. Favour done! Just as he reached up to peel off the mic, there was brisk tapping on the door. That could be only one thing: the two heavies on cue making their checks, like Nick had warned. Despite being warned this could happen, Harry began sweating, his heart also beating rapidly as he fumbled for a few seconds, trying to calm himself down while he hid the mic and the recorder, with his shaky fingers getting tied up in the cord. He decided to make loud snoring noises but rather than stopping, the tapping turned into heavy knocking, followed by several bangs that made the flimsy door shake on its hinges, sending Harry's pulse sky-rocketing. While making the noise of someone waking up, he checked that his cock was peeping through the towel before taking a deep breath and opening the door.

'Oh, hi, big boys. Want to come inside and spend time with daddy?'

He tried sounding gruff while looking the two towelled heavies straight in the eye, keeping his mouth open so that saliva could drool in two parallel streams. Sweat was pouring down his forehead as the two intimidating men unnerved him.

The sight of a dishevelled, pot-bellied septuagenarian with suspect fluid control did the trick, and the heavies left without a word or backward glance and Harry shut the door. He needed a few minutes to calm down and the slump in stress prodded the blue pill into action, creating a towel teepee in his lap. He chuckled and went to the changing room to put away the recorder in his locker, determined that would be his last favour for Nick, ever. It had been a while since he'd felt so vulnerable. With a still slightly shaky hand, he fished out a blue pill from his trouser pocket and gulped it down with water from the cooler before heading back to the maze of dim corridors and steam rooms, wondering if he would ever find a boyfriend in the time he had left on this earth.

10

THE DIRECTOR STARED INTO THE middle distance as he absentmindedly fidgeted with his phone. His companion would be late so he had a bit more time to think things over, though he already knew instinctively what had to be done.

Not surprisingly, the club was quiet given it was a week-day afternoon. He was sitting in one of his favourite leather armchairs near the expanse of floor-to-ceiling windows that looked over a wasteland criss-crossed with rusted railway tracks, all that remained of a once-bustling goodsyard. Bordering it was the new railway line which, after looping above the high street, disappeared into the long, concrete box tunnel in front of him. If the developers get their way, the sun he now saw would be blocked by a gargantuan mass of glass and steel, sucking the air from the Old Nichol below.

Shuddering at the thought of more change to a familiar landscape, the director watched the orange and blue railway carriages enter one end of the tunnel and exit the other, all in total silence thanks to triple glazing. Two cranes stood motionless behind the station, waiting for their orders to build a bright, shiny world of unique penthouse suites in the sky. Oh, no doubt, there would be a sprinkling of affordable housing to keep local councillors on a leash, hermetically sealed behind a poor door to avoid cross contamination with the luxury flats. Ah, *plus ça change* since those Victorian philanthropists threw our forefathers out of the rookery. And to think how our soon-to-be-sold Postie properties will be no more than a historical curiosity in the shadows of towers. But then again, hadn't Shoreditch always gone about its business away from the disinfectant of sunshine since the Plague?

'Bloody good malt,' the director thought, looking approvingly at the tumbler in his hand. He'd ordered a small one to avoid clouding his thoughts as he lamented at how the new generation of Posties were revolting, in every sense of the word: no sense of tradition, no patience, no clue, no taste. The greedy buggers wanted it all now and weren't going to listen to him one iota. He was obsolete, like his title and the clapped-out cabinet that came with it.

What a tiresome joke it all was.

He looked out of the window again, thinking how mixed signals from the property market should prompt all sensible Posties to wait a bit before selling out. Or at least drip feed to minimize the risk of flooding the market. But no, it was not to be. Counsel from an old fart like him had fallen on stony ground. The prospect of cashing in on frenzied gentrification had turned their heads. And maybe they were right to get out now, before Shoreditch inevitably became vanilla. Doubtless there would soon come a day when the young and the innovative who flocked here would crave a less synthetic Zeitgeist, and somewhere that charged cheaper rents. How times had changed for today's Postie! They could spend hours over a glass of bubbly, agonizing over which leafy street to live on, not like their forefathers who were flushed out of the rookery like vermin. Shouldn't that make them think twice before selling their ancestry so quickly?

Fat chance.

He shook his head so vigorously in disgust that the manager came over to check if everything was all right. Of course it was. Another whisky wouldn't go amiss. Better make it a double, please. And seeing his short, fat companion entering the large sunlit room, he ordered a large gin and tonic too.

'You sounded a little out of sorts on the phone earlier, Mr Director,' his companion said with a playful emphasis on the title, as he sat down with a grin in the opposite armchair.

'Let's forget the director shit. What are we going to do about Hope Wharf? The troops are rebelling in the trenches, so we can't sit on our backsides and do nothing any more,' the tall ginger-haired man said sharply, before shrugging his shoulders in an apology.

'I'm inclined to agree. The new-build going up next door to Hope Wharf will make it look a little dated if we hold back too long,' the companion said. 'I see the estate agents are calling the development a contemporary luxury waterside experience. To you and me, that's a flat by the canal in old money. We could keep renting out Hope Wharf, but as you say, that's no longer an option given that a loud majority is screaming for cash.'

'How this whole area is changing so quickly. Takes my breath away at times,' said the tall man. 'Do you know I almost got run over by a bike on the towpath the other day?

Don't they have bells? And I agree. Keeping Hope is not an option any more, given what most Posties want. We also run the risk of ending up with wet feet like Canute if we try holding back the inevitable when all around us is being tarted up and sold off.'

The two lapsed into silence and sipped their drinks as they looked at the red cranes against the the blue sky.

The short, fat man picked up the conversation: 'Look, let's step back a bit. We haven't actually had a formal vote yet on whether to sell Hope, or anywhere else in the portfolios for that matter. And before we actually hold a vote we could try and persuade enough Posties to see how risky it would be to sell everything in one go.'

The director waved his hand to dismiss the idea. 'To be honest, I'm not convinced that tactic would work. We'd rightly be accused of stalling for time. The younger ones want out and there are enough of them to swing the vote. They're not remotely interested in the past, nor do they want the dubious honour of preserving a crummy cabinet. In some ways I don't blame them as there's nothing to keep them here, and most have already buggered off to posher places anyway. I would probably do the same if I were in their shoes,' the tall man said. He stretched out his long legs to reveal a pair of shocking pink socks. After attracting the waiter's attention, he pointed to their glasses and mouthed 'Same again, please'.

With fresh drinks and a small bowl of unsalted cashews on a pink glass cube between them, they carried on talking, with the director starting this time: 'Trouble is, if we do sell the freeholds, we'll have lawyers all over the deeds like a rash. I fear we may see some hundred-year-old skeletons tumbling out of the cabinet, so to speak.'

'So you are saying that we should proceed cautiously?' the small fat man said. 'Sounds eminently sensible. But we'll need to find a way to, how shall I put it, reassure buyers over any discrepancies in the deeds. I think it would be useful to test the water with Hope Wharf before selling anything else.'

The director nodded in agreement. 'Absolutely. We must be totally professional, be whiter than white, or we'll get some cocky mobster from north London saying we can't keep our house in order. Alas, the days of using the darker arts of persuasion are long gone. I suspect we both know who should handle this.'

'We do, Mr Director, we do. Our very own Thomas Fry, of course. He's a very experienced property lawyer even at his age, and knows developers' tricks like the back of his hand. Surely we can find a discreet way for him to gloss over imperfections in the deeds. A generous thank you on top of the lolly he'll get from his share of the sales wouldn't go amiss, either. And, Mr Director, as you mentioned from your last chat with him at Jock's, he does seem eager to help in whatever way.'

The director giggled. 'Yes, you can certainly say he's eager to please. Let's set up a meeting with him, though not at Jock's. I have this strange feeling that I'm being followed there, and I know the place isn't Tom's cup of tea.'

'Very wise,' the fat man said. 'Why don't we use your grace-and-favour pad at Hope for the meeting, while we still can? I do love the view from up there. That place will sell in a heartbeat, and being *in situ*, as it were, keeps us focused on our historic but sad job at hand.' He sank back into the armchair, and his eyelids drooped while he began racking his brains about what to get his picky wife for her birthday that would fully reflect the woman's unfeasibly generous forbearance of late.

11

TED HAD BEEN PAID CASH on the nail for making the cabinet.

It had been a while since he'd felt so flush and, having been back at work for a week, the unease from toiling away in Hope Wharf on his own had all but faded. The cabinet looked good, despite the shortcuts. Amazing what a bit of elbow grease could do. It was another gleaming reminder of his carpentry skills, as if any were needed. More to the point, Elsie was impressed with his craftsmanship, even though her final inspection lasted barely a minute before she shoved a brown envelope filled with cash into his hand. He'd taken the trouble to point out the felt lining inside the drop-down writing leaf. The bottom drawer was also lined, as requested. It had been fiddly getting the material to stick evenly with the glue they'd given him, but it looked fine in the end. He hadn't bumped into Frank once, which was the biggest relief of all. Just the thought of that bloke and his outsize balls gave him the collywobbles. Now he just hoped the proud owner of the cabinet would laud his handiwork to high heaven: word of mouth was the best way of bringing in orders in this trade.

A few more jobs like that and he could afford a television.

It was Saturday morning and he whistled his way towards the high street, a shopping list tucked into his back trouser pocket. He'd volunteered to fetch the groceries as the wife was short of time, having to nip to the Smethwicks' for a couple of hours' overtime. He'd been tempted to say she could skip it this time round, now that he had some spare cash, but what if she asked where it came from?

Still, it felt good going shopping with notes in his wallet, and not just coins rattling in a pocket. Shopping had become much easier now that rationing was finally over, no more who-you-know when it comes to stocking the pantry. The wife was making spotted dick for supper and it had to be Bird's custard to go with it, which meant going all the way to the bottom end of the high street to Folgate's, the best grocer round here, where they stocked the custard powder. Wonder if he had time for a quick pint at the Ten Ancients? Maybe not, but he'd buy a bunch of flowers on the way back to put a smile on her face. She'd been a bit distant lately.

He stopped outside the post office to buy a stamp for his brother's birthday card. In he went, to join the queue that ran all along the back wall and then curved round to the counter. As he shuffled along, he picked up a few leaflets and looked at the posters on the wall. He was tempted to open up a national savings account with a guinea now that he was flush, but thought better of it. He'd do so once a nipper was on the way. Something caught his eye as he glanced at a large poster of mugshots. He couldn't quite put his finger on it straightaway as the picture had been taken somewhere different and the man was wearing a tie. But no doubt about it, though, it was definitely the same toothy smile and fair hair. The caption underneath said: 'Missing: Charlie Pooter of Islington'. There was an unspecified reward from his family for information that would uncover his whereabouts. The photo looked more recent than the one he'd found in the wallet at Hope Wharf. The word 'missing' triggered a rushing noise in Ted's head, forcing him to lean against the wall for a few seconds. He left the queue and went outside to breathe in the cold air and steady his racing heart, before walking back up the high street towards home, forgetting about the custard powder as he wondered how much of a reward they were offering.

12

'COULD YOU MOVE OVER A bit, Mr Director? This end is a bit sticky, for some reason.'

'Can we drop the formalities, Thomas? Tell me what you're hearing.'

Nick could just about follow the conversation Harry had recorded at Jocks' Hangout if he closed his eyes and concentrated hard, using the headphones to focus on each word against background pop music and his friend's wheezes and coughs.

He was in the flat's quietest corner: sitting on the toilet in the en-suite with the extractor fan switched off, leaving him cocooned by thick marble tiles from traffic hum and railway screech.

'It's clear that most Posties want to sell up. With gentrification and property prices peaking, they want to get out now,' Tom was explaining in a clear, businesslike voice that flagged meticulous preparation for the meeting. All that was missing was a power point presentation.

'Greedy little shits: they were lucky enough to be born Posties and now they want to flog it all off, having done diddly bloody squat themselves. No sense of history.' The director was snarling so loudly that Nick didn't have to replay any of that section either. Then there was a short lull in the conversation, leaving him miming a catchy Michael Jackson song that was punctuated by some barely audible moaning from another cubicle down the corridor.

'Well, that may be true up to a point, Mr Director, but I'm not quite sure that's the full picture,' Tom continued, in the tone of a parent humouring a stroppy teenager. 'You and I know that not a penny was actually paid for any of our properties. Let's just say they were acquired for a very worthy cause. Sadly, the younger Posties don't buy the history bit and want to cash in now before any skeletons come out of the cupboard, or should I say, cabinet,' Tom said with a forced laugh that was not reciprocated. 'Anyway, I think we have no choice but to divest now while we're still in full control, rather than risk something from the past leaking out and ending up in court. That could mean we possibly lose the lot. That's the consensus thinking I've been asked to pass on to you.'

It was clear where Tom stood, and it wasn't on the side of the ginger dinosaur he was speaking to, Nick thought, shoving a towel under his bum to soften the convex toilet seat cover.

'Oh, goody. So I get the honour of being the director that ends it all and shuffles off into the sunset with a crummy cabinet as a souvenir. Don't they realize it's my neck on the line if anything dodgy is found out because I'll have to sign the sales contracts? Bet the spoiled brats won't be visiting me in the clink!' The director's voice was getting hoarser.

Louder groans from a neighbouring cubicle made the two pause until Tom resumed: 'I'm happy to go back and express your concerns, and stress again some of the rather delicate legal challenges we could face, but I must point out that opinions are generally rather firm on this. At the very least, I think we'll have to dip a toe in the water and sell Hope to placate everyone.'

'You're probably right, Thomas. Sorry to be so tetchy. But we mustn't do anything that isn't thought through carefully or we could end up in a very sticky situation and, as you say, risk losing everything we Posties have built up over a century. We're going to need all your legal nous on this one, Thomas. Fear not, you will be handsomely rewarded.' The director's voice was now weary as well as hoarse.

'I'm always happy to help. You look a bit worn. Perhaps I could ease the tension a bit while we're here, Mr Director?'

'I'm very flattered but you can take your hand away, Thomas. I make it a rule not to mix business with pleasure. Appreciate the thought. Right, let's focus our efforts on persuading our dear young Posties to see the folly of their ways. Or at least be patient for a bit longer. Fancy a quickie in the bar? Only cooking lager, I'm afraid, but it will refresh our spirits.'

There was a sound of people shuffling about, a door being unbolted, and then just the background music. He was about to switch off the recorder when he heard sharp tapping. Ah yes, the two heavies, on cue as ever. Pretty impressive, the way Harry handled them, though there was a definite quiver in his friend's voice. The old trouper deserved an obscenely expensive dinner for doing all that. He turned off the recorder and sat on the toilet lid to let the conversation sink into the recesses of his brain, but it wasn't long before a broad smile lit up his face as a plan formed in his head. He would sleep on it first. Just as Gingernuts had wisely advised, some things need patience and careful thought before execution.

13

FRANK'S FEAR WAS PALPABLE, AND Elsie was at a loss to know what to do or say.

It was Saturday morning and they were in Hope Wharf, the cabinet dispatched to the director and Ted paid. Frank was sifting through the cupboards and cubby-holes for a third time since she'd arrived, the two rooms already looking as if they'd been ransacked by Teddy Boys on the rampage.

'Look, just give it back and I won't say anything about it ever again!' he shouted at her while looking around, as if he were hoping to spot a corner, drawer or cupboard he'd overlooked.

'Some cheek, calling me a thief, Frank. I've never seen this bleeding wallet of yours. I've no idea what you're talking about!' she snapped, her patience running thin.

'Oh, come off it, love. Do it for a living, don't you?' he hit back, this time his voice lower and laced with a hint of menace which made her stand still and hold a breath for a few seconds.

The armchair was on its side, the cushion ripped open. All the glue pots had been emptied out, their contents flushed down the drains. Everywhere had been searched endlessly, but still no sign of the wallet. Breathing heavily, with the back of his kilt dark from sweat, he sat down on a stool, looking defeated.

'Why the hell are you worrying about it? Those Posties look after you, don't they? There couldn't have been more than a few quid in it, Frank. Anyway, I can get you another one 'cos I'm going up West this afternoon, as it happens,' she said, trying to sound chipper than she felt.

'It's not the money or the wallet, Elsie. It opens a can of worms if I can't find it,' he replied, so quietly that she had to crane her head to catch the words. Sensing it was best if she left, Elsie picked up her shopping and headed for the door, half expecting him to call her back, but he remained seated on the stool with his head bowed as he breathed heavily.

After the door shut and he was alone, Frank thought hard about where the wallet might be. No, he hadn't taken it home, or anywhere else outside the wharf for that matter. Nor had he thrown it out. He remembered putting it under the armchair cushion, meaning to deal with it later, but in the rush to make glue he'd forgotten about it.

He should have burnt the bloody thing straightaway.

With a weary grunt, he got up and went over to a window to let in some air. He caught himself looking down at where he'd let slip the sack of bones into the dark water. The surface was still, the prolonged freeze having created thick sheets of ice for the coots and ducks to use as pontoons. He calmed down as the bitterly cold air and clear blue sky brought a sense of perspective, helping to lift his spirits a little. Now, he thought, how the hell was he going to get out of this pickle?

14

FRANK HAD NEEDED A COUPLE of days to decide what to do about the missing wallet.

Standing inside the wharf, he rubbed his hands in glee before putting on a pair of tan leather gloves in anticipation of stepping into a sulphureous cloak of invisibility. No doubt about it, the pea-souper was perfect for what he needed to do. If only it were permanent, he could go about his business without the quizzical glances and half-smiles he put up with every day wherever he went.

He'd felt stupid after that tantrum in front of Elsie over the missing wallet, but by now he was back to his old self and thinking clearly, not like the filthy smog that was about to envelop him. He locked the door and, with a spring in his step, headed across what he knew to be a wide stretch of grass and weeds bordered by poorly maintained terraced houses. The smog was so thick that he couldn't see his feet, but he knew the way like the back of his hand. The long fawn mac, and a thick layer of greasy vapour rub smeared over his chest, would keep away most of the damp chill. Although the coat was long enough to cover his kilt, it left a seven-inch gap of exposed shin above the tops of his heavy black boots. But he was already feeling the warmth of the yellow balaclava his mother had knitted for him, along with a matching scarf that was now wrapped tightly round his neck. The wide brim of his black fedora hat was pulled low over his head, covering his eyes from any passers-by who came too close. He was confident of being anonymous, though he reckoned it wasn't quite as dense as the Great Smog of a few years back, which now seemed a lifetime away. And in many ways it was. He'd heard tales about the wild events that went on during that pea-souper, and the many who coughed themselves to death. It was a time when he had a very different way of earning a living, working behind the counter at Woolworths, though already realizing all was not fine and dandy down below.

'Tickety tock,' he whispered to reassure himself as he walked down streets he recognized from touching garden walls, broken fences and chipped iron Posties, tracing a map inside his head since childhood. And there it was, Cheshire Street, on the right. He knew that the house was the seventh on the left-hand side and within a minute he was outside its front window, relieved that all was quiet as he pressed his nose against the glass. Good, no lights either. Tuesday was darts night and Ted would be down the Cock and Cardinal with his mates from the furniture factory. Frank had also learned from Elsie's blathering that his wife worked over-time for a posh family in north London on Tuesday and Thursday evenings. Best be careful in case she came home early because of the weather.

He carried on walking down the street until he reached the end of the terrace where he took a left, shortly after-wards turning left again to double back along a parallel, narrow path that was sandwiched between the backs of the houses and the railway lines which the smog had long silenced. He stopped at number 15 and pushed gently on an unlocked wooden gate, making it swing inwards with barely a squeak. He entered the small narrow yard which, having checked a day earlier, he knew had the toilet and shed on one side and a low brick wall along the other. The back door would be just a few feet ahead but before reaching it the neighbouring yard light came on, followed by the sound of a door being unlocked and pushed open. Taking no chances, he crouched at the base of the wall from where he could hear someone step out, followed by the sound of a match being struck. Within a few seconds he could smell cigarette smoke as he crouched so low that his scrotum pressed against the cold flagstones, making his creaking knees slowly give way.

'Just spending a penny, love. I'll make you a cuppa in a minute!' a man's voice shouted. 'Never stops, does it? Always something. Get this, get that. Thinks she's Princess bloody Margaret.' The voice continued, this time quietly. Frank heard a different door bang shut: must be the toilet. A high-pitched squeal of a fart was followed by irregular squirts of urine hitting water, ending with the chain being pulled. A few seconds later Frank felt something bounce off his back and land at his feet: a cigarette stub, still glowing. The back door slammed and the man was gone. The lights went out, leaving him once again in the clammy dark as he had to grip the top of the wall to haul himself up, trying not to groan as his knees clicked straight.

He stamped hard on the cigarette with his right boot, annoyed with the delay.

Ted's back door was locked but after banging his shoulder hard against the frame several times, it splintered to allow him in. Why the hell did they need to lock up in the first place? Let's face it, who'd got anything worth nicking round here? Inside, there was the stale smell of the fry-up Ted had had for his tea. After a few fumbles in the dark he switched on a light and got to work, checking first if anyone was in the house. Empty, as far as he could see. Then he began a systematic search for Charlie Pooter's wallet, certain it would be in the bedroom, probably under a pile of socks in a drawer, but he decided to start in the kitchen and work his way up through the house, including the attic if need be.

There was no sign of a wallet among the pots and pans and bowls in the pantry, so he began to search the living room, which looked oddly bare for a matrimonial home. The place needed a woman's touch. Elsie would bring a bit of life and warmth to this bleak hole, he thought, looking at the withered spider plant in its cracked clay pot on the dining table. The grate hadn't seen a fire for days, by the look of things. Shivering, he drew the curtains and turned on the main light to continue with his search.

The cupboards were empty apart from a china tea set still wrapped in its original box. Probably a wedding present they didn't like or from someone they couldn't stand. Why didn't they display it in the glass cabinet over there, like anyone else would? Above one of the cupboards was a set of shelves with books and a couple of small ornaments, some of which looked like prizes from a fair. The toby jug was nice, but he left it alone. Can't be thieving. At first glance the top shelf looked empty, but then he noticed a thin and flat volume was on its side, wrapped in brown paper that barely stood out in the thin, yellow light.

He stood on a chair to examine the shelf properly and there it was, leaning against the back wall. Rifling through it he found no money, but then again he'd already spent it on beer. Pooter's snapshot was missing, which meant Ted must have seen it. He ripped the brown paper cover off the book that was lying on its side; it was stuffed with loose papers which he recognized as the designs Ted had used to make the cabinet.

Still no photo.

He picked up the book, intrigued by the title's old-fashioned typeface compared with the near-mint condition of the volume itself. 'The Gentleman and Cabinet-Maker's Director by Thomas Chippendale': he read out the words embossed in gold leaf. He found smaller bits of paper between the pages, one of them with the name and address of a man in Leeds. Losing patience, he shook the book hard by its spine, sending the plans and scraps of paper floating to the floor. A small shiny square landed at the foot of the chair: Pooter's picture.

'Hah!' he shouted, throwing the book violently to the other side of the room.

With a gleeful flourish he stuffed the photo into the wallet, which he tucked inside his coat. The clock on the mantelpiece showed it had only turned seven, giving him plenty of time to finish the job that night. He left the house by the back door, not bothering to turn off the lights. There was no sound from next door this time, and the alley-way also seemed empty, with the railway tracks still silent and invisible in the smog.

Relieved to be out of the house with the snapshot and

wallet back in his possession, he tightened his scarf and pulled the fedora low as the smog clung to his face and shins, drawing the heat out of him. Back on Cheshire Street, he retraced his steps and heard a shrieking child being stilled by the reassuring voices of two or three adults. The smog was too thick for them to see him, and his rubber soles muffled his footsteps. He soon reached Brick Lane, where he turned north and walked to a main road which he crossed to cut through a series of backstreets, once again using fences, walls and corners to guide him, though finding it hard at times to stifle a cough brought on by the acrid air scouring the insides of his throat and lungs.

He tried to hurry in case Ted's darts match was ending early because of the weather. The pub would be coming up soon on the left-hand side and he slowed as his fingertips felt the smooth whitewashed wall of the Cock and Cardinal. He stopped to listen in case someone was in front or behind him, or having a fag outside. Not a soul, nor stray dog. One of the pub's doors opened and Frank stepped back a few feet to make doubly sure he was out of sight but close enough to remain within earshot.

'Nah, no sign of it lifting!' a man shouted, before going back inside and shutting the door.

That didn't sound like Ted.

He edged further along the wall to a window and peered inside, making sure not to draw attention to himself. Taking off his hat made it easier to move his face closer to the glass. The place was almost empty apart from eight blokes clustered round the bar. The darts match must have ended but Ted was still there, his back turned to the window. Deep in conversation, he was clearly enjoying himself as his hands and shoulders jerked up and down before a bout of laughter erupted. They all had near-full pints lined up on the bar. It would be a while before any of them left.

Three-quarters of an hour later, Ted was the first to put on his coat and cap and bid farewell to his mates before leaving. Frank followed as he headed home, whistling in hesitant bursts while making his way slowly. It was a popular song from the war; for the life of him Frank couldn't remember the name, but its jauntiness soon fizzled out as Ted had to give his full attention to finding his way through the pea-souper, bumping into bollards and recovering from missteps on the kerb and potholed streets as he went. Frank, a few yards behind, heard a groan and a sharp curse when Ted must have tripped, but thankfully those steel-capped boots of his resumed their irregular tapping on the cobbles.

As expected, Ted veered right down a narrow lane, a shortcut that would take him past a row of lock-up garages that were well away from the main streets. Frank picked up speed and got so close that Ted could smell minty vapour rub through the smog, making him stop in his tracks.

'Who's that then?' Ted called out. 'Bill, is that you having a laugh?'

Frank smashed a cosh down on Ted's head, cracking the skull and making his legs buckle so that he hit the ground with a thud. It startled a cat, which let out a loud meow, followed by the sound of claws scratching on brick as it fled. After a couple of heavier, direct blows to the head, Frank slid the cosh back into the long narrow pocket he'd stitched for it inside his mac, bent down to grab Ted by the lapels, and dragged him across the tarmac to the door of the garage at the far end of a row of five. He took out a key to open the padlock and lifted a brass flap to pull open the door just wide enough to bundle the body inside. It took a few seconds of fumbling in the dark to find the matches he'd left with two candles on saucers. The flames puttered in the clammy smog that had seeped inside, but they gave off enough light. Sweat was now dripping off Frank's face despite the cold weather. His chest was heaving, sending more wafts of vapour rub upwards, its smell comforting and familiar, helping to calm him down. By holding a candle close to Ted's head, he could see blood oozing out of the left temple and onto the concrete floor, but there was no pulse when he squeezed Ted's still warm wrist.

'Ah tickety-tock,' he said to himself. 'Nice and tidy.'

Knowing he had to get a move on before the body stiffened, he grabbed the wooden cart parked at the back of the garage and wheeled it over, its axle creaking when he hauled Ted onto it. Hope this bloody contraption is sturdy enough for the short journey ahead, he thought. The two sets of pram wheels had been oiled after all that squeaking the last time he'd used the cart, which had almost given him away.

He covered the body with bundles of straw, shavings and other rubbish he'd collected and left there a few days ago, but it was a good ten minutes before he was able to breathe normally, though his sodden balaclava stuck uncomfortably to the sides of his face, his shirt also glued to his chest by an emulsion of sweat and vapour rub. And he was ravenous, but the job needed finishing before he would be getting hot grub. After a final check of the loaded cart, he snuffed out the candles and slowly opened the garage door while listening hard for passers-by. Not a whisper from either direction. Good. He decided it was safe enough to open the door wide enough to wheel out the cart into the alley-way and padlock the garage. He checked again that he had everything with him before pushing the cart forward, relieved that Ted wasn't too unwieldy. Lucky he wasn't a tall feller. And the wheels were staying in place on the axles, doing their job nicely. He pushed the cart back towards the Cock and Cardinal, avoiding main streets as much as possible, though the smog was still thick enough to keep most people indoors.

Ah, soon be rid of you, Ted, he thought.

The streets that were cobbled made the cart bump about and jettison some of the straw and bits of rubbish, forcing Frank to stop and check every few minutes to see if Ted was still hidden properly. He wheeled it past the abandoned train station on his right, knowing the town hall would be coming up on his left, on the other side of the street. The pea-souper meant he could see none of its large stone columns or the word 'Progress' carved high up on its soot blackened façade. Well, Frank my lad, you've made some tidy progress yourself tonight. Yes, everything was finally falling into place, and it felt good to be wheeling away a problem that had gnawed at him for days.

Bloody hell. There were many people out on the street here, darting out of his way at the last minute to avoid the cart. 'Make way, make way. Emergency fuel delivery!' he shouted, pushing the cart along the pavement, past the Electricity Showrooms on his right. Not far to go now, but with Ted's head just a few inches below the handlebar he was gripping hard, he now knew what it was like to be a hermit crab crawling along the sea floor between shells: vulnerable and easy prey.

'Emergency fuel, have we? Well if it isn't our law-abiding citizen Frank Pollock. And where are we off to at this hour, if you don't mind me asking?'

Frank stopped the cart and his shaky hands kept a tight grip on the handlebar; his bowels were on the cusp of contracting as he began sweating heavily again. There was no mistaking the face that was now within inches of his own, its booming voice laden with scorn: PC Arthur Crisp, who was already bending down to inspect the cart.

'Ah, Officer Crisp. I'm just making me way as fast as I can with this batch of fuel here. We'll be needing all we can get in this terrible weather. Bit parky out here, wouldn't you say?' Frank said, unable to stop stumbling over the words as his fingers trembled inside the tan leather gloves. A stream of sweat was already trickling down from the fringe of his balaclava and into his eyes, making them sting. He was having difficulty focusing on the policeman.

'Bloody hell, that smells almost as ripe as you do, Frank,' the policeman said, straightening himself up quickly after barely a glance at the cart. 'You'd best be off then.' PC Crisp walked away into the smog without another word, his silhouette disappearing well before the echo of his heavy, steel-capped boots had faded.

Shaking, Frank breathed in hard several times before starting to push the cart as fast as he could and leave the square to get away from the policeman. He manoeuvred it into a short, narrow lane and then veered right into a cobbled street and brought the cart to a juddering halt outside large iron gates. The smog was still too thick to see the building's red brick façade with its arch over the entrance that had an inscription he'd learned when he was a boy even though he wasn't sure what it meant: *E Pulvere, Lux et Vis*. What the hell was the connection between soap and electricity? He rang the bell in four short bursts, pushed open the gate, and wheeled the cart inside, ramming it against a wall so that Ted's head briefly rose above the straw.

'You took your bloody time, Frank. I can't be keeping the coast clear all night,' the head supervisor, a short, stocky white-haired man in filthy overalls said, unable to conceal his fear of the sweaty face peering at him from under the fedora. He glanced at the mound under Frank's mac, the hairy bare shins, and boots covered with dried brown splashes that had bits of straw stuck to them.

'Keep your hair on, Harold. I won't be long now. Why don't you go for a nice cuppa while I deal with this batch of fuel and we'll be none the wiser, will we?' Frank spoke quietly with an insistent, hard edge to his voice, making the supervisor cross his arms before turning on his heels and going into the works office without another word.

This building had always fascinated Frank, with its subterranean, rhythmic hum which he could feel vibrating through his boots when the furnaces operated flat-out, as they were now. He wheeled the cart to the goods lift whose concertina-grilled gates were open and ready for the load, though it took a while to grind its way to the top, where Frank dragged the cart out onto a flat roof and back into the smog. After pushing it along a few feet, he lined up the cart next to a two-yard-square shimmering hole and yanked up the handlebars to tip the contents down the hot, metallic throat of the dust destructor.

'Enjoy the warm welcome, Ted,' he chuckled as he heard the body and rubbish scrape and bump their way down the chute to the furnaces below. He wheeled the empty cart to the far end of the roof and parked it out of sight behind the maintenance shed.

After taking the emergency stairs to avoid being seen, he walked off into the smog filled streets.

Exhausted and dirty, Frank was also elated that Ted would not be bothering him ever again about Charlie Pooter. Without a cart to steer, he made much faster progress, thinking what a close-run thing it had been with PC Crisp. But the job was done, and just in the nick of time by the looks of things, as the pea-souper was thinning in parts, which would coax more people onto the streets.

Within a couple of minutes he was walking up a flight of stone steps and pushing open a large glass door. Inside, it was quiet, not surprisingly on a night like this, though he could see a couple of regulars sitting on a bench chatting. He nodded at the young man behind the counter, who sat bolt upright in shock when he realized who it was under the hat and balaclava. Frank took the small bar of grey soap and threadbare towel handed to him without a word, and gave no money in return. As he looked for his cubicle, he thought how nice it must be to have your own bathroom, and not having to drag a tin tub in front of the living-room fire every week. After running the taps for a few minutes, he eased himself into the big, full bath, the warmth quickly melting away the tension in his stiff neck and shoulders. With eyes closed and only his face, scrotum and big toes breaking the surface, he mouthed a silent thanks to Ted for heating the water.

III

1

LIZZIE SPOTTED A COBWEB IN the far corner of the bedroom, the band of silk spanning several inches between the
wall and pelmet. There was no sign of its spinner, or of any
trapped prey. She wondered why she hadn't spotted it until
now as she took pride in her work as a cleaner for the
Smethwicks. While making a mental note to dust it to
oblivion later, she shuddered as an inquisitive tongue
explored her inner thigh, leaving a trail of drool that trickled
onto the fresh linen sheet she'd put on the bed that very
morning. She was finding it hard to relax despite the twitchy
pink muscle doing its best to distract her.

She knew why, of course.

Ted had been missing for four days, with no sign of
him. Not a dicky-bird. She was at a loss over what to do
since arriving home late three nights ago to find the kitchen
and living room in a mess. The bastards. Why were they
burgled when there was so little of value to take? Strangely,
the rest of the house was untouched and, as far as she could
see and remember, nothing was missing. She still reported it
to the police, though she and Ted were too skint to afford
insurance, and repairing the smashed back door would not
come cheap. Bloody typical. Just when she needed a

carpenter, Ted went and disappeared.

His workmates had no clue where he was, either. She decided not to get in touch with his relatives in Yorkshire. Not yet, at least. Maybe he just wanted time to himself. He'd been a bit distant lately. She'd brushed off that pushy woman who had called round twice asking if he could make her some shelves. Needed to avoid that one, and her dodgy friends. She'd seen them drinking and laughing their heads off in the Ten Bells. Nothing but trouble, the lot of them.

She breathed faster and her buttocks pressed hard into the mattress as the tongue and its owner worked their way to the top of her thigh, near to their final destination which was already being stroked in thoughtful preparation. She was going to be strong and stick to her work routine in Highgate. Besides, if Ted was not coming back, she would need every penny of her pay from the Smethwicks, what with rent day fast approaching.

Just as she was arching her head into the lavender-smelling pillow, there was a hammering on the front door.

'Who the hell's that?' Denise Smethwick asked hoarsely, sitting bolt upright on the bed with her long auburn hair dishevelled.

The loud knocking continued.

Denise rose, put on a black and gold Chinese silk gown, and went to peep through the bay window that overlooked the gravelled driveway.

'It's the bloody police! What the hell do they want?' she said, turning to Lizzie. 'I hope to God it's nothing to do with Christopher again. I tell him to be careful in Soho, but he never listens.

Denise tightened the gown's cord around her slim waist

with a rapid tug, wondering what her husband had been up to this time. 'I'll go and answer the door. I think you'd better get dressed and pretend to be cleaning the bathroom or something,' she told Lizzie, who was already picking up clothes that were scattered across a large, powder-blue Persian rug.

There were three officers standing outside: a rotund, middle-aged, balding inspector who looked in a bad mood, and two young, smiling constables, one on either side of him.

'Please come in, officers. How may I help you?' she asked, keen to show willing. 'Please excuse my appearance. I've not been feeling too well today, and was resting. I hope nothing serious brings you here.'

She took them to the drawing room.

' 'Fraid it's very serious, ma'am. Very serious indeed,' the inspector said, cradling his hat in the crook of his arm and glancing longingly at the nearby whisky decanter, before facing her to explain himself. 'We're looking for a Mrs Lizzie Datchett, who works here as a charlady, if I'm not mistaken,' the inspector said.

'That's me,' a voice behind them said, and all four turned to see Lizzie walk into the room, wearing a plain navy dress and flowery pinny. She had a feather duster in one hand, the other holding an empty pail with a damp dishcloth draped over the rim.

'Mrs Datchett, I know you've had conversations with the police in Stepney about your missing husband. I'm here to tell you that after making further inquiries, I am arresting you on suspicion of murdering Ted Datchett. We're taking you down to the station straightaway,' the inspector said, prompting one of the constables to bring out a pair of handcuffs from his pocket.

Lizzie, silent, turned to Denise, who looked away almost immediately.

'Officer, I can't believe what I'm hearing. Lizzie wouldn't hurt a fly. What evidence do you have to make such dreadful accusations?' Denise said, her voice now less composed.

'I'm not at liberty to discuss that with you, ma'am. The facts will be disclosed in due course in the appropriate place and manner. Right, Mrs Datchett, I think we'd better get a move on.' The inspector placed a hand firmly on Lizzie's shoulder.

Handcuffed, and the pinny folded over the arm of the Chesterfield, Lizzie was escorted to the end of the driveway, where a police car was waiting. To Denise's relief, the car reversed into the main road and took a right down the hill, without a blue lamp flashing or siren blaring to draw the neighbours' attention. She stood in the hallway for a few seconds, her legs shaking, before going back to the drawing room, where she poured herself the first of several large whiskies.

2

TURNING THE CORNER ONTO PARK Road, Julie caught her reflection in the window of a large, black four-by-four. The angle and bright morning light lent enough depth for the glass to reflect her taut face that failed to hide a truth she was struggling to deny: Richard probably wouldn't get in touch. So far, no text, email or voicemail blinked or vibrated on her new pink phone. It had been two whole days since they'd met over dinner with friends at Pete's house on Friday, when Tom had stayed the night in town. Since the meal she'd made a point of wearing red knickers, her default lucky charm, but Richard's silence was becoming more unsettling and harder to ignore as time passed.

So, back to square one after barely a chase, let alone a thrill to go with it, she murmured, kicking a crumpled, empty beer can onto the road, forcing a cyclist to swerve and curse.

It wasn't as if she hadn't made an effort.

During the meal she'd been careful not to appear too keen or desperate in her witty exchange with him. She'd held it together well, switching to white wine to avoid Gothic teeth and tongue. And stopping after five glasses. Each time he'd said he was already a partner in his law firm at his age, she'd made a point of looking admiringly. She'd also complimented his Thunderbirds cuff-links.

And here she was on Monday fucking morning with another predictable start to the week. She cut through the park and headed for the tube, thinking how she found this green space uplifting before taking the underground for the City. Getting in early before the markets open at least meant the trains weren't too packed. A big advantage, given there were so few men these days who gave up a seat for her. Did she have to be pregnant or a cripple?

Thinking back to Saturday, she remembered how she'd been close enough to run a hand along Richard's broad, denimed thigh, but had finally thought better of it. Only slappers move that fast, and she also needed to think through what to do about Tom.

The morning was sunny but her mood still dark as she left the grassy stretch and walked down the hill, past a tall terrace of elegant, yellow-brick Victorian houses whose large sash windows offered a glimpse into tasteful suburban domesticity. This part of her daily commute made her wonder what it would be like to have a real marriage, to swap her veneer of coupledom for authentic, multi-dimensional living. Richard had promised to call and there was no doubt that he fancied her, that much was plain to everyone that night. Even Pete, Miss Cynic Bitch par excellence, had eventually agreed with her after she'd dissected Richard's responses and body language into the early hours. After telling Richard twice about that new film, the zany one by that stylish Spanish director, he'd finally nodded. And she'd been quick on her feet to recommend that upmarket Sichuan restaurant near his flat, a deft ploy which made her look attentive after he'd gone on and on about the great Asian food he'd eaten during his last trip to Bangkok and Hong Kong. Spicy food gave her heartburn, but there was always room for compromise. No point being dogmatic on a first date.

She was in full agreement with the girly mags that counselled waiting a bit before calling. But for how long? She'd given him her business card but unfortunately he was out of his. It had been easy to find out where he worked, and funnily enough his office was just a few streets from hers – maybe another sign this was meant to be? She could easily drop by, perhaps for a lunchtime coffee? No, best if the bloke called first. She didn't want to end up being a quickie for someone of that quality even though those sorts of nights were among the best sex she'd ever had.

It must be different this time, before she was too old to care or for anyone to notice. He looked the mature type, not wanting to appear in a hurry to score. She liked the way he spoke about past girlfriends in a positive way, saying it was best to let things go before they drag on too long, to be honest when there's no chemistry.

Classy.

She stopped for a few seconds to send Nick her second text of the day, suggesting they meet up later in the week to discuss what happened on Friday with Tom and his overnight stay. Why hadn't her friend called back to brief her? She needed to pin down what he was up to after gleaning from the paperwork in his study drawer and snatches of telephone chit-chat that he was selling buildings in the East End. It didn't sound to do with his day job.

If divorce was on the cards then she needed quality intelligence for her lawyer asap.

Richard could have called last night. He had no excuse as she'd watched him for almost an hour through his wide-open, first-floor French windows in that dinky back street in Pimlico. It was so obvious that he wasn't busy because she could hear pop music from her vantage point at the base of a large oak tree. Maybe he was still tired or hungover from Friday. She doubted it, somehow. She would pay him a second stealth visit after work, and this time try the video camera on her new phone. Had to be better than the crap photos she took last night.

3

ELSIE SAT SMOKING AND SIPPING tea in the living room, convinced things were not what they appeared to be. Reading fresh revelations behind James Dean's death in a newspaper spread out on the table in front of her deepened her sense of unease. Bloody unbelievable that so much could happen in a year, what with Churchill throwing in the towel and poor Princess Margaret calling off the wedding to that tasty captain because he was divorced. Beggars belief, really. No, things weren't going well these days except for that stuck-up Postie lot, flashing their cash up West, with Frank running after them like a poodle on heat.

Walking up the high street that morning she saw cops on every corner, making her stomach churn. They were asking if anyone knew anything about Ted Datchett, a local man who had not been seen for days. 'Can you help? You live round here, don't you, madam? Did you know him?' one of the policemen had asked her, knowing exactly who she was given the number of times she'd been in the nick. Here's the address and telephone number of the police station in case you've forgotten, another policeman said, with a wink. She thought that second one was Crisp, the smuggest of the lot round here. Barely able to say a word, she had just nodded, not speaking a word for fear of giving something away.

With so many bobbies on the prowl, she gave the shops in the high street a miss and carried on to Hoxton market, where she made a point of buying the food for her supper. Not that she was short of a bob or two after the Paris trip. The Ovaltine tin in the attic was stuffed with enough notes to keep her fed and watered for a while yet before she and the team would have to go gallivanting again.

A few quickies in the West End would keep things ticking over nicely for now.

Elsie didn't need cops to tell her that Ted was missing; she'd heard almost straightaway from Brian at the factory after he failed to turn up for work on Wednesday. Did he get lost in the pea-souper, Brian had asked. She wondered if anyone had seen her talking with Ted in the street when she was offering him the cabinet job. By the end, the poor devil had been so happy to be done with it. He hadn't bothered haggling for more money after the extra evening work he put in. Told her he was keen to get back to the factory before they could manage without him, now that furniture-making was starting to move out of town to better premises. The wife was in no mood to up sticks, Ted had explained to Elsie with a sigh.

She took a big slurpy sip of tea and pulled her cardigan tight as the wintry nip in the air made her shiver, despite having lit a fire. At least James Dean left a body, she thought, glancing down at the newspaper again. It was as if Ted had vanished into thin air.

'Nah, it's definitely not her,' she said, loud enough for her voice to echo. She'd buttonholed Lizzie on the high street to check if there was news, but got short shrift. Not surprising, given what's happened. Instinct told her that Lizzie was clueless about Ted's whereabouts, let alone that Elsie may have had a hand in his disappearance.

Hearing that the cops had arrested Lizzie on suspicion of murder had been a shocker for everyone. It was all wrong. Surely even Crisp and the other cops could see the idea was plain barmy. The bloke had no money, and she wasn't the type.

As she sucked heavily on her cigarette and stared into the fire, the conclusion was inescapable: Frank was the reason why Ted was missing. It was so obvious. He and his postie masters were clearly up to their necks in it.

But why?

She'd never seen Frank so panicky that morning down the wharf when he was all het up about a stupid missing wallet. And he'd accused her of nicking it, the bloody cheek. She tried to erase from her mind's eye a picture of Lizzie Datchett swinging from a rope like that Ruth Ellis not that long ago, for murdering her gorgeous lover.

The thought of Frank and the gallows made her get up to check if the back door was locked properly. She put a sixpence in the meter under the sink and filled the kettle. Tea and fags were the only company she wanted.

4

TOM LEANED BACK IN HIS black-leather swivel chair in the study and used a finger to navigate up and down a spreadsheet on his tablet computer. There were 112 names on the list.

'How simply dreadful. To think that the heirs to the Old Nichol are nothing more than a bunch of greedy little shits,' he said out loud, mimicking the hoarse voice of the director with its volatile mix of plummy posh and raw East End, with the latter overriding the former when the pompous git drank too much whisky.

Pitch-perfect. Tom sniggered.

'And it's about time too that we sold up and moved on,' Tom added under his breath and in his own accent. He placed the tablet on the desk and rubbed his hands together, smiled, and poured the remains of an astonishingly fruity pinot noir into his glass. He picked up the tablet again to re-read the familiar names, pausing occasionally as he recalled their faces, memories of parties, run-ins with relatives and distant conversations. It was incredible how things had changed since a bunch of paupers agreed to a do-or-die postie pact after being kicked out of the rookery. Fast-forward a century and here we are, about to enter full liquidation of accumulated capital gains, as his accountant pithily put it.

The director was right, of course, but for the wrong reason: the Posties were indeed revolting, determined to turn piles of Victorian bricks into hard cash, but not because they were turning their backs on who they were. All that sentimental guff about loyalty and heritage being dumped by a feckless younger generation was bullshit, and the director knew it. Heritage was an alien indulgence for those whose DNA comes from the gutters of the Old Nichol, where they only had their wits to live on.

It was simply a matter of hard-headed business. It was time to take profits, to secure value for future generations from what had been built up over years. Is that not a sensible, respectful nod to our postie pioneers, Mr Director?

He'd always admired that first generation of Posties, the real social trailblazers round here who'd effectively founded the world's first urban regeneration agency. Admittedly it may not have been done in any conventional or lawful sense. Still, they were ahead of their time in gentrifying bombed out corners long before Ivy League trust-fund kids and scruffy art graduates opened pop-up galleries and shabby chic organic, fair trade cafes. What was it he'd read the other day? Yes, that stupid sign in the artisanal bread and marmalade bar which said the milk was from a single herd in Kent. Fuck me. And what's the carbon footprint on a pint like that? Anyway, who cares how the Posties did it? Reckon the end justified the means after being priced out of that spanking new Boundary Estate by a bunch of north London philanthropists not sure what to do with their money.

Not that the Postie pile was any match for the Grosvenor or London's other uber landlords – but still, it had ticked along nicely, having morphed into a hyperactive hole in the wall as property prices rocketed. To think how even a shite derelict warehouse purloined in early years would be making them a mint. And that was just for starters. Not bad for the boys of the Jago.

'Timing is all in markets, my dear boy, timing is all,' he said with the director's accent again. 'But those dreadful, greedy shits want more! They always come back for more.'

He drained his glass, thinking how it should come as no surprise to anyone that most of them wanted to grab the cash and piss off while the going was good. Well, nearly everyone, he corrected himself, as he recalled his meeting with the butt naked director in the sauna. That man had no bloody clue how most Posties think. The twat.

At least he could go back to the director and tell him truthfully that he'd canvassed all living, accessible, compos mentis Posties about selling Hope Wharf, and anywhere else that might find a taker. Nearly all of them wanted out, to sell up now rather than keep on collecting rents and ground rents year after year. Not that he'd bothered trying to persuade them otherwise. Let's face it, once you'd slapped an extra floor or two of glass lofts onto the warehouses round there, the extreme outer limit of planning permission had well and truly been maxed out, especially when you had to deal with the annoying vigilantes from the local conservation societies as well. Conserving what, and for whom? Admittedly, there were a handful of Posties who suggested that flogging the stuff over a few years to limit unwanted legal scrutiny might be an idea. Well, stuff that, you unimaginative wankers. Now he was going to be single again, he was quids in.

'To a brave new world,' he said out loud, thrusting the empty bottle into the air.

'Sorry, darling. You said something?' Julie asked, her head appearing from behind the half-open study door.

'Nothing, darling. Just rambling again,' he replied with a jump.

He heard her sigh and go to the kitchen where she slammed the microwave door. A couple of muffled pings followed a few of minutes later. Good. Now it was his turn for din-dins.

Cripes, he thought, remembering his cack-handed attempt in the sauna to soften up – or rather harden up – the director for the sale of the century. He'd been so glad to be out of that steam pit and get home for a hot shower and think about Sunita from the office while having a wank. When was the last time he'd pictured Julie's face when coming? Aeons ago. There was no hope in hell of getting off with Sunita in real life; she was way too smart to fall for someone like him. And, she already had a boyfriend in tow who was big in advertising, and no doubt cool and good-looking too. The jammy bastard.

Anyway, before getting involved with other women he had to clear things up with Julie first, to draw a humongous red line the size of the Berlin Wall between them, and then he could move on. They both knew the marriage was over but he was buggered if she was getting her mitts on his postie dosh. Bet she's trying to line up some bloke before jumping ship – she hates being on her own as well, he thought. Perhaps she'll shack up with that underachieving, clueless dickhead she bribes with booze to tail me. Some private eye. A fucking disgrace. He snorted as the last of the ruby-red liquid coursed down the back of his throat. It had been so much fun to drag him to a queer sauna a few times. Wonder what he made of it all? The twins had such a laugh hassling him. Their idea of shoving a bollard in his bed was an inspired touch of The Godfathers!

Yep, Hope Wharf would be the first to go, and a great way to test the market too. How did the estate agent describe it on their website? 'A luxury live-work canal-quarter experience'. Bet it took a media studies graduate a whole morning and a spliff to think of that one. He rose unsteadily from his chair and had to grip the walnut desk to maintain his balance, toppling a silver-framed picture. 'Sorry, auntie Elsie,' he slurred, putting the photo back on its stand. The kitchen would be clear by now. Time to get some grub.

5

FRANK WAS HAVING A BAD day, and was holed up at home in bed.

He was used to the occasional fever, chill and headache; they were part and parcel of his condition, but today all three had ganged up to keep him flat on his back. He hadn't been himself since the pea-souper night; all the willpower and concentration poured into making glue, keeping an eye on Ted and cleaning up a mess of his own making had taken a heavy toll, draining away his energy.

Listless, he lay between the sheets for the whole day, pushing his spirits even lower.

He knew he'd been lucky so far, and couldn't depend on things staying that way. If PC Crisp had searched the cart and found Ted, then he'd be swinging by the neck in no time. But the policeman hadn't, and a nosy carpenter ended up in a puff of smoke. Problem solved. Or should have been if it wasn't for the bleeding cops swarming all over Shoreditch and arresting Lizzie Datchett.

'What yer on about? She won't hang. The cops haven't got an ounce of proof to convince a jury. And what makes you so sure he's dead? They haven't found a body, have they, so he must be still alive,' he'd told a persistent Elsie several times during her unexpected visit to the warehouse the night before.

'I reckon someone's done him in, and it should be obvious to the thickest cop it wasn't her. All I need is one of Ted's mates to tell the police they saw me talking to him, and I'll be arrested in no time,' she'd snapped back. 'Enough people must have seen him, you and me coming to this miserable place. You only need one nosy parker to squeal and we'll all have some explaining to do down the nick.' Before turning to leave, she looked at him long and hard, and he couldn't stop himself from going sweaty in the face and red in the neck. Did she know more than she was letting on? Doubt it, as he'd been careful to cover his tracks. Every drop of the blood spattered outside and inside the garage had been washed away. The cart was clean as a whistle, too. He'd checked it again the other day.

Despite all these precautions, he felt permanently on edge, made all the worse as undisturbed sleep stayed out of reach, his temperature rose and the continuous drip of gastric acid etched away at his entrails. What should he do next? Only a fool would mess with Elsie and he'd regret it fast; the stupid Posties had a soft spot for her, and he never could work out why. He suspected she spoke with them directly sometimes, going behind his back. The bloody flirt needed putting in her place.

He shifted to the other side of the bed, where the nylon sheet was cooler and drier.

There was also the problem of what to do with the new manager at the dust destructor. He needed educating in the postie ways pretty damn quick. Should be a doddle, though. Bit of a foreigner, coming from Manchester, but he'd soon learn which side his bread was buttered. Just as well there wouldn't be more batches of fuel to cart along there and burn. Frank chuckled.

In the meantime he would keep a close eye on Elsie now her pretty head was getting all bothered about Lizzie bloody Datchett. We'd see how long that one lasts. She'd soon be back to stuffing knickers with those fingers of hers and their bright red nail varnish. He smiled, triggering a sharp stabbing pain in the back of the head that dulled his fledgling erection. Don't fret about what hasn't happened, he told himself. And when the fever subsided in a day or two, as it always did, then he would feel much better too. The Posties had already given him another job to do after the cabinet went down a treat with the new director. Well, talk about new brooms sweeping clean. This one had made it clear he wanted to bag more buildings as if there was no tomorrow. Another deeds job it was, then. Kept the tallyman from the door, thank God.

He closed his eyes and slipped into a fitful doze, but not about a smiling Elsie as it usually did these days, but about Lizzie Datchett, who'd come to Hope Wharf in a red dress. Why was she bending over to open the cabinet Ted built? Her dress was tightening around her backside, revealing a faint knicker line he wanted to trace with a chisel in his hand. She stepped aside so he could see the cabinet's interior with its felt-lined shelf that displayed a row of small metal pots brimming with warm honey. He wanted to dip in a finger and smear the sweet liquid over his parched lips, but he couldn't quite reach, no matter how far he stretched. Breathing rapidly, he woke up in a heavy sweat, with both sides of the bed now damp.

6

THE MUSIC STREAMED AT FULL volume from the curved grey speakers as Nick, stretched out on his black-leather sofa, let the pulsating rhythm course through his body. The bright sunshine flooding into the room through an expanse of French windows also helped to lift his mood. He could see the potted bollard on the balcony from the corner of his eye. It looked like a half-finished, first-year art-school installation.

Listening to the music in his urban eyrie high above the streets made him feel connected to life on a deeper level, but blissfully shielded from the siliconeastas, mass millennials and office workers out on the piss below. He turned onto his side and glanced down at the remains of a curry lunch he'd assembled from a row of aluminium containers, lined up like an empty cargo train on its way to a depot under the coffee table. He grimaced at the sight of a blue-leather handbag poking out from under the sofa; another reminder to throw away Amanda's stuff. It was time for a clean break. His piecemeal efforts so far had been like slowly peeling off a damaged fingernail; it was best to yank it off to let the new growth emerge from underneath.

He noticed that the two unopened letters on the floor

were spattered with ghee, the orange oil making stains like psychedelic 1960s wallpaper. He was feeling very full and very contented. Listening to the tape of Tom and Mr Mystery Man had cheered him up no end. It was mind boggling how a century-old social microcosm could stay invisible to the untrained eye in an internet age.

They sounded like a version of the Freemasons. Wonder how people come to join?

He'd looked up Hope Wharf online and found a link to Nichol Estates, a property firm that during the 1980s had converted the place into flats that doubled up as business units, part of the same pioneering wave of gentrification as his own home. Hope Wharf was obviously Victorian, and had been used by joiners since well before the Second World War, according to the rose-tinted reminiscences of now-dead locals he'd read online. The place had been empty from the late 50s, and brought back to life by squatters in the 70s, before they'd been chucked out, no doubt, by Nichol Estates. He'd drawn a complete blank over who owned it before them, or how ownership changed in earlier years.

A recce had yielded little apart from a pleasant stroll.

He stood on the towpath to see Hope Wharf from the other side of the canal, and liked its large windows with their authentic wooden shutters pinned to the outside walls. The place must have been used for loading goods on and off barges with the crane whose remains was fixed to the outside wall, a historical charm that gave estate agents a hard on.

Should have checked if the place was listed as there would be more information in the public domain if that were the case. Shame about the rubbish in the canal. You'd think the council would dredge the crap given how much council tax the tenants were forking out. He'd counted at least two traffic cones at the bottom of what was surprisingly clear water. The wharf's main entrance on the street side revealed little, just the usual code-entry system to open a reinforced glass door into a narrow lobby with mail boxes down one side, a lift on the other, and a big mirror on the far wall. He'd already paid for searches at the Land Registry and all seemed fine, if not informative.

So far, so dull then.

He tapped his fingers to the urgent, repetitive rhythm of the music on the cushion pressed against his chest. Trouble was, he thought, no news editor was going to be remotely interested in a story about descendants of slum dwellers flogging off a canal-side wharf to cream off a profit when everyone else and their mother were doing the same thing as fast as they could before the market crashed. A housing bubble lifts everyone's boat, right? Yep, there was a big credibility hole when it came to showing that not only was all of this dodgy, but gobsmackingly and criminally so, to make it interesting to a reader. Grainy black-and-white pics of warehouses and cloudy eyed biddies banging on about the old times wouldn't cut it with an editor. And he needed cast-iron intelligence, not just on Hope Wharf but also other places to show a pattern of flouting the law that went back years. And where was the public interest in all this? Where indeed.

Ah well, give it a bit more time to stew, and if nothing came of it then Julie would have to pay an obscene fee to a forensic accountant, or private eye, or both. Her hunger to fleece Tom was unbridled, but she'd be needing the very best of luck to come out on top of all that.

He stretched out to pick up the two stained letters. One of them had a Swiss postmark and was the quarterly statement from his private bank with its fee for what he'd long called wealth mismanagement. The other letter was embossed with the logo of the block's managing agents, the mere sight of which triggered his usual response: here we go again, another hike in service charges to repair the lift. He threw both letters so forcefully that they hit the window and crash landed in the empty newspaper rack underneath. His thoughts turned back to Hope Wharf and the recording from the sauna, wishing he had a better grasp of what was going on beneath the surface of his own borough. He would try and pump Julie for more information on the postie empire. Should he tell her about Tom's offer of a hand job? Maybe not. Well, not for now anyway. Wonder why Gingernuts turned him down? Tom was pretty good-looking and in great shape, even if a bit up his own arse at times. If he told her about Tom's goings-on in a gay sauna, she'd confront him, and the last thing he needed were two heavies pounding on the door or getting seriously heavy with Harry if they ever put two and two together, which they would eventually.

He let rip a satisfyingly long fart, tapped the zapper to turn down the music, and closed his eyes, thinking of way to wipe that cocky smile off Tom's face. In less than half an hour he woke up, anxious after stumbling through dense forest while being stalked by the silhouette of Amanda on the border of his peripheral vision. He blamed the curry.

LIZZIE DATCHETT WAS SITTING ON the edge of her small, worn sofa at home, not even bothering to draw the curtains or turn on the light. The room was still a mess from the burglary, and she was on her second glass of neat gin since being released by the police barely an hour ago. Thank God for the Smethwicks, who'd sent Pierce to do the talking.

'Mrs Datchett, please don't worry. They don't have a shred of evidence against your good name to convince a jury,' the short, balding solicitor had said before they both sat down for a long interview with the sweaty inspector, who'd chain-smoked throughout, not offering her a fag once. She would have screamed at them had she not been so tired and scared. Throughout the questioning, her thoughts kept returning to that woman they hanged less than a year ago for murder. What was her name again?

'Oh, they'll keep trying to bully you into admitting something, anything, to close the case,' Pierce had said. 'With what they've got so far, they'd be laughed out of court. I'm quite sure of that, and I suspect they know it too.'

After the interview, he was scribbling notes in his file with a black fountain pen. He was like a doctor trying to reassure a patient the affliction was not terminal. That

Denise had insisted on paying his bill was also a relief, because if Ted didn't turn up soon, she wouldn't be able to afford to live here much longer. On her own, the rent was beyond her means, and she wouldn't go begging to her parents. 'I did warn you. We told you he wasn't good enough,' her mother would be eager to say, seizing any excuse to reiterate her low opinion of Ted since their courting days.

How long ago that felt. And which courting days would she remember a few years from now? Those with Ted or the time she met Denise at the Gateways in Chelsea? She was instantly attracted to her. Denise was sitting on a stool and leaning over the bar, talking to one of her confident and loud university friends. She felt nervous in the company of those people, conscious of not having the poise that money and education conferred. She'd stared at Denise from the back of the long, narrow room, not having the nerve at first to make a move, though it was only an hour or so later they were jigging in and out of each other's orbit on the dance floor. It wasn't just Denise's vivacity that was attractive, but also the way she dressed in her own effortless style. Most of the women in the bar, including herself, wore what one of Denise's friends called 'sexual semaphores': a man's jacket or pretty dress. Well, nothing wrong with either because underneath they were all women to Lizzie.

The gin was making her light-headed and she sat upright to focus better on the situation at hand. She leaned over to stub out her cigarette on a saucer that was already overflowing with twisted stubs. It was dark outside though the sky was clear, a relief after that horrible, choking pea-souper. The glow from a street lamp gave out enough light for her to see the papers strewn across the floor and to notice how the spine of Ted's favourite book, the large, flat one on cabinet designs, was badly buckled. The burglar must have thrown it against the floor after rifling through the shelves for valuables they could never afford. If Ted had walked out on her, that book would have been the first thing he'd pack, along with the sketches of cabinets that now lay around her feet. She used her right foot to slide one of them across the lino towards her, and switched on the standard lamp next to the sofa, making her eyes burn briefly until they got used to the brightness. That was definitely Ted's stubby handwriting in the left-hand margin, she thought. 'No engravings, plain finish'. Further down the page he'd added 'Two coats'. Across the top, in capitals, she read: 'Need by Feb 5. Cash from Elsie. MUST use only materials from Frank!!!'

The date was barely a fortnight ago.

Trying to tame her thoughts, now racing from gin and Ted's notes, she couldn't for the life of her remember him working on a cabinet out the back, in the kitchen or anywhere else, in the past year, let alone month. She would know about it. He hadn't taken any time off since Christmas and she was sure he'd been working as usual in the factory, and coming home in the evenings. Well, except for darts on Tuesday nights, of course.

She downed the remaining clear liquid, poured herself another, and lit a fresh cigarette.

Easing back in the sofa, it dawned on her how Ted's notes went some way in explaining the look on Elsie's face on the high street, why she'd kept on asking about him and his whereabouts. 'When do you think he could come round to take measurements for the shelves? You don't think it would be any trouble for him, do you? He's not gone away on holiday, has he?'

It was the words of someone who knew more than they were letting on, who was worried that something had gone wrong, who wanted reassurance that Ted was fine.

She must confront Elsie to get to the bottom of it all, but it was best to treat her with kid gloves, given she was always holding court down the Ten Bells, all dolled up in fancy clothes with stupid men falling over themselves to buy drinks for her and her big-mouthed friends all night. But who the hell was Frank? Probably some harmless bloke doing the donkey work for Ted to get on with the cabinet. Maybe she should have had a word with him first before tackling Elsie. Couldn't do any harm.

She rose unsteadily to her feet, stubbed out her cigarette and folded the cabinet drawing carefully. Must keep this safe, she thought. Perhaps she should show it to Pierce. Best not to complicate things when it looked like she was in the clear. Well, if the cops knocked on her door again, she wouldn't be going down the station without Elsie being dragged there by the scruff of the neck as well.

8

FOUR FLOORS BELOW, THE WATER was being tugged imperceptibly east by the Thames and its waning tide. The canal reflected a cloudless sky in July, apart from where patches of bright-green bloom trapped plastic bags and spent beer cans.

Not surprisingly for a hot Saturday afternoon, the towpath was choked with people out strolling, trying not to get run over by cyclists weaving their way along, with few bothering to slow down.

Funny how nobody ended up in the water for an unplanned dip, the director thought as he looked down, noticing that the old brick shed on the towpath was now a cafe with customers squeezed into small, uncomfortable 1960s classroom chairs, trying to look relaxed. 'Pete's Pop-Up', read a board leaning against the shed. What on earth does that mean? Shaking his head, the director turned away to sit down at a long glass trestle table whose chunky chrome legs left him unsure where to fold his own.

'I think you're going to miss this place!' his short, balding friend shouted from the galley kitchen. 'Quite a perk, don't you think, Mr Director? Makes it worthwhile putting up with the drudge you power brokers have to deal with.'

He was pouring freshly brewed coffee from a small cafetière into two powder-blue porcelain mugs.

'Indeed. Well, to work, then,' the director said, flipping open a bulging box file in front of him on the table that was crammed with printouts and frayed legal documents. 'I've been studying the stuff Fry emailed us this morning. The phrase "resistance is futile" springs to mind for some reason.' He looked out of the window again. His friend was right, of course, he did love this glorious glass box the board had decided to build on top of Hope Wharf a few years ago. And very true. Not bad at all for a grace and favour pad. From this watchtower he could pick out most of the buildings that would soon no longer be theirs, if all went to plan. The director had tried stamping his own, albeit temporary personal touch on the place, such as that Haring print he'd bought in New York, set off perfectly against the large white wall. One of the younger Posties had asked why he was so keen on Mr Men posters at his age.

Bloody philistines, as well as greedy shits.

'I suspect Fry's heart was not quite in it when he asked our fellow rookers to reconsider selling,' the companion said, sitting opposite the director after placing the two mugs of coffee on a newspaper article about the increasingly mixed prospects for commercial property in the capital. The director had circled several paragraphs but his friend ignored them, believing – like Fry – that most of the Posties were keen to wade across this inner-city Rubicon to a shiny post-Shoreditch world of vomit-free suburbs and Waitrose shopping.

'I doubt his cock was up for it either,' the director chuckled, the coarseness of the quip catching his friend off-guard briefly.

'Ah yes, the meeting in the sauna. Bless. He was only trying to please,' the short man said.

The director took out a tablet computer from the brief-case at his feet and called up the spreadsheet Fry had sent him the previous evening, his heavy finger jabs making the gadget jump around on the table. 'I had a funny feeling it would end up like this on my watch. Let's face it, the signs were there from the start. I'm sure you won't be surprised to learn that I've already put out a few feelers about Hope. When we sell here, and I think it's now a case of when rather than if, we shall need to push things through quickly, and not just to avoid legal potholes. A little bird tells me some rather extensive planning applications for new-builds and warehouse conversions are in the pipeline round here. Exactly what we don't want to be competing with, especially when it comes to letting go of our more tired properties.' The director reached for his coffee and glanced round, as if he had expected biscuits too.

'But Mr Director,' the companion asked with a raised eyebrow, 'would we not look a touch desperate, let alone risk a weak hand in negotiations, if we put several up for sale at the same time? The big developers and not to mention the prospective buyers would put two and two together pretty quickly. We don't want to get shafted where it hurts, do we?'

'I've thought of that one,' the director replied. 'Apart from Hope, the other two I have in mind for selling straightaway aren't part of Nichol Lofts but come under separate companies. Just as well one of my cannier prede-cessors muddied the ownership trail. Prescient, in fact.'

'Yes, of course, now I remember,' his friend nodded. 'Though that wasn't without a spot of bother at the time, I believe. Didn't some anal solicitor ask awkward questions about the deeds?'

'That was certainly the case, though all was quietly sorted out without a soupçon of dirty Calvins washed in public. But yes, you're right, we must be more careful than in the past now we don't have a Teddie – or was it a Frankie or Freddie – to glue careless lips, as my father would say. Where on earth did he get such idiotic sayings?'

The two men laughed out loud.

The director sipped his coffee and leaned back in his chair, the sight of spreadsheets on a screen giving him that uneasy feeling of not being fully in control, coming as he did from a generation that preferred reading paper printouts. Predictive texting triggered similar anxiety.

Sensing the director's waning interest in the data, his friend reached over to grab the tablet and went to sit in a leather armchair that overlooked the canal. He began swiping his finger lightly over the screen to make the spreadsheet scroll up and down, the names conjuring up familiar faces and events.

Ah, Jim Sands, the man who sees us as the last bastion of true East End heritage, votes in favour of selling the lot, he thought. Yes, the final farewell to their spiritual home won't be long now. And it won't be a bad result for a venture whose rents brought riches the Old Nichol tenants could only dream of.

What more was there left to do, anyway? Don't all good things eventually come to an end? And wasn't it more sensible, profitable even, to get out while they could and avoid the inevitable decline of what they had?

'Do you think Posties will still want to keep in touch once the quarterly cheques stop?' he asked the still silent director, who was rifling through his box file glumly.

'I doubt the alumni will be holding a tombola any time soon,' the director replied drily. 'But we should end it all with the mother of all knees-ups and raffle the cabinet. Once the spoils have been divided, I think it's just going to be you and me reminiscing over drinks at the club.'

They sat without saying a further word as they waited for Thomas Fry to arrive and tell them what they already knew, before discussing the detail of what had already been decided. The small fat man began checking a website selling lofts in Manhattan while the director stared out over Shoreditch, savouring a view that would soon belong to someone else.

9

IT WAS DADDY BURTT'S FOR a slap-up dinner and Frank's
appetite was back, the chills and headaches gone.

He always did these deeds jobs better on a full stomach
as he could never be sure quite how long they'd take. As he
was about to step inside the Christian Mission food kitchen,
he looked across the square at the dust destructor humming
like a well-oiled machine, its permanent plume of white
smoke rising perfectly straight into the clear, windless night.
What a relief he would not be paying another visit to that
place any time soon, he smiled, as daily routine and health
were back on an even keel. He turned and walked down a
short, wood panelled corridor to the main hall, the smell of
freshly cooked food becoming stronger with each stride. Ah,
must be cottage pie. Perfect. That would take his mind off
that tiring pea-souper night and Ted. His tongue was
champing to suck up the gravy and soften the burnt, crispy
mash he loved so much. Bleeding heck, this place was
packed. Couldn't complain, though. A full house meant
there'll be plenty of people who could, maybe grudgingly,
vouch that he supped here tonight. The volunteers nodded
nervously at him, making only fleeting eye contact, but he
smiled back before taking one of the few empty seats that

was right in the front of the serving hatch.

'Been a while, Frank. Found yourself a fancier restaurant?' shouted Jack, who was pouring tea into a row of cups from a large aluminium urn on a trolley. His left forearm was missing, the result of a war injury. How Frank wished his physical ailment was due to a Jerry bomb as well; people would be all friendly and invite him to their homes, and the cocky kids from round the corner would listen respectfully to his tales from the front.

'Been a bit poorly, Jack. Had a chill, but that's gone now!' he shouted back, and sat down, not waiting for any sympathy. The regulars always kept their distance, fearing his postie paymasters would tap them on the shoulders if they upset him. It was good to feel that sort of power over this rag-tag and muffin lot. It made him swell with pride as he sipped water from a battered metal tumbler. If this lot only knew how squeamish the Posties really were, it would be a different story. Let's face it, would the boss of a real mob fret about a stupid cabinet? Nah, the perks would be more of the big tit and blonde kind. The Posties were a bunch of paupers who'd struck it rich. Big fish in a piddling sea, that's what his mother called them, and she was right. But as she also said, you don't go biting the hand that feeds you, even when it's as limp as a dead eel in summer.

The mash and carrots were barely warm, but the gravy was thick and hot. With the meal downed and two mugs of tea drunk, he sat for a while and thought over what lay ahead in the coming hours. Unfortunately this could be the last deeds job as the real mob round here was tightening its grip, and had no patience with amateurs like the Posties. Still, there would always be tidying-up work of one kind or another, especially as the rookers upped sticks to live in posher parts of town. The squeamish little lambs would still be needing him to keep things in order.

He rose and buttoned his mac, lifting the collar to cover the nape of his neck, and walked down the central aisle and out the door with barely a goodbye or a nod. Outside, the evening was still crisp and clear and within minutes he was walking down a narrow alley-way between two scruffy warehouses just off the high street. There was no street lighting but like on the pea-souper night he could feel his way while humming to himself. He knew there was little risk of being seen or heard as nobody in their right minds would be venturing onto these back streets at this time of night.

The fingers of his left hand traced a brick wall until he felt a wooden door which would be unlocked. From inside his coat pocket he pulled out his tan leather gloves and put them on before turning the handle and pushing open the door to step inside a small yard that lay in front of a large five-storey brick warehouse. With the door shut gently behind him he switched on a torch, but kept the beam pointing at the ground to stop it catching windows on the upper floors.

Couldn't be too careful.

The yard was empty apart from a couple of dismantled sawing machines waiting to be taken away to the scrapyard. He made a sweep with the torch beam, catching the tail of a rat disappearing down the narrow space between the building and an eight-foot perimeter wall that was topped with metal spikes. Following the rat's path, he came to a side door which he opened using a key left for him on the lintel.

Inside, the lovely sweet smell of wood and shavings was as comforting as home cooking, putting him at ease. He shone the torch round the workshop with its rows of sawing machines, most covered in old tarpaulin, a sign of how a once-thriving furniture industry was on the wane. Large offcuts of wood, and screws and nails of all sizes, littered the floor.

The place was a total mess.

'Dear oh dear! What would a spark do here, I wonder?' he asked out loud with mock concern, his voice echoing in the room. He'd worked out the answer several days ago with the desperate owners, Calvert Fine Furniture, which had long ceased to make money – or good enough furniture, by the looks of things. Its best carpenters had been lured further east to work for the big boys. Shame, really. At this rate there would only be a few small workshops and one-man-band upholsterers left, giving the rag trade a clear run. And then what would happen? All the jobs would be doled out by the Bengalis to their own. Well, that was no different from the carpenters, or the silk weavers before them. Keep it in the family, as they say, just like the Posties, too. Some things never bloody changed.

Wonder how long the Posties had been turning the screw on the owners? Maybe the company just wanted an easy way out by pocketing the insurance money and handing over the deeds to the Posties. Still, a bit of old fashioned East End persuasion was needed to move things along. Those photos of the owner's son being spanked to within an inch of his life in a brothel on Cable Street had helped. The thought of sex made him recall that warm moment of intimacy in Hope Wharf with Elsie. Oh, how those deft little hands of hers could be so tender. No cat in hell's chance of that happening again. He still kept her knickers under his pillow as a memento, though their smell of French perfume had faded.

The workshop owner had shown how to create a power surge to ignite carefully placed paper and sawdust, assisted by petrol. The kindling would be enough for the blocks of wood and cuttings already laid out in rough lines across the floor to catch fire. He zigzagged between the machines and piles of timber to a cupboard on the far right-hand side of the room, inside of which was a row of five levers that he had to push down simultaneously to generate a burst of sparks. First though, he checked if the stripped wires hidden by one of the machines were close enough to the paper and sawdust. Good. He unscrewed a small bottle of petrol left there for him, and tipped out just enough to avoid detection by the fire brigade. Satisfied everything was ready, he slipped the bottle into his mac pocket.

What a palaver.

He'd suggested lighting a match and legging it but the owners were insistent, saying they knew what the insurance company and the cops would look for before signing any compensation cheques. Back at the mains cupboard, he used a stick to push down all five levers together and it worked first time, a two-foot flash lighting up the dark, quickly followed by small flames that grew in size and strength as they spread along the floor.

Nothing beats meticulous preparation and a cool head.

He waited a few minutes to make sure the fire had spread enough to engulf the sawing machines and work-benches before he headed for the side door. The rest of the warehouse was empty, the business too weak to support stocks of timber, let alone finished chairs and tables in the forlorn hope of new orders. Out in the open air again, he buttoned up his mac and tiptoed back down the narrow path, turning round to check the fire was still taking hold. Excellent. Flames were already creating a glow in the fanlight above the door he'd used.

What the hell was going on?

Back in the main yard he froze when he saw the outdoor lights had been turned on. How could that be? Sweat began to form on his forehead, his stomach cranked out acid and his balls felt heavier when he spotted the back of a stocky man standing by the now-open door onto the street. Why on earth had the night-watchman turned up so early? It wasn't the usual one either. And where did that large cosh propped up against the wall come from? Surely the man couldn't be that scared working round here. He must have been deaf and blind, though, not to notice the fire. Thankfully, the bloke was having a fag before checking the premises. Frank knew if he spotted him he'd have no chance of escape, because all the night-watchman would need to do was step into the street, lock the door and shout for help. With these high walls, he would be like a rabbit in a cage.

Rivulets of sweat were now running down Frank's forehead and into his eyes; his bowels were threatening to become uncontrollably loose as he racked his brains about what to do next, knowing he could not afford to mess up, otherwise the Posties would hang him out to dry if the cops caught him. He'd be done for arson and end up in prison. Shuddering at the thought of how the lags would treat him, he took off his boots and walked in his woollen socks towards the street door, making sure he stayed outside the man's peripheral vision. The night-watchman gave out a muffled yelp when two tan leather-gloved hands gripped his neck and yanked him inside. Frank then kicked the door shut and forced him to the ground, pressing his thumbs harder on the man's windpipe. Despite his advantage of surprise and strength, the night-watchman lashed out several times with his legs and fists until he was suddenly still, his open eyes staring upwards at the clear, starry sky. Frank was dripping sweat onto the man's face and could smell cigarettes on the last, rattling breath that condensed in the cold air.

Frank hauled himself up and went to turn off the yard lights, though he knew this would soon be pointless as flames were already beginning to light up the building from within and thick smoke was belching out of the gap between the warehouse and the perimeter wall. Glass was beginning to crack from the heat, the noise loud enough to be heard in the street.

Where the hell could he hide the night-watchman until he fetched the cart and find enough straw and rubbish to cover him? He looked at the building and then up to the sky, shaking his head in disbelief: everything was a mess again, and all of his own making despite the best-laid plans.

IV

1

JULIE WAS GRATING ON NICK'S nerves as they sat at an outside table of the restaurant, determined to maximise every minute of summer. Everything and everyone was pissing him off at the moment and he knew she was just a convenient lightning rod for a bout of unfocused ire. But he loved dining alfresco, even if it needed the flickering and hissing bottled gas heater next to them to take the edge off an unexpectedly chilly evening air. Wasn't global warming meant to make summers hotter? The restaurant was on a quiet, scrubbed square lined with an architectural hodge-podge of buildings. Next door had a blue ceramic plaque with something about Daddy Brute written on it. Had to have been a famous East End wrestler in his time, a sport his granny loved watching on Saturday afternoons when he was a kid. Years later he'd read that many of the matches had been routinely fixed, a cornerstone of his childhood memories suddenly crumbling.

The wide red-brick building on the far side of the square with its Latin inscription over the main entrance also drew his eye because of its simple elegance and clean lines. Clearly another Victorian technical college or school converted into luxury lofts. He'd lived long enough round here to get a good sense of its history. Wonder if the Posties had owned it?

'Been bloody manic today from the first Americano. Anyway, any news on what Tom's been up to?' she asked, looking him in the eye as she bit into a fleshy green olive. 'Give it to me straight, warts and all, baby. I'm a grown-up girl, as you well know.'

Nick laughed and grabbed an olive himself.

'Well, frankly, it's all a bit dull so far. I really don't think he's cheating on you. There's not a whiff of extracurricular nooky, and to be honest, all this is starting to get on my tits. I must admit it was fun at first, but I'm not cut out for this private-eye thing.' He was trying to sound light and jokey, avoiding her gaze by focusing on running his thumb and forefinger up and down the stem of a large glass of warmish red wine. They should have gone for rosé, a chilled no-brainer at this time of year.

'Shit, Nick. He must be up to something, right? He's rarely home in the evenings. He must be doing business then on the side. You know, a private transaction of some sort.'

He noticed that she'd lost a bit of weight and her breasts looked fantastic under that tight, classy, wraparound summer dress. She really was cranking up the sexual energy – or pussy preps as one of his college friends would call it. Wonder what the equivalent would be for a bloke? New boxers and flossed teeth?

'Well, he does have a pretty demanding day job that involves a lot of wining and dining clients to keep them sweet,' he said. 'By the way, you look great. You and Tom getting back in the *luurv groove* again? Let's drink to that!'

She ignored the remark and started fiddling with her phone, checking for messages again.

A scruffy, lank-haired man in his forties was making his way past the tables, begging for money. He stopped to show diners his gashed left forearm, spattered a little too liberally with fake blood to be credible outside a West End theatre.

'Got any change, mate? I need a couple of quid to get meself to the hospital,' the man said.

Nick barely looked at the man, and Julie pretended to be reading a text. He'd seen the bloke a week earlier, the gash that time on his right forearm and the wound a bit more convincingly painted. The guy must be left-handed, Nick thought and sipped his wine. 'Tom's probably closing a deal for a client who wants to be discreet. You know what these rich twats are like. Meet in private dining rooms and hotels. Keep the competition in the dark all costs.'

She didn't look convinced.

'I'm sure I heard him mention on the phone the other evening about the majority agreeing to sell the wharf. It doesn't sound the sort of sale he usually handles. Any idea what he could mean?' she said, finally putting the phone back on the table. 'It sounded more like a group of share-holders than some publicity-shy tycoon.'

A waiter was now standing by their table, armed with a gadget to beam their order to the kitchen. The distraction gave Nick more time to think of a plausible response without revealing too much about Hope Wharf, or else she'd leg it back home to confront her husband. The guy would know instantly where she'd got her information from, giving the heavies a fresh reason to bump into him again. Painfully.

'Look, as far as I can see he's not shagging some hot young bimbo, or any bimbo for that matter, which I think is what you wanted to know, and now it's time for Poirot here to call it a day. And as far as property sales, what's the big deal anyway? The two of you can spend more cosy nights in Zermatt with the commission he'll get.'

She fidgeted in her chair, unwilling to let it go.

'Tell you what, I reckon I'm going to get a consultancy job any day now, but with the time I've got left, I'll give it one last go to see if there's something I've missed. But just bear in mind that he'll spot me a mile off. Again.' He began tearing off chunks of warm pitta bread to scoop up globs of pale-pink cod roe the waiter had put on the table. 'Then I call it a day and you can hire a real private eye. In the meantime you can chip in for my air fare to Hong Kong. I'm going to need a bit of R and R with old mates there once the next consultancy project is finished.'

'Thanks, Nick. I know I can rely on you. Bestest mate. Let's get another bottle, on me. My little pre-thank you,' she said, swiping her phone screen to check again for messages. He noticed a brief pout but didn't press her as his mind turned to ordering a really chilled rosé to flush away the palpable tension from Julie's inner turmoil.

'Anyway, that's enough about little old me. What's new with you? You feeling better about Amanda now?' she asked.

'Thanks for asking, but let's lets talk about her another time,' he replied, instantly annoyed with himself for sounding so defensive. 'It's so nice being out here, though you wouldn't think it was summer having to sit next to a heater! Anyway, just nipping in for a pee. I'll order a rosé for us on the way back.'

2

ELSIE WAS HOPING THAT BAKING would calm her down, help her get a sense of perspective after the day's events had left her almost suffocating with worry, like when she was alone in a police cell for the first time, or during those long evenings tending to her dying mother.

She knew exactly how she wanted her Chelsea buns. Her lips pursed, she whacked the lump of dough with a rolling pin, sending puffs of flour into the air which rained a white mist onto the grey lino on the kitchen floor.

'You bent her ear, didn't you, you nasty little bitch!' Frank shouted that lunchtime, pinning her against the metal vat in Hope Wharf. 'Why can't you keep that pretty mouth of yours shut, and stick to filling your knickers in the shops? The cops aren't after Lizzie any more, so stop interfering.'

He was in no mood to see reason.

'I'm only here to give you some friendly advice, Frank. She could call on you at any time. For all we know she may have even told the police that she suspects one of us did him in.' By that stage of the conversation she was stuttering, finding it hard to breathe as her feet barely touched the flagstones. She'd tried wriggling from him, but the curve of the vat dug into her back and his scrotum was pressed against her belly. His breath reeked of whisky and she could see bits of orangey food in the gaps between his teeth when he brought his face right up to hers.

She saw now that she'd been stupid to see him on her own; she hadn't fully appreciated the careful handling he needed in his volatile state. She told him Lizzie had visited her that morning and within minutes was screaming her head off: 'You're up to your fucking neck in it, aren't you? What have you done with Ted?' Elsie was glad the windows were shut at the time, to stop the neighbours hearing. Lizzie had gone on and on about how she had proof, it was all on paper, and then shoving what looked like a half-folded drawing in Elsie's face. 'And who's Frank? Where is he?' she kept asking, pointing to where Ted had written the name in pencil. 'I want to know, or I'll tell the cops.' Lizzie had then burst into tears and slumped on the sofa for a few minutes before leaving without a word, utterly broken, while Elsie stood there, unsure what to say, and not even daring to put a hand on Lizzie's shoulder.

Recounting this confrontation to Frank in the warehouse was, she now saw with hindsight, a mistake as it had given him an excuse to vent his frustration. She'd never felt so relieved as when he backed off, leaving her still pressed against the vat as he walked into the other room, kicking metal pots out of his way.

'So you didn't tell her who I was?' he asked a few seconds later with his back turned to her. Even from several yards away she could see the waistband of his filthy green kilt was dark with sweat, his muscular shoulders heaving as he tried to steady his breathing. He was in a real state but he got no sympathy, not after the way he'd treated her.

'She doesn't know who you are, but she can easily find out by asking anyone round here. It wouldn't take long, would it, for the cops to put two and two together. That's all I'm saying.' She spoke quietly, while edging towards the door. Strange how the workbench was laid out with tidy rows of shiny clean chisels and mallets. Thought the cabinet was finished. Maybe the Posties wanted another one. The sound of her heels clicking on the flagstones made his face swivel round like a demented hawk about to swoop on a dormouse.

'You think I did him in, don't you?'

'All I'm saying, Frank, is that I wanted to give you a bit of advice, a quiet word in your ear. I think it would be better if you lie low for a while and keep away from Lizzie until the dust settles.' Keeping her voice low calmed him enough so that he shrugged in response, and then sighed and sat down in the armchair, easing the tension between them enough for her to open the door without so much as another glance from him. Instead, he was winding up the gramophone.

'Sorry, Elsie, I'm a bit out of sorts at the moment. Why not close the door and sit down with me for a while? I'll get a fresh brew going. No rush, is there?' He looked at her with that cheeky, behind-the-counter-at-Woolworths smile spreading across his face, making her pause, but only for a split second.

'Sorry, Frank, but I'd best be off. There's stuff I need to do,' she replied, and left.

It had been a lucky escape in many ways, she grimaced, and put the rolling pin down on the table to stare out the back window into the yard, trying to make sense of her jumbled feelings. The harsh words with Frank and Lizzie within hours of each other had been heavy going.

Angrily, she picked up the rolling pin, raised it high in the air and brought it crashing down onto the yellow Formica table, just missing the ball of dough and smashing a bag of dried fruit she'd nicked for the buns. She put the rolling pin back down and bent low to scoop up the currants and sultanas off the floor, gathering them in a mound on a dirty dishcloth.

She didn't even want to guess what was going on in that man's mind.

'Lizzie can't touch me and don't you forget it, Elsie. Besides, you know as much as I do about all this if our day in court ever comes,' he said. 'You offered Ted the job and you paid him. You can't wash your hands of this that easily.'

She grabbed the rolling pin and thrashed the dough as hard as she could several times, each blow a direct hit, and then she sat down to have a cup of tea and a fag, furious with Frank for crossing a line and threatening her in that way. The bastard was right on one thing though: the cops clearly had no evidence against Lizzie, who would soon be gone from Shoreditch. She doubted the poor love could afford the rent without Ted bringing in money too. She was bloody lucky her employer was helping her out while she found her feet.

Frank was a problem now, and it wasn't safe to be around him any more, especially on her own. Sooner or later he'd come calling again, full of charm and smiles as if nothing had happened. What he didn't know was that a couple of messengers had been round to tell her what was on the director's mind.

She cut the dough into pebbled-sized lumps, laid them in rows of four on a floured tin tray, and left them to rise as she went out the back to get some air and have another cigarette. Once the dough had risen enough, she sprinkled the buns with sugar and slid the tray onto the top shelf of the oven. Shame she couldn't make more use of her new cooker. Well, find a man to feed, she thought, while checking her hair in the mirror, making a note to try a new style.

As the buns baked, she set about making the glaze. Bleeding heck, time to get my skates on, she muttered, glancing at the clock on the mantelpiece. She stepped into the yard and picked up a blackened saucepan that had been there for months after her attempt at making scrambled eggs went wrong. Rain had dislodged much of the burnt crud, which she poured down the drain to make a gurgling noise that woke up next door's cat, which was stretched out on top of the yard wall. She stroked its tortoiseshell head, and the cat turned on its side, as if inviting her to rub its fluffy belly.

'Ooh, you little floozy. Just like yer owner, aren't you?' she whispered.

Back in the kitchen she turned on the hob and heated a mixture of milk and sugar in the pan until a thickened liquid was simmering gently, which she stirred with a stick picked up from the yard. Right, where was that paint brush? Ah, there it was, on the mantelpiece next to the clock. After turning the heat down, she poured white powder from a small brown cardboard packet into the bubbling mixture, using the stick again to stir it in thoroughly. Then she took the tray of golden buns out of the oven and placed them on the table to cool.

'My little beauties!' She beamed.

After another couple of fags and a bit of tidying up, the buns were cool enough for her to paint on the glaze with slow, careful brushstrokes to avoid spattering the liquid across the kitchen floor. When she'd finished, she put the brush in the pan and took both outside to rinse under a tap.

'No, no, no, poodlipoos,' she said, pushing away the cat, now agitated by what looked like milk being gratuitously flushed down the drain. She stuffed her apron, the saucepan and paint brush into a sack which she tied up tightly with string. After rinsing her hands for several minutes under cold water, she went back inside, humming her favourite Elvis song.

3

'I THINK THIS CALLS FOR champagne, don't you?' the director asked his short, fat companion.

It was mid-afternoon and still too early for the after-work crowd; they would have the pub mostly to themselves for a while. Bliss.

'I was just thinking how we were never in their league, nor were we stupid enough to try,' the companion said, nodding at a pop-art depiction of two notorious and long-dead East End gangster twins above the bar. 'Yes, champagne would hit the spot, as my pretty young intern would say.'

They had given the club a miss that afternoon because it would be rammed with a private party full of media types, commandeering their favourite armchairs by the window, shouting into their phones and furtively vaping fruity clouds on the balcony. Ghastly.

'But you must bear in mind,' said the director, 'that those two are long dead, along with their racket while our modest endeavour carries on. Well, for a bit longer. We can toast to that if our hirsute friend behind the bar wakes up. I like to think that we Posties are the bona fide caretakers of the old East End, though there's no chance of us being immortalised in trendy art.'

A few minutes later, after realising they would have to order and pay for their drinks at the bar, they were finally drinking the pub's best bubbly.

'Silly me, but I forgot to ask, what's the occasion, if there is any?' the short man said.

'The sale of our century has officially begun. Believe it or not, I've just sold Hope Wharf on behalf of the baying masses,' the director replied, raising his glass. 'I heard that one of our developer friends wasn't having much joy lately, what with the council not too impressed with his plan for a ninety-storey glass tower next to the conservation area. Beats me how he thought he could get away with it just by funding a druggie drop-in centre in the basement. To cheer him up I suggested he could take Hope Wharf off our hands and develop the industrial plot that goes with it. Didn't need much persuading, I can tell you. Spare brownfield is a wet dream for those types.'

'Ha. Brilliant thinking, as ever, Mr Director. All they'll have to do is promise reconditioned brick and a few warehouse-style windows, and their unique and exciting work-live retail project will sail through planning, just like the other hutches along the canal.' The companion nodded.

'Quite,' the director replied with a knowing nod and a long sip. 'And with spare land round here finally attracting a premium, our friend won't be in a hurry to fret over the odd wrinkle in the deeds that a lawyer may uncover while padding out the hours.'

'Have they signed on the dotted line? Can we tell everyone the good news? Good to have the first dollops of cash on the way to silence the restive masses, as it were. Onwards and upwards, that's what I say.' The companion beamed, topping up their glasses with a flourish that sent foam cascading over the rims and onto the distressed oak table.

'We can indeed. And I've already put in calls about our other properties. With heavy heart, of course, but I'm getting accustomed to the idea. What doesn't kill you makes you stronger, as they say. So, one down and another twenty to go. Or is it twenty one? I've lost count.'

They paused to sip champagne and look out of the window at workmen erecting scaffolding on a derelict industrial building opposite the pub. The director remembered it as a textile sweatshop for years, and it was now clad with a hoarding that promised a suite of exclusive flats, all with free fibre-optic 4G broadband, a communal gym and a free Fiat 500 car. There was an international freephone number for foreign clients, and details of a marketing day in Shanghai.

'Shame we never managed to nail down that place over the road. I suppose there's always one that gets away,' the short man said, as if reading the director's thoughts. 'I'll ask our man Fry to pass on the good news about Hope and make sure nobody is left off the list, otherwise they'll be screaming blue murder. You'll be flogging the cabinet next at this rate.'

'Oh, I doubt I'd get more than a tenner on Brick Lane,' the director laughed. 'Seriously, I think the next sale should actually be a lot easier because it's that former furniture factory off the high street. Funny, really. Hope was our first acquisition, and the next building our last. A nicely disguised insurance job, apparently, though I do remember Daddy mentioning a hired hand failing to fix the fixer. I've no clue what he meant. He could be rather cryptic in his twilight years.'

A group of bearded young men in checked shirts and khakis entered the pub and sat at a large oval table by the door, close enough to be within earshot. They were discussing a new app and trying to outsmart each other without being overtly competitive. The director and his companion tuned into the verbal jousting for a few seconds, the former thinking wistfully that it had been years since he himself had radiated such youthful, raw enthusiasm.

'Fancy another bottle?' the director asked.

'Absolutely, but why don't we go to the rooftop bar off the high street and order a nicely chilled Chablis? We can toast our thanks to the pioneering Posties from the Old Nichol below, and see the roof of our next sale. How's that for a trip down Rookery Lane?'

'I see there's no stopping you today. Need a pee first. Champagne goes through me like nobody's business,' the director said, getting to his feet while glancing over his shoulder at the animated siliconeastas, who were ordering a round of micro-brewed pints and bowls of organic pistachios.

4

Nick was seated at the back of the restaurant, his fingers worrying the weave of the crisp white tablecloth as if he were desperately trying to crack a coded message in Braille to save his life. The waiter had given up hope of taking a drinks order after being waived away three times.

Must keep a clear head to avoid gaffes when the guest arrives.

From his table by the large window that looked onto a side street, he could see the whole restaurant at a glance. It was a popular haunt of the veteran siliconeastas, those in their thirties who still clung to the helm of a wannabe unicorn, petrified of bankruptcy before the IPO. What were the odds that one of the millions of newly-minted Asian maths graduates would invent that killer App before this lot does? Shortening by the day, no doubt.

Even though it was barely noon, the place was already living up to its reputation as one of the best restaurants in the grid of rapidly gentrifying streets he rarely left these days. On the few occasions he went to the West End to meet friends or to shop, he felt like a tourist in his own town, amazed at the changes since his last foray. He needed to get out of Shoreditch more often.

Ah, here we go. A waiter was escorting his guest to the table.

'Hi. I'm Jack. Sorry I'm late. Central line buggered up again,' the twenty-something, short, dark-haired bloke said with a handshake and a shrug, before sitting down without waiting for a response.

'No sweat. Just arrived myself. I hope you like the food, it's had rave reviews in your magazine,' Nick said. The reporter had taken some persuading to meet up for lunch. Hacks must get inundated with freebies, he thought. Wonder why he didn't bring a notebook to make the neighbouring tables curious?

'Mind if I use a tape? Bloody awkward trying to write and eat at the same time,' Jack said, placing a Mars-bar-sized digital recorder near Nick's glass. It was a cheaper version of the one Nick had thrown against the hotel bedroom wall a few days before, setting off a cringe-inducing flashback that was enough to make him beckon the waiter to order wine.

'Er, don't you guys use shorthand any more? No, no recording. All this is a bit sensitive. Old-fashioned notes or nothing, I'm afraid. As we agreed on the phone, this is all definitely off the record.' Nick looked Jack firmly in the eye until he pocketed the gadget.

'Sure. No problem. I can always check back on stuff with you,' he mumbled.

Nick had deliberately kept things vague over the phone in case the conversation was being taped. Can't be too careful, given the heavies had a habit of turning up at some point.

'As it happens, I've been thinking about what you've

told me so far and between you and me, my editor's a bit picky on this one. He likes a human angle we can play up. I mean, we need to think people, pain, tears and trauma, that sort of thing. Let's face it, big property developers and nasty landlords aren't the page-turners they used to be, unless you've got blind grannies or pregnant women turfed out on the streets, which means better pictures.' Jack was explaining with the palms of his hands opened outwards.

Nick was half-expecting this after browsing the reporter's articles on the web. The one about a single mum from eastern Europe being forced to give her scummy landlord a weekly hand job in lieu of a massive rent increase stuck in the mind. It certainly was competitive out there as far as property stories were concerned. Casually, he began recounting his carefully prepared spiel, trying to make it sound as natural, off-the-cuff and reader-friendly as possible. It was all about slums-to-bums, pausing a few seconds for the golden quote to sink in, but it failed to trigger any obvious reaction, though Jack did scribble a few words on the back of the daily specials menu.

'My best mate has a tattoo of a shark on his arse but that's not a story, is it?' Jack said after Nick's flow fizzled out. The reporter was also trying to catch a waiter's eye to ask about the Merlot refill he'd ordered. The restaurant was getting very noisy, forcing them to repeat things, slowing their conversation, and increasing Nick's anxiety levels. They edged closer across the table and lowered their heads to avoid having to shout so much.

'Why are you telling me all this anyway?' Jack asked. 'Can we get a pic of a pastie, I mean postie, tattoo? That would kind of go down well with our gay readers.'

At least the reporter was trying to tick another box to grab his editor's attention.

'Hi, Nick. How's things? It's must be at least four days since I've seen you out and about. Isn't the weather steamy?' Tom was standing next to their table, having slapped Nick on the shoulder, making him lunge to within an inch of his wine while Jack stared, waiting for an introduction.

'Tom,' Nick said, 'It's great to see you. I had dinner with Julie the other night.' Nick's hand was clasped hard round the tumbler of water to stop himself shaking. 'Oh, by the way Jack, this is Tom. His wife Julie is an old colleague of mine. God, we've been friends for years, haven't we? Anyway, Tom, mind if we pop outside for a minute? It's hard to hear anything in this place, and I want to run something by you.' Nick sprang to his feet and gripped Tom's forearm.

'He's cute!' Tom shouted over his shoulder as he was led to the door, forcing Nick to roll his eyes at the reporter, who was checking his phone.

'That's so funny. No, he's interested in a career in finance, a nephew of an old school friend of mine, though I'm not sure what to tell him now that bankers are at the bottom of the social heap,' Nick flannelled when they were outside on the pavement. 'Look, I just wanted to check if you're planning anything special for Julie's birthday. I know it's not a big one but you know what she's like, always up for a party. It would be a great excuse to get old colleagues together.' He knew he wasn't fooling Tom but, what the fuck, no matter how fake he sounded, it was miles better than giving him any inkling of what he was up to with that increasingly annoying rookie reporter.

'I'll get Julie to let you know if anything's happening. Well, I should be getting back to my table, as I don't want to leave my guest waiting. I'm sure we'll be bumping into each other again soon,' Tom said with a grin that raised Nick's pulse-rate even further.

They went back inside to their tables which, to Nick's relief, were several metres apart. He didn't recognize Tom's lunching partner, a short, fat balding man with a cheery smile. Thank God, no sign of Gingernuts from the sauna or the two heavies. Would have put him right off his squid ink risotto when it arrived. Good, at least Jack was working his way through a fresh glass of wine, and hadn't walked out. Progress of sorts, then.

5

LIZZIE WAS DOZING IN BED, cocooned under a beige eiderdown, where she could feel the warmth radiating from Denise lying next to her, engrossed in a paperback and every now and then breaking the easy silence with a sigh or a giggle.

The intimacy failed to quell a gut-feeling in Lizzie that Ted wasn't coming back.

How different it felt lying next to Denise, compared with sleeping with her husband. There were none of the grunts and snores she'd hear from Ted, though since his disappearance, she would do anything to hear those sounds again to know he was safe. She'd taken it for granted that he would always be there, despite her double life. Was she now paying the price? She was already making it clear to anyone who dropped by the house, or stopped her in the street, that she must now give up her home to work for the Smethwicks as a live-in maid. There was simply no choice, you see, especially with no cheque from the insurance man to tide her over. Well, couldn't afford the premiums. When you're childless and young, why buy a policy, she'd told the pushy man from the Pru after she and Ted married.

With the police off her back, she could reflect on her

circumstances more calmly. Shouting her head off at Elsie released much of the tension that had welled up inside her. That woman must have an inkling of what had happened to him, she could see it in her eyes: it was guilt, plain as can be. But when she mentioned seeing Frank to ask about Ted, she'd looked at her differently, almost scared. Why? That Frank didn't look like he would harm anyone. It was shameful how those kids made fun of his balls while she followed him through the back streets to that decrepit wharf on the canal. He looked so sad in that kilt. It needed a good wash. It wouldn't take her long to get him tidied up. Perhaps she could do his laundry to get him talking.

'Evening, ladies. Shall I be master and lock up?'

Charles was still in his striped City suit, the top button of his white shirt undone, and a green mark on one cuff; his varsity tie was loose and oddly twisted.

'Been working hard in the office, darling? There's cheese and ham in the fridge, if you're peckish,' Denise said, barely looking up from her book.

'No thanks, darling, I had dinner at the club and then caught up with chums in Hampstead. I'll see you both in the morning, bright and early.' He smiled and was gone. Lizzie snuggled further under the eiderdown and Denise moved closer, continuing to read.

Lizzie was realizing how much she had loved – still loved – Ted, in a certain fashion. It made her heart pound not knowing which tense to use when thinking about him. Could he really be dead? No. That was hard to believe. People don't just disappear like that. Her husband didn't have an enemy in the world. She would have a chat with Frank to see what he thought, as not trying to find answers would rankle for the rest of her life. She would do all she could to find him before the trail turned cold. Anything less would be an insult to his memory – if indeed it turned out he was dead. Ted was a good bloke, and she'd never deserved him. Alone in a cell, she'd realized that more than ever.

'You look as if you are about to burst into tears, my darling,' Denise said, squeezing her arm through the blanket.

'Oh, just thinking about Ted and wondering what the hell's happened to him. Why would he disappear like that, without a word to anyone? I can't even remember the last time we had a row. He didn't, I mean doesn't, have a bad bone in his body.'

Denise frowned and shut her book.

'Maybe he crossed the wrong man. You know what things are like in the East End. What's important is that you're safe here, and the police have gone away. I hope you're not still thinking of meeting that strange man you mentioned. Let sleeping dogs lie, I say. We don't want the police turning up here again, do we?' Denise squeezed her arm again, this time harder.

But Lizzie's mind was made up. She had to go back home for a few days to empty the house and sell what pieces of furniture they had, before moving in permanently with Denise – and Charles, of course. Living with her lover was something she'd barely dreamed of, and certainly in not this way.

'Don't worry, Denny. I'll have plenty to keep me busy, what with emptying the house and all that. No idle hands for the devil,' she said with a forced smile. Denise turned on the radio and clicked off the bedside light before wriggling closer to Lizzie. They lay still in the dark, listening to the Home Service, and Charles whistling to himself in the next room.

6

TOM RUBBED MORE OLIVE OIL into her perfectly hairless belly, making the skin glisten under the harsh office lights. Her navel was a shallow, overflowing green pool, topped up by Tom's slow hand strokes. The oil lent lustre to her crease-free thighs as she smiled, her bright white teeth contrasting with the dark blue silk of her dislodged bra. Her panties were already speckled with Italy's finest extra-virgin.

'You didn't have to work late just for me, Sunita,' he said above the hum of cooling computers which displayed the company's red logo ricocheting across screens in perfect synchronicity.

He didn't have much time left.

The security guard was doing the rounds and the blinking panel above the lift at the far end of the room showed he was already patrolling the second floor, leaving just another three to inspect before he would find them.

A few minutes max, Tom calculated. But he felt in complete control of time, Sunita and all around him. The flow was good, the momentum with him.

'I wanted to thank you properly for my performance review, and show how passionate I am about meeting the goals you've set me,' Sunita told him in a low voice as her left hand rhythmically crunched a wad of yellow Post-it notes, as if it were a stress ball. He smiled and rubbed in more oil, this time vigorously as he worked his way down the slope of slippery skin towards her partly clad and neatly clipped triangle of uniformly black pubic hair.

'Let's see how quickly you can meet my targets,' he said in his most managerial voice. 'I want 110 percent.'

Their quickening movements made an orange plastic pen and pencil holder wobble and fall off the desk, with a stapler soon following.

The lift panel was now flashing their floor number, a ring and a tinny female voice confirmed its arrival and the opening doors. He mounted Sunita, making her breathe in sharply and twist her head to one side so that her shoulder-length hair hid all her face apart from those deep crimson lips that were still locked in a smile.

'Oh, fuck!' Tom shouted, bolt upright in bed, as spunk spurted over his legs and the black silk sheets.

'For Christ's sake, can't you have a wank without waking me up?' Julie mumbled next to him, and turned onto her side to face away.

Whoa! Best one yet, he thought as he slid out of bed. It was nearly six in the morning, and with his semi-hard cock swaying like a dousing rod tracing a line to the loo, he picked up his boxers and went to clean himself up. After making tea, instead of going back to bed he went to the study, switched on his tablet computer and clicked open a spreadsheet to bring up the list of Posties. He often thought how incredibly different their lives must now be compared with their piss-poor forefathers, who were forced out of the Old Nichol with nowhere to go. Well, none of this lot would have to nick an apple or a piece of bread to survive.

Yep, it probably was the right time to wind up this profitable co-operative of theirs, created from the unintended consequences of selective Victorian philanthropy, with a little help from the Luftwaffe and the now rich pickings it left among the ruins. These days there would be student sit-ins and a storm of tweets against such social cleansing of the rookery. But you had to hand it to those pioneer Posties, a classic case of first-mover advantage in gentrification and perfect fodder for a social history PhD. He sipped his steaming Earl Grey and smiled at how coming first thing sharpened his powers of expression.

He opened an app to check on the overnight currency markets in Asia. Ah, good, cable still nice and steady. Could be a good time to turn sterling proceeds from Hope Wharf into dollars for our expat Posties in the States. Bugger, the Swissie had shot up again; best not to shift any dosh to his own account in Zurich until the franc cooled a bit. No sweat.

The lawyers had strict orders to park the cash in their account until they heard from him, as there was no trusting good old Julie Marple. She'd shag the most expensive forensic accountant on earth if it meant a bigger divorce settlement. The 'D' word punctured his upbeat mood, as no doubt it would all be messy in court. Sad in a way, too. But what then? Perhaps it was just as well that Sunita's affections were all in the mind, as that was about as far they would go in real life. Not only gorgeous, but pretty hot in the brains department too. A stupid move that could jeopardize their professional relationship was a big no-no, as he needed to delegate more high-level work to her while he dismantled a century-old property empire. It would be an intensive, hands-on task, a description that made him giggle as he recalled the director and his shrivelled wiener in the sauna. The big developers would no doubt be scoffing in the boardroom at the sight of the Posties' ragbag of lofts and warehouses coming onto the market. Well, stuff them and their poxy plasterboard hutches.

'Any tea left, darling?'

Julie startled him, but luckily it was only a graph of sterling and the Swiss franc on the tablet screen.

'It's cold by now, dear,' he said. 'You go back to bed and I'll make us a fresh pot.' He went to the kitchen, put the kettle on and grabbed a couple of tea bags. He saw that she'd left her mobile on the table. Funny that. It was usually glued to her right hand these days. Wonder if she's testing him? He had to stop himself from picking it up. The video clip she'd taken outside the guy's house the other evening could have been the work of a first-year film student on speed. And the preliminary report from his private eye had been worryingly thin on detail, given the fat fee he was paying her. The bloke that Julie was keen on sounded pretty decent, but had zilch interest even in a quickie. Shame, really. A traceable fling would be great ammo for the inevitable bun fight between their lawyers. No sign yet she was going off the rails in other ways. As far as he could see she wasn't stuffing prescription drugs or worse down her gob, only the usual gallons of vino with that Detective Plod mate of hers.

He poured tea for Julie into a mug with 'The Maldives are Magic' printed on its side in letters almost totally bleached away by dishwasher salt. It was a souvenir from their honeymoon and now a metaphor for their marriage. 'Don't think I'll be contesting this, M'lud,' he said under his breath, and headed for the bedroom.

7

FRANK WAS POORLY.

Swaddled in a yellow viscose blanket he'd brought from home, he sat in the armchair in Hope Wharf, the gramophone next to him playing Vera Lynn for a second time that morning, but the songs were no balm for his constant nausea.

He thought hard about what he'd been up to in the past twenty-four hours, trying to pin down why he would be feeling so ill. It wasn't because of his condition – those symptoms he knew a mile off. Perhaps it was something he'd eaten or drunk?

Much of the day before had been quiet until he was summoned to meet the top postie – the one they call the director – in a private room upstairs at the Cock and Cardinal. The bloke was polite enough, though his persistent questioning about Ted put him right off the cold beef and mustard sandwiches they'd ordered. To make him feel even more uncomfortable, the director kept asking about the night-watchman at the last deeds job Frank had done. Had he seen him? Any idea why the man would disappear like that? He could see how the director and his two side kicks were listening hard to his answers, but by then Frank was losing his rag, telling them he couldn't do their dirty work for them *and* have to answer all these stupid questions. 'You'd think I was the bloody Ripper. When have I ever let you lot down?' Even the landlord had nipped upstairs to check what all the noise was about, only to retreat in silence after being glared at by all.

'Take it easy, Frank. We don't want any nasty tittle-tattle sending the boys in blue our way, do we? You're family and we take care of you. Am I not right?' The director turned to his two sidekicks, who nodded vigorously, before continuing. 'Perhaps it might be wise if you lie low, that's all. Get away from Shoreditch for a while. Why not take a holiday?'

The director talked as if it was the height of bleeding summer, Frank thought. He remembered taking several sandwiches at that point in the conversation – everyone could see how his hand was shaking with anger – but the director had tucked in, too, and Frank would have heard by now if the director was sick.

'You don't have to worry about money. We'll take care of that. Why not visit the family on the coast? The sea air would do you a world of good,' the director had tried again as they both scoffed more sandwiches. 'Let's just say that when you get back we'll need your invaluable assistance to keep things in order for a long while yet.'

There was no way he was going anywhere at this time of year.

From the pub, with a fiver from the director in his pocket, he'd gone home for a kip before going over to the post office to send his mother a birthday card. At least the director had reminded him to do something useful. Maybe he was right, and it was time to pay the parents a visit. Margate wasn't that far, though God knows why they retired there. Any further and they would be in the sea. The house felt empty after they'd left but it was still home to him, though there was probably no chance of getting Elsie or anyone else to share it with him. Nah, he'd go and see them in a couple of months' time, in the spring, to mark the anniversary of his poor sister's early death from TB. They'd like that. How he missed her. While queuing in the post office for a stamp, he'd tried hard not to smirk while looking at Pooter's picture on the poster of missing people. Funny though, no photo of Ted despite the cops swarming all over the place. No photo of the night-watchman either, come to think of it. Too soon, probably. Gawd, those coppers – so bloody slow. Frank wondered why the director was so interested in him.

Still no idea, then, why he was feeling sick.

Leaning back in the armchair, he mouthed the songs to try and lift his spirits, and pulled the blanket tighter round himself, still thinking hard about the past few hours. Had he overlooked anything? After the post office he'd come straight to the wharf, where he'd dozed in this chair to catch up with sleep lost during all those nights making glue and dealing with Ted. The last port of call had been Daddy Burtt's for supper. Far too many kids there last night, and those useless volunteers wouldn't lift a finger to control them, especially that cocky shit from Vallance Road who'd flicked bits of shepherd's pie at him. 'Big balls, big balls,' the little bastard had taunted him while the volunteers looked the other away, scared of catching his eye. He'd shrugged it off, as he wasn't going to give that Christian Mission lot a reason to kick him out, not that they'd have the guts to try. After downing his jam roly-poly and custard, he'd grabbed the usual food bag they'd left on his seat while he was in the toilet. What else? Well, that was about it.

He leaned over the side of the armchair to change the record on the gramophone but before he could lower the needle he had to get up and race to the lavatory, just making it in time to vomit down the pan before opening his bowels for the umpteenth time that day. Half an hour later, he felt better and a lot less shaky as he rose to his feet. The nausea and high temperature eased even more after he downed a pint of water. Time to get some fresh air now the legs weren't so wobbly. Perhaps the worst was over.

It was quiet outside, nothing unusual for that time of day. In the distance he recognized a couple of women who were carrying shopping bags. He walked round the side of the wharf to lean on the railings and look out over the still, cold water as a barge passed by on the way to Limehouse and the open river, its black exhaust a reminder of the night Pooter brought the bones and planks. How it all felt so long ago. Why on earth was the man at the tiller shrugging his shoulders and pointing to a patch of water? Frank looked down to his left to see a tight circle of ducks and coots bobbing up and down as the boat's wash reached them.

They were stone-dead.

Taking a closer look, he noticed white bits floating in their midst, the remains of the Chelsea buns he'd torn up and thrown into the canal that morning. Bloody hell. He could feel adrenalin start to course through him as he recalled how he'd brought the Daddy Burtt's food bag to the warehouse that morning, but noticed that the buns were too stale to eat. Shame really, as they looked pretty with that milky, sweet glaze he loved. He'd tried a tiny piece but then reluctantly threw the lot into the canal for the ducks, just where the wet, feathered mound now rose and fell in the water.

He went back inside to sit in the armchair, the image of the dead birds seared into his mind. He was shaking again, but not from nausea. Who the hell had left the buns on his chair at Daddy Burtt's? Well, he certainly won't be going back there until he found out who'd tried to poison him. He turned on the gramophone and wrapped himself in the blanket. After the Posties had asked him to lie low for a while, he would have to be quiet and careful about his next move.

8

THE SUNDAY FLOWER MARKET WAS coming to a colourful and perfumed crescendo on the stall-lined street of refurbished Victorian terraced houses. Caught in one of two parallel conga lines of locals and tourists shuffling in opposite directions, Nick was forced to take his time. He leaned over to sniff the pots of herbs neatly packed in square cardboard trays, a subtle bouquet garni of oregano, rosemary and sage that was slowly being overpowered by the intense perfume of the large white lilies on sale at the next stall he was approaching. 'Come and buy the best lilies in town and help me feed the mother-in-law!' the stallholder shouted with gusto to his semi-captive audience.

Not that he wanted to rush as he had to keep a good distance between himself and Tom, who had stopped to run a finger up and down the twisting trunk of a potted bay tree that was crowned by a perfectly clipped ball of corrugated leaves. Julie's husband was accompanied by a well-built dapper man in his fifties, who seemed genuinely interested in the plants and flowers as they walked along, a few metres ahead. Tom's boredom, however, was palpable as he rubbed his forehead vigorously with the side of his hand each time the other man stopped to admire a display of greenery or blooms.

Two hours earlier Julie rang to say she'd overheard Tom on the phone saying he would be more than happy to meet up for a chat to discuss the project, as her husband had cryptically put it. Meeting in person wouldn't disturb any plans, and an early lunch upstairs at the Arnold Arms by the flower market was just the ticket.

'So at the drop of a fucking bunch of petunias he scraps quality time with me for a pub lunch with a property developer or whoever the hell the man is. And I assume it was a man,' she moaned into his ear. 'On a weekend. What do you make of that then? Believe it or not, I was actually getting a chicken ready for a trad Sunday roast à deux, and the bastard swans off with barely a word of explanation.'

With no brunch, lunch, or any other plans and – strangely for a Sunday – no hangover either, Nick was up and about early because of the sunny weather when she phoned him.

'What the hell, I need plant food for the ficus anyway. You know he'll spot me again, don't you? Never met anyone like him. That man has eyes as well as a tattoo on his arse!' He laid it on down the phone line.

'OK. I hear you. You know we agreed this is the very last favour. Promise,' she pleaded back, and then ended the call before he could think of something witty to say.

Perhaps this last-gasp pursuit would reveal other buildings Tom was flogging for the Posties. That would give him more ammo to toss the cub reporter's way now he was going decidedly cool on the story. 'Tell me why my readers should care,' the jumped-up pen-pusher had texted the other day.

Nick had put on a New York Yankees cap and sunglasses to blend in with the crowd. He went straight to the pub to bag a table at the back with an unrestricted view of the main door, and wait for Tom and his lunch date to arrive. And now, an hour later, he was tailing them through the flower market, feeling a little exposed, despite the heavy crowd. He was determined not to give Tom any more excuses to take the mickey. It had been a few weeks since Julie asked him to spy on her husband, and it had been a bit of a wheeze at first. Always worth trying something twice, as they say.

Having his hands tied up by two pairs of Calvin Kleins to a water pipe in a gay sauna for twenty minutes had not been comfortable, but it was hardly life-threatening, and would make for a great dinner-party story. The receptionist at Jock's Hangout was pissed-off when a cleaner had found him.

'No bondage here, mate. There's plenty of other places for that sort of thing. We take health and safety very seriously here.' The receptionist had pointed to a list of house dos and don'ts on the wall behind him.

That, and the ball-breaking embarrassment of what happened in the hotel had hardened his resolve to dig up something about Tom now that the bloke's utter self-belief was grating like hell. He also wanted to know how the two heavies fitted into all this. Very tightly, he sniggered to himself, making a woman next to him in the line turn and stare.

Worried that Tom would spot him, Nick took out two tenners from his wallet, handed them to a stallholder, and pointed to a bay tree. Out-of-the-pot thinking. He could follow Tom plus one with his face hidden by a ball of leaves.

The plant would be perfect for the balcony, next to the bollard.

He saw that the two men had stopped and joined the line of people moving in Nick's direction, forcing him to squeeze through a narrow gap between two stalls to hide until they crawled past. He was soon tailing them again, though his arms were beginning to ache from having to constantly keep the bush at face height. The two men finally reached the last stall and then carried on at a faster clip, leaving the street to head down an alley. Nick knew it would take them to the high street after passing that orange-brick estate which now seemed part of his daily life these days. In a couple of minutes Tom was pointing out the raised bandstand at the estate's centre. Then they continued and turned right into a broad avenue that ran alongside a large church to connect with the high street. Nick decided to hold back for a few seconds, reasoning that they would need a bit of time to cross the busy high street before he could catch up to see which street they'd taken next.

'Well, would you believe it? It's our friend Nicholas. I see those green fingers are busier than ever. What a lovely coincidence. We were beginning to miss you,' said one of the two heavies, both of whom were standing in front of him, blocking his line of vision to the high street.

'Tell you what, Nicholas, why don't we go and sit in the bandstand and enjoy this fine weather. I think that plant of yours could do with some sunshine,' the other heavy said. He felt himself being gently turned 180 degrees and semi-marched, the bay tree's ball of leaves swinging from side to side as his feet barely touched the ground.

'Been down the sauna after our brief encounter last

time?' heavy number one, in a white T-shirt, asked. 'So sorry. Please excuse us, Nicholas. We shouldn't be intruding on your private life.'

'Then again, you don't seem to worry about butting into other people's affairs, do you?,' heavy number two, dressed in a navy shirt and cream linen jacket, chipped in like a well-oiled double act. They mounted the steps to the bandstand, where a group of youths were drinking beer at the far end, leaving room for Nick to sit opposite, sandwiched between the heavies and out of earshot.

'We haven't been formally introduced, have we?' Nick said, making a point of putting on a cheeky grin as he stuck out his right hand. The bay tree was on the ground, its slim trunk sticking up between his legs and the round bushy bit hiding his paunch.

'Ah, he wants to get to know us better. Isn't that nice?' the T-shirted heavy on his left said. 'Maybe you'd like to come to dinner. You know where we live. We could give you some slum-to-bum stories to pass on to your reporter friend. What do you think, Nicholas? You could even take a photo of our tattoos.'

'Er, I'm a bit busy at the moment. Big job coming up. Perhaps some other time,' Nick replied. They fell into an awkward silence as the heavies checked their phones and he stared straight ahead over the top of the bay tree, ignoring glances from the youths who were downing beers.

'Well, it's been a pleasure, Nicholas, but we can't sit here all day chatting. You be careful now, there's already a director buried under here. Make sure you water that plant and remember, it needs a sunny spot. Perhaps on that big balcony of yours,' the heavy in the jacket suggested, without a trace of irony. They left him sitting on the bench and walked towards the high street, not bothering to check if he was following them. He took off his sweat-soaked baseball cap to allow the light breeze to cool his head. Looking down at the bay tree he smiled at the sheer stupidity of it all. 'Looks like you need something to do!' his mother would have said. Ah, that reminded him: next week would have been her seventy-fifth birthday. He would replay the last voicemail she'd left on his answering machine, as he did each year.

He got up and headed for the high street too. Tailing Tom was making him think more and more about his own life. The man oozed confidence from every meticulously groomed pore on his body. Meanwhile, here he was, reduced to killing time by doing Julie stupid favours. He did owe her one, though. Dealing with Amanda would have been a complete nightmare without her support.

Nick crossed the high street and continued down a narrow side road to his flat, seething at the thought of the heavies having a laugh while telling Tom about their latest effort to thwart him. But then again, at least he knew for certain that Julie was really on to something, that Tom had begun to flog Postie properties, and not even they could keep that quiet or totally hidden for long if people knew where to look. These weren't the pre-internet, pre-public record days of the Old Nichol slum. But apart from Hope Wharf, he still couldn't identify other Postie properties. And why sell now? Were they in dire straits?

He keyed in the code to enter a walled courtyard to reach the main door to his building. Just then, all thoughts of Tom, Julie, rookeries and bloody bollards evaporated, as he began ranting under his breath about something far more important: the wheelie bins were all over the place, and not lined up against the wall as they should be according to the managing agent's signs, which any dickhead with half an 'O' level could read. Bet it was that hipster lot from the third floor again. Worse, some twat or twatess had dumped a mattress in the yard instead of arranging for the council to pick it up from the street.

Christ, where was Harry? Time for another residents' meeting.

He let himself into his flat and, after a quick, nervous check for intruders, put the bay tree on the balcony at the furthest point from the bollard, and then went to run a bath. With his favourite pulsating music on full blast, he slid into the warm water and began sipping a glass of cold rosé wine. Shame he was out of bubble bath, but he wasn't going to let petty things like that upset him.

9

ELSIE SUCKED HARD ON A cigarette as she stared at the embers glowing in the grate. She wasn't going to shovel on more coal as she was about to take a bus into town, glad to get out of Shoreditch for a few hours and lose herself in the West End crowds. It would be a breath of fresh air in more ways than one as her nerves were frayed since she found out that Frank was still very much alive, and screaming foul play to anyone who would listen.

She'd flinched when Maisie related how he'd stormed into Daddy Burtt's and almost punched one of the volunteers, shouting like a madman, demanding to know who had baked the Chelsea buns. Who had left them on his chair? Who was trying to kill him? Again and again he'd asked the same questions, only to be told nothing. They had to manhandle him into the street and tell him not to come back until he treated people proper.

Elsie knew it was only a matter of time before Frank suspected her, if he didn't already. Better not cross his path for a while. Only the other day she'd stepped into a grocery store when she saw him walking up the high street in her direction. Her presence in the shop had startled the assistant, who told the owner in a loud voice that he would keep an eye on her. Bloody cheek. Nothing worth nicking from there anyway, just miserable sprouting spuds and a few limp lettuces that she could get at half the price in Spitalfields market. What worried her was Frank's knack of winkling information out of people, and she'd be a fool to underestimate that. He'd already put a note under her door that morning asking if she fancied dropping by at the warehouse for a brew and a chat. All harmless and friendly, of course. There was a job the Posties wanted to put her way but best to explain everything in person, the note said. The sight of his handwriting in thick black pencil had made her flesh creep. It would take more than tea to coax her over there. She burnt the note straightaway in the fire that was now slowly dying in front of her.

If only she had a bloke to keep him away.

Most of all, she was angry with herself for allowing, engineering even, their brief moment of intimacy in the wharf. She'd let herself down, made herself vulnerable. Still, she knew better than to keep the Posties waiting and had already chatted with one of their pissed henchmen down the Ten Bells. A strange request it was, too. The director was wanting a nice pair of black silk panties. For a respectable young lady friend it was, mind you, the bloke had slurred between gulps of stout. And he'd pay handsomely. The director was too busy to buy them himself and besides, such purchases were best left to a lady, the henchman said with a smirk. Pull the other one, Mr Director. Well that little job would be easy-peasy. She'd get her hands on a nice pair of knickers up West that very afternoon, and be paid by tonight without going near Frank.

Yes, it was good getting more work from the Posties. It

meant having more irons in the fire. The Posties had money to burn as them properties Frank talked about must have been bringing in a penny or two. Not that pounds, shillings and pence would make them respectable because under their fancy clothes they were still a bunch of slum-dwellers that got lucky. Not one of them could cut it as a costermonger or even a mudlark to save their life. Her grandad had been pearly king of Limehouse. That's what you call proper respect. She got up to put the fireguard in front of the grate, and lit a fresh cigarette. While putting on her new coat she stroked its bright red buttons, a reminder of the boiled sweets her grandad gave her as a treat down the pub while she stroked his shiny, pearly jacket before a parade.

No, Frank was not good for the nerves, she thought, catching her pale, tense face staring back at her in the mirror above the mantelpiece. She went to check the back door to make sure it was locked and bolted, before stepping out into the street and turning the front door key with a determined twist for peace of mind. With a bit of luck and careful planning she could avoid Frank for weeks. She'd be busy organizing the next trip with the team and testing her new panty-pouches. Had to be worth a go with their entry through a slit in the side of the skirt. Stuffing things down the top could be a bit hit and miss at times. Some of the smaller items had ended up tangled in her fanny. Not very ladylike. Wonder what would her grandad have said about that!

She would give half the afternoon's takings to Doris, a sales assistant in the Bond Street department Elsie was heading for. Worth keeping her sweet as it might lead to other things, though hopefully not the clink again, she laughed, attracting a quizzical look from the swaying clippie who was taking her fare on the top deck of the bus. Going into town on a Saturday brought back memories of her teenage years when she visited the shops and cafes with her friends, hoping to meet good-looking, demobbed soldiers killing time while they waited for a better life, but happy to make do with a bit of fun in the meantime.

By the time she reached the department store the crowds would have built up nicely, and the assistants run ragged. Should be a piece of cake – or even a Chelsea bun. She cackled until Frank's face flashed across her thoughts, killing her smile stone-dead. Never would she let herself be on her own with that man again. He couldn't be trusted. It had only just dawned on her that even the Postie messengers rarely called at the warehouse when he was there. It was always her they asked to check on the cabinet, as if she was some bleeding antiques expert. They always met him in the pub. Funny that. She was glad that Lizzie Datchett was leaving Shoreditch because out of sight and out of mind was the best way to deal with the Franks of this world.

The bus stopped outside Tottenham Court Road underground station where she got off, thinking that if she walked straight to Bond Street she would be too early, as Doris was on her break for the next forty minutes. Not to worry, she would run her other errand first. She headed down the Charing Cross Road and turned right into one of the scruffiest streets of Soho, instantly feeling more at home. She stopped outside a chemist with its dusty windows protected by iron mesh. Opening the door rung a shrill bell.

'Angie, how are you, my love? I had a nice little chat with your mother yesterday. I think she was going to mention it to you,' Elsie said to the young, red-haired girl leaning over the counter. The chemist himself, dressed in a white, crumpled coat, was sitting in a glassed-off room at the back, sipping a cup of tea as he read the back page of a newspaper, making occasional notes with a pen.

'Auntie Elsie. It's been a while. Thanks again for all your help with the wedding dress. Me and Jim won't forget that in a hurry,' the shop assistant whispered, before shouting, 'You take your time, madam. We have a lovely range of hair brushes for you to choose from.'

Elsie was fascinated by chemists and their displays of coloured glass bottles, mortars and pestles, all labelled in a funny language. The trays of soaps and perfumes smelt fresh and clean like the powder room of a posh hotel. The assistant ducked from view to pick up something from under the counter and, after checking the chemist was still weighing up racing tips, she slid a small, plain, brown bottle across the counter, which Elsie put straight into her handbag. They chatted a bit more, making loud comments on the best shampoo for dry hair, and ended with Elsie buying a small tube of toothpaste and saying goodbye. Outside, she walked at a leisurely pace towards Bond Street, the small bottle rolling in the bottom of her handbag with a tube of lipstick and loose cigarettes, lifting her spirits no end.

10

'WELL HELLO, P.C. NICK. DON'T tell me you've got more undercover work for me, or should I say no cover at all?' Harry said in a husky, southern-belle accent on the doorstep of his flat.

He really was the perfect tonic after smug Tom and the obnoxious heavies, Nick thought.

'Sorry to disappoint, but it's just a social visit this time. No more freelance work from me. Don't tell me you actually need an excuse to visit that place?' he teased while walking into Harry's pristine flat.

Nick was annoyed he had missed the residents' meeting and a chance to rant about disorderly wheelie bins in the yard, but then again it was a lot easier being briefed by Harry, who always hoovered up juicy titbits about what was going on in the block behind closed doors. Nick had already seen the email circulated by residents about the planning application for a green alternative-energy centre on disused land behind their building. He'd also heard about the electronic petition to oppose it, but had decided that he quite liked the idea in general. Quite worthy in fact, as it would heat a public pool and primary school the power company promised to fund in return for planning permission.

'What did everyone make of the generator thing? I've read about them in Sweden where they heat up whole districts. It should be quiet and nicely landscaped, and let's face it, it would be miles better than another boutique hotel and basement bar for vomiting pissheads,' he said, making himself comfortable in one of Harry's sleek black-leather dining chairs.

'Well, we didn't really talk much about it as many of us felt the same way you do. Something will fill the space, and that would be better than a butt-ugly residential block of steel and glass overlooking us,' Harry said as he poured Nick a glass of chilled prosecco, adding a squirt of blackcurrant cordial. 'Pauper's Kir Royal, darling. Hope you like it,' he said. 'Anyway, at the meeting which you called but did not attend, we avoided talking too much about the generator to stop Jake banging on about some famous incinerator round here millennia ago.'

'Well, the energy centre would come in handy to burn the crap idiots dump in our yard,' Nick interrupted.

'Cheers. Yes, we ticked that one, so moving on swiftly to the topic twisting everyone's knickers. It was the letter from the management company saying the freeholder is selling out. A can of worms, if ever I smelt one, if that's the right way to put it,' Harry said, downing his drink and preparing another one.

'Not sure I got that letter,' Nick said, thinking back to what he'd collected from his mail box recently, apart from takeaway menus, estate agent begging letters, and business cards from cleaners who couldn't spell. 'What difference does it make who owns the freehold? Thought we were going to buy it ourselves, once everyone's quids in?'

'Well, that's just it. We want to make sure Mr or Ms New Freeholder doesn't pull any dirty tricks like jacking up the ground rent or whacking another floor or two on top of the building like everywhere else round here,' Harry said. 'Anyway, four bottles of Marjorie's tannic Aussie plonk later, and by some tiny fucking miracle, we actually agreed to chip in for a solicitor to look at the whole thing. Happy with that?'

Nick felt his eyes glazing over from talk of freeholds and lawyers. He took a large sip of Kir. 'Of course. Sounds good to me. Let me know how much dosh you want and I'll transfer it to your account, or to whoever is collecting it. Got to be worth a try, hasn't it?'

He smiled to himself, thinking how he would have manned barricades to stop this sort of nonsense in the past, but for some reason his inner revolutionary spark had fizzled out. Temporarily, no doubt, while he was up to his eyeballs with work and Julie's demands on his time.

'Any more steamy encounters down the road lately?' he asked, trying to change the subject.

'Possibly,' Harry smiled back, and crossed his legs with a flourish. 'One has been enjoying a late-life renaissance, thanks to daddy's little blue helpers. Wish I'd taken them years ago.'

'Bloody hell. I'm not sure I'd remember what to do if the opportunity came along,' Nick laughed, downing his second glass almost in one go.

'Thanks for the drink. My turn next. Let me know how it goes with the freehold thing. Sounds like nothing to worry about.'

Nick headed for the door, determined to call the consultancy: it was weeks since they'd promised him a project. As he'd already concluded the other night, work would be a perfect way to forget about Julie, Tom and, most of all, Amanda. It would be good to put his mind to something else.

11

FRANK HAD A PLAN AND it felt good to be back in control.

The vomiting and runs had stopped and he was keen to start sorting things out, good and proper, to tie up loose ends. He was certain who had tried to poison him. He could kick himself as it should have been obvious from the start, but he'd been blinded by anger, weakened by illness, overly trusting to see it at first.

'I'll bring her down a peg or two,' he'd concluded after sitting all night in his armchair at Hope Wharf, feeling calmer for the first time in days and now sipping a mug of tea as he stood by the open window to look out over the canal. The sight of those dead ducks and coots bobbing in the water the other day would stay in the mind forever, a cold and soggy reminder of how close it all came. Then again, if he hadn't left Pooter's wallet in the warehouse then none of this would have happened. Bleeding waste of time worrying over spilt milk, as his dad would say.

He was dog-tired, having slept fitfully since discovering that someone probably less than a mile away was out to get him for no good reason. How evil was that? Better watch your back in future, matey, because there's no telling what people are thinking. At least the post office had removed

Pooter's picture from the wall; the cops must have given up on their search, the lazy bastards. Well, they hadn't tried very hard, had they, not like with Ted when all those bobbies were stopping everyone and their mother on the high street. Making a big show over a local man, no doubt.

Ha, it made him smile to see how the Posties were so nice to him now, sending a cooked chicken, tins of fruit salad and enough evaporated milk to sink a barge. He had a plateful last night, his first proper meal in days without running to the lav within minutes.

Yes, things were looking better but there was still work to do, still loose ends to tie up, though it was a pity he couldn't go back to Daddy Burtt's. Not yet, anyway. He missed the hot food and warm fug like the kitchen at home used to be on Sunday lunchtime. The ban from the Christian Mission would soon be forgotten, no doubt about that. It was only because of that posh volunteer from Kensington getting narked that they dared to confront him in the first place. Most of them goody-goody volunteers never lasted long anyway, just a few weeks until they buggered off to enjoy feeling smug in their big houses. Just like those pompous councillors who visited once in a blue moon, smiled and pissed off in a hurry, leaving their food untouched and checking their hands for lice.

Damn, there was something he needed to do.

He knelt down next to the main door to work one of the bricks free so that his hand could reach into the cavity and pull out Pooter's wallet. After tapping back the brick with his foot until it was flush with the wall he went to the side room, where he poured petrol into an empty pot under the vat. After making doubly sure Pooter's picture was inside, he dropped the wallet into the pot and set it alight with a match, the leather taking a few minutes to smoulder into a charred lump, the fumes irritating his throat. Spluttering, he used a rag to pick up the pot and carry it to the open window, where he tipped the burnt remains into the canal. A pair of swans looked up, hoping for crusts, but when none came they glided elegantly away, shaking their orange beaks in disapproval.

Evening was drawing in, the towpath empty, but he could hear a barge in the distance puttering towards him and so he pulled back from the window, leaving the shutters open just enough for the breeze to rid the place of fumes. He was pleased with how tidy everything looked; lining up the polished tools on the workbench had restored a sense of order. The Posties could come round any time to check up on things, though he was usually out when they did.

After the barge motored past, he closed the shutters and opened a tall cupboard at the back of the side room, where his fawn mac hung on a nail. It was still dirty from wheeling the night-watchman to the dust destructor, but he'd give the coat and his spare kilt a good wash once this last chore was done. In fact, he may as well give the whole place another scrub from top to bottom, just in case he'd missed anything.

Perhaps the director was right, and it was time to take a few days off.

He checked his boots to make sure they were securely tied, the laces trimmed to the right length to avoid tripping him up. Yes, he'd thought of everything this time; wouldn't be leaving anything to chance again. The thick rubber soles gripped well on the flagstones, giving him a heightened sense of security as he put on the mac, promising to treat himself to a new coat once everything was sorted out by tomorrow. Chilly shins were getting on his nerves, though with the weather not quite as parky of late, he left the balaclava in the cupboard. No vapour rub or fedora tonight either, but definitely the tan gloves. He buttoned his mac, turned up its collar and checked that all the lights were switched off before opening the door and walking purposefully into the night, feeling at peace as he hummed his favourite Vera Lynn song.

12

'BUT WHY GET NICK TO follow me? What on earth do you hope to find out that you can't ask to my face?' Tom said in the most neutral tone of voice he could muster, to show he was being his utmost reasonable self, that he was a mature adult and expected her to behave that way in return. That was his plan, anyway.

They were in the kitchen; it was late but still humid despite the open windows which let in birdsong and distant sirens but failed to create a draft. They'd just opened a second bottle of rosé in the unspoken hope it would ease the tension between them, but knowing deep down it would at best temporarily anaesthetize them to the irreparable damage being wrought. Given they both had long passed the point of no return in the accusatory stakes, more of Provence's finest would simply force them to think longer and harder about their responses, in case something slipped out that would signal a loss of control or could be used later.

Then again, perhaps he should just go with his gut feeling and scream his head off.

Julie didn't look at him directly but glanced downwards at the floor as she kept twirling her phone on the crumb-strewn kitchen top, the pink oblong colliding with an empty microwave-meal container, sending it flying into the sink.

'Aren't you going to say something? You think I'm hiding things from you?' he continued, this time sensing she was cornered, and with no ammunition to launch a counterattack.

'I just feel you've lost interest in us as a couple. You've been distant. I rarely see you, what with work and all that postie stuff,' she said, flicking back her fringe and making eye contact to gauge his reaction.

He breathed out and half smiled as he leaned back in the dining chair and crossed his arms, glad he'd already rehearsed his lines after sensing that a showdown of sorts couldn't be far off. It would have been good to defer this a bit longer and let her make the first move, but he'd given up waiting. The postie sales were going well, with a second building gone in as many weeks and offers already coming in for a third, thanks to the surprisingly proactive director who was putting out discreet feelers to all the right people in the market. That man was zooming up in his estimation, someone worth keeping in touch with after the grand sell-off was done and dusted. Perhaps the occasional dinner, but not that fucking sauna again.

As for Julie, closure was overdue and it was time to move on in his personal life, draw a line, and any other cliché the agony aunts could offer. First of all he wanted regular sex again, to straighten out his increasingly twisted thinking and to get a few nights of undisturbed sleep. Time to unleash the beast, as one of his recently divorced mates once said, though to have sex with someone whose heart is in it would be even better. Perhaps he might fall in love again. Stranger things had happened. There was, of course, also the question of what to do with the oodles of moolah he was going to get from his share of the Postie sales, but that was something to decide at leisure in a new, post-Julie era which he now wanted to start in haste.

'Look, I'm happy to give things another go, to start afresh, no questions asked,' she said, stopping mid-sentence when her phone vibrated with a new text.

'You think I've been shagging on the side, don't you?' he said, turning up the hurt volume a touch. 'Not all men see the world through their dicks.' He instantly regretted the corny phrase, but barely paused. 'As for the Postie stuff, as you call it, what's there to say? As I've told you before, it's just a glorified local history society that's long past its sell-by date.'

He knew she would have to be totally delusional to accuse him of playing away, because all he had to show in the adultery department was Sunita as wank fodder. Shit, he could feel a twitch in his boxers just thinking about her, forcing him to casually cross his legs. No need to go nuclear just yet, though, by revealing he knew about her saddo middle-aged pining for that hotshot young lawyer, who unfortunately had the nous to give her a wide berth. And she'd never really explained the weird bond she had with Nick, who'd made him feel like a spare prick at their wedding. He couldn't believe the bloke had gone on her hen night.

'Are you still angry I didn't want children? Is that it?' she asked.

'That was your choice, and to be fair you made that clear long before we got married,' he replied quietly and without any hesitation, prompting her to start fidgeting with the phone again to avoid looking at him.

Interesting she was trying that one on, he thought, having often wondered what kids with Sunita would look like. Truly stunning, no doubt. And super-bright. Julie had left it too late anyway if she was changing her mind, but his sperm would still be in fine fettle for years, ready to produce the next generation of Posties, or rather post Posties. He glanced down casually at his crotch to check that his hardening cock was hidden properly under the folds of his plum coloured khaki shorts. The closer he was to splitting up with Julie, the hornier he was becoming. It was like being eighteen again, with anything possible. In his semi-pissed mind, at least.

'So, what are we going to do, then?' she asked, while reading the new text message that was not from Richard, just Nick arranging dinner. 'Jeez. No escape! Someone from the office reminding me of an early meeting with one of our top clients in the morning,' she said, then casually locked the phone and tossed it into her open handbag.

'How about we have some space for a while? If we still think it's not working then we can sell this place, or one of us can buy the other out. Sounds fair?' he asked.

Despite the inevitability of it all, the casual-sounding arrangement felt like a hammer knocking her sideways, causing her breathing to become erratic for a few seconds: years of life as a couple had irrevocably shifted from the present to the past in the space of a few seconds.

'I suppose it's a plan,' she said after a moment, unable to think of anything else to say. Had their marriage ever really begun, she wondered. She had been genuinely happy on her wedding day almost nine years ago, walking down the aisle with her eyes definitely wide open and convinced they had all the makings of a lasting relationship. What had she missed?

'Agreed, then. I'll start looking for somewhere temporary to live. And perhaps you can call off Nick. That guy ought to get a life as well as a job,' he said, trying to sound jokey as he headed for the study, taking the near-full bottle with him.

Retrieving her phone to check for new messages, she found none.

13

THE CHERRY LIPSTICK WAS NICE and sexy, Elsie thought, half dancing to a song belting from the radio. If only she could get the hair right then maybe Phil from behind the bar at the Ten Bells might sit up and notice for once. Maybe even ask her out. Some chance! He was more interested in greasing his quiff half the time, and looking for a woman to hang on his arm and every word.

She pouted in the mirror above the mantelpiece. 'Time to get a bloke!' she shouted, before dabbing on more lipstick. Shame she couldn't nick one, like the tin of corned beef that morning. She threw back her head to laugh, took another long drag from a cigarette and blew a concentrated stream of smoke that bounced off the mirror and swirled around her face, just like in films.

The disgust with herself after that stupid intimate brush with Frank in the warehouse had finally gone. His attentions had at least reminded her that she was still a looker, in her prime. But it was time to get her skates on and find a husband if she was going make babies before her oven got cold, as her mother's sister kept saying. Couldn't argue with that. For God's sake, she was nearly twenty-five and heading fast for the nearest shelf, with two of the team packing it in soon. Doing a runner wasn't easy, with a kid on the way. The next generation of panty-pouchers had to come from somewhere.

'Oh, yes they bleeding well do!' she shouted over the music.

She sensed that Phil was a bit wary of her. People talk, but what was holding him back? She was determined to try out a new hairdo that evening just to show him and anyone else who cared that she was no different from the other girls: looking for a lad with sideburns like Phil, all nicely clipped down to his jawline. After flicking through magazines, it had came to a toss-up between rolled bangs, or big curls like Lauren Bacall had.

Having decided on the big curls, she'd already washed her hair in the kitchen sink, sneezing as droplets of soapy water trickled up her nose while still trying to sing along to the radio. Her glossy black hair was now in curlers and dry enough for the next step. The hairspray she'd bought for this had better work as it wasn't cheap, but she was worth it. Sneaking an aerosol into her knickers or handbag had been too tricky in the chemist. The polka-dot hairband or fake flower behind the ear? Plenty of time to decide on that one.

Nothing was going to stop her having a good time to-night.

She'd smiled while hearing about Frank's latest tantrum since they let him back into Daddy Burtt's, though she was relieved that he still had no clue who had baked the Chelsea buns. No regrets: they helped banish her fear of him. That man could scream blue murder but nobody would be squealing on her, she was sure of that.

Jigging to the song she began removing hair clips, leaving the curlers to drop to the floor one by one, and roll around her stockinged feet. She gave a tube of dried hair a quick squeeze to see if it held up. Perfect. Well, if that didn't get Phil's pulse racing then nothing would.

As she turned down the radio she glanced round the living room she still found hard to call home since her mother had passed away. For some reason the china cabinet by the far wall brought Ted rushing into her thoughts. Funny how all that business about his disappearance had died down, but her intuition screamed that something was still going on beneath the surface. Wonder how Lizzie was coping by now? Maybe she could talk her into joining the team – could she think on her feet in a busy shop? Best leave her alone. She had a job and she'd be fine now the cops had backed off, but what the hell had Frank done with Ted? It was as if the man had vanished into thin air. Probably chucked him in the canal. About the limit of Frank's imagination.

Finally, all the curlers were out and she was shivering in her pink petticoat, the coal fire no longer stoked enough to keep away the deep chill outside that had lasted for weeks. No way was she putting on her new dress until she was done with hair spraying. Didn't want unsightly stains spoiling the look. She put on an old cardigan to warm herself up, its collar still smelling of the perfume she'd brought back from Paris – another reminder to get the team's tickets for the next trip in a month's time. Plenty of orders were coming in on the grapevine. Must choose a different city this time, just to be on the safe side.

Nearly there. One more squirt on the left-hand side, and then time to get dressed. The hair looked good, stiff enough to last an evening, and it set off her lipstick nicely. Perhaps she could stash a few rings inside those curls? Silly girl!

She heard a screech from her yard gate opening and banging shut.

Who the hell was that?

She peered through the kitchen window just in time to see an outline of someone approaching the back door. With the yard light switched off, it was impossible to see who it was. Had to be one of the girls checking what I'm wearing tonight, the nosy minx. And without as much as a knock, the door handle was turning. 'Manners,' she smiled, and checked herself in the mirror. Picking up a tissue, she pouted and began sharpening the outline of her lipstick. Where the hell had she put the mascara?

14

It REMINDED NICK OF HIS father's funeral, the bit at the graveside where the vicar spoke about man bringing nothing into this world and taking nothing out.

It was late afternoon and he was sitting at the dining table, poring over the map of Shoreditch he'd bought from the local history shop. The Posties came from nothing and made up for it big time, he thought, using his index finger to trace the boundary of an empty box Victorian cartographers had inserted to mark a rubble-strewn patch of land after London's most notorious slum was pulled down at the behest of well-meaning philanthropists. Now it was Britain's first council estate, a revolutionary milestone of sorts in a municipal battle against squalor, and one that stood the test of time until Thatcher's right-to-buy counter-revolution eviscerated the estate's social foundation. How history had turned full circle for locals, who once again have little choice but to leave. Wasn't it Ahmed from the Indian takeaway who said the other evening that his son had finally found a flat he could afford – in zone 5? It had almost made Nick hang his head in shame as he walked back to his Grade II listed loft.

But there was no risk of Tom or any other Postie return-

ing to the financial nothing their forefathers came from.
The rents and ground rents from God knows how many
properties must have felt like riches from heaven in the early
years. Like the Jews and the Huguenots before them, it no
doubt meant they could leave behind the East End grime
and head for leafy suburbs. Impressive really, how a bunch
of paupers could build up a money-spinning property
empire. Where did the finance come from? And now, for
some reason, they wanted to cash in. To think he'd been
clueless for so long about what was going on under his nose,
on his own – or should that technically be the Postie's? –
doorstep.

It all made him an ignorant dickhead in anyone's book.

The mobile had been flashing for days as he avoided
checking messages. It was the same number for three
unanswered calls and voicemails: the reporter, who wanted
more stuff for his story. 'Just need to run a few things by
you. You can trust me with your sources. Won't even name
you in the article. Promise,' he said in his first message. No
way, of course, and Nick didn't bother listening to the other
two messages.

After what he'd just learned, the last thing he needed
was a scoop on the Posties.

The light bulb moment came after he'd bumped into
Harry in the lobby four days ago while binning the takeaway menus and valuation offers from estate agents clogging
up his mailbox. They had fancied a quick coffee at the
remaining independent cafe on Curtain Road. Not fre-
quenting a chain was one of the few acts of social rebellion
Nick could muster these days, and even that was getting
harder in the face of rampant gentrification.

'Guess who I saw in the building yesterday?' Harry said, stuffing a Portuguese custard tart in his mouth after they'd sat down. 'It was that tall ginger bloke you asked me to follow in the sauna. Almost didn't recognize him with his clothes on. Spooky, eh? There he was, showing this rather tasty stud round the building. You know the type: young and pushy in a pin-stripe, silk tie, immaculate brogues and pocket square. Dreamy. Well, until they open their mouth, that is.'

The mention of Gingernuts had a far bigger kick to Nick's brain than the double Colombian macchiato he was sipping. The jump in his blood pressure was such that all he could do was nod at Harry to continue.

'Well, it turns out that the young bloke was from our soon-to-be new freeholder. I told him I was a long-standing resident and hoped they wouldn't be pulling a fast one, because there are at least two solicitors living in the building and one of them was me. He was so annoyingly on-bloody-message, all tripe about Triangle Prime Lofts wanting to reach out and consult with stakeholders, to have a constructive dialogue with interested parties. Anyway, he did let slip they were thinking of adding another floor to the building, just a couple of penthouse flats on top of your place. I think your balcony could end up in permanent shade, but you'll need to check that if they ever put in a planning application. But he did say all communal areas would be refurbished without a hit to the service charge. I think they call that a bribe in old money.'

At this point, Harry glanced at the cafe counter as if he wanted another cake, but decided to continue with what he was saying. 'I think Jake was right in the residents' meeting.

We need to have another go at buying the freehold, and this time really get some merde hitting the fan to stir up interest. We have to show everyone in the building what it means if we don't have full control of our destiny, as it were. Fancy another coffee?'

All Nick could do by that point was shake his head, as the rest of his body was frozen. So game, set and match to Tom. From the day he'd moved in, his ground rent had been going straight into the Posties' benevolent fund. While trailing the fuckwit through the streets of Shoreditch to find the location of Postie buildings, he'd been living in one all along. No wonder the knobhead always smiled whenever they'd met.

'Drink. Now,' he told Harry. He needed something more cathartic than coffee as he realized that raising the merest hint of doubt in the press over the legality of Postie properties would hurt himself where he'd feel it the most: in the pocket.

Over the road at the Hops Arms, it had taken him less than a couple of minutes to down his first drink after they'd found a table, squeezed between two sets of siliconeastas, who were nursing halves of micro-brewed beers in their lunch break.

'Your round next, Harry. A large pinot noir this time, if you don't mind. I think they do a decent Kiwi one here.'

Staring out of the pub window, he wondered how many other clueless buggers like himself were cash machines for the Posties. Doubt if any of his ground rent would end up in Julie's bank account, given where her marriage was headed. No, Tom would be way too smart for that to happen.

Where the hell was that drink? He could see Harry jostling with hipsters for the barman's attention. There should be a fast-track queue for locals, he thought, finally smiling.

'While I remember, that ginger bloke was asking if we'll campaign to stop the energy centre next to us. He said he and another local developer were thinking of building luxury flats there, with a private basement pool we could use free of charge.' Harry had returned from the bar with a full bottle of pinot noir and two fresh glasses.

'You looked in need, my son. Auntie Harry is balm to your troubles. Anyway, I told Mr Triangle that we actually quite like the idea of an energy centre because we wouldn't have loads of late-night parties to keep us awake. That last bit didn't go down too well.'

Nick remembered laughing out loud at that point, as the wine and Harry had begun lifting his spirits. Impromptu binges were certainly the most best, he thought, leaning on his dining table to stare down again at the map of Shoreditch after it had taken him twenty-four hours to get over his monumental hangover. But at least it had answered the nagging 'what next?' question as far as he and the Posties were concerned: diddly-squat, if he wanted to keep a roof over his head. He traced again the outline of the empty square on the map with his finger, amazed at how much history was crammed into that urban acre. As he stared down at the map, to his intense irritation his mind began picturing Tom's face just where the Metropolitan Board of Works built the bandstand from Old Nichol rubble in an act of Victorian social cleansing, setting in motion a Postie crusade that was being cashed in a century later.

And there was absolutely nothing he would do about it.

15

LIZZIE DATCHETT WAS OUT THE back, in the wash house.

It had been a late start, but never mind, it wouldn't be the first time she was doing the laundry so late in the afternoon. Why care any more about what people think, after what she'd been through? She'd soon be gone from here.

It was unsettling picking through their belongings and deciding what to take to the Smethwicks. Ted's clobber was the most painful to handle. Not willing to believe she wouldn't be seeing him again, she stuffed his Sunday best and some work clothes in a bag to store in north London, for a few months at least. And she wouldn't wash his dirty work shirt, underpants or vest: she'd sniffed them again that morning to remind herself of him. The boots he'd left in the hallway were filthy, all speckled with globs of dried glue that were covered in a film of fine sawdust. She'd keep those for now, too.

The kindling in the small furnace was igniting the larger pieces of wood to heat up the chipped enamel tub of water cradled in an iron frame over the flames. She was going to boil her whites, a dolly ready to poke and prod away the grime. It would be the last time she'd wash her clothes in this way for a while, perhaps for good, as the Smethwicks sent theirs to the laundry, even though they had a spanking-new washing machine in the utility room. The thought of her and Denise's knickers and slips being washed together had made her blush at first. Their relationship was moving to a deeper level of intimacy, and faster than she'd ever imagined in her dreams.

But why had Ted walked out on her? Did he suspect the truth about her all along? And what could sour her new life now that she was in the clear with the police? She couldn't afford to stay here any longer and wait for Ted to return.

She was finally getting her breath back, though still marooned between two lives, no longer knowing where she belonged, which was was real. What on earth had happened to him? It was so completely out of character. What the hell was she meant to tell everyone? Some neighbours and friends were still popping round with packets of tea or cigarettes for a chat, as if she were a widow, lost in bereavement, in need of consoling. In some ways she was. There was nothing new she could tell them, but the chats were opportunities to mention again that no insurance money was coming her way, just in case they thought she was somehow involved in all this. To think she would be starting life afresh in a part of town even her mother would approve of. Not that her parents would ever see the real picture, or even want to, given there was no prospect of grandchildren.

After another fag and a cup of tea, she grabbed the dolly to swirl the clothes in the simmering water, which was murky with dirt. Better get this lot rinsed straightaway or I'll never finish today, she thought, bending down to pick up a pair of wooden tongs for plucking out the steaming clothes, and dunking them in the galvanized drum of cold water. The heat from the fire and vigorous jousting with the dolly was bringing her out in a sweat, the physical effort soothing after the strangest fortnight of her life.

While prodding the clothes she compiled a list in her head of what needed doing before she locked the front door for the last time and handed the keys to the rent collector. It was Denise who had suggested she pack a box of Ted's books to store in the basement with his clothes. Funny how he drove her up the wall by going on about bleeding Chippendale, but the Cabinet-Maker's Director book, bashed up by the burglar, would be first into the box, along with sketches for the cabinet he had just made. Better hang on to them in case the police come calling again, her inner voice whispered.

There she was again, twisting her wedding ring round her finger, though not taking it off completely like she briefly did last night. There was no question of putting it in a drawer; wearing it would stop most blokes pushing their luck.

Plunging her hands into the drum of freezing water focused her thoughts back on the chores she needed to finish. She gave her underwear, petticoats and slips a few more twists and a tight squeeze before throwing them into the wicker basket, ready for the wringer. Should she have a bite first? In that case, better put a shilling in the meter to keep the lights and cooker on as darkness began to fall outside.

'Want help with the mangle, Lizzie?'

The voice made her turn round so fast that she had to lean on the dolly to steady herself.

It was that Frank standing in the doorway. The sight of his grubby kilt and swollen groin under a mac streaked with dirt made her stare, open mouthed; there was something vulnerable, even childlike about the band of white, hairless flesh between the tops of his filthy black boots and coat hem. Behind him in the yard she could see the front wheels of a cart that was piled high with straw.

What the hell was he doing?

'Well, I've finally found the nasty bitch who bakes poisoned buns. Say something, Lizzie. Can't believe you're surprised to see me.' He spoke in a slow, hoarse voice that was barely above a whisper.

Without waiting for a reply, he stepped into the wash house and slammed the door behind him.

'Get out of here or I'll call the police!' she screamed.

He shrugged, smiled and stepped towards her, grabbing the dolly before she could lift it high enough to hit him, as her other hand reached for the tongs.

16

'SO STILL NADA ON WHAT Tom's been up to then?' Julie asked with a rising note of desperation in her voice. 'What about that bloke he was talking to in the flower market? They must have been up to something, otherwise he wouldn't have looked so bloody pleased with himself when he got back. He was glued to his laptop for the rest of the day. I told him to roast his own fucking chicken.'

It was late evening, and their conversation was having to compete with 1980s disco music that had just been turned up a notch as the bar became more crowded. They were standing near the centre of the room, right on the edge of what had once been the dance floor but was now a standing area for those too late to bag a stool or one of the brown-leather sofas.

'As I've already said, it wasn't exactly Poirot's finest hour. Tom and whoever that bloke was managed to disappear down a back street before I could see where they'd gone. There were just too many people from the Sunday markets to stay close enough without him spotting me. Again.'

She ignored the barb and took out her phone to check for messages, a frown suggesting there were none she wanted.

'Sorry, Nick. I don't mean to be so pushy,' she said.

'Shhh. It's Amanda in here, remember?' he hissed into her ear, making her jump.

'Of course. I mean Amanda,' she continued, squeezing his arm. 'Sorry. Really sorry. Look, I'm not blaming you for what's happening between me and Tom. You've done everything you can to help, and I won't forget that. It's just that I'm feeling a bit mixed-up at the moment. Anyway, that's enough of my crap. You look great tonight, and a lot happier than when we were here last time. I'm glad you're finally sorted now. I'm really happy for you. But what made you change your mind about Amanda? I thought you'd decided you didn't want to do this again. Did those books I gave you help?'

He turned to look at himself in the large mirror on the wall. She was right, Amanda did look good, and felt it too. The dark blue dress he wore hung more loosely and elegantly than that uncomfortable, clingy frock he'd chosen the last time. This one was also much better at disguising his paunch. Also saved tucking his prick out of the way as well.

'Thanks. I think I'm getting my head round things, finally. A large part of that is down to your support. I couldn't have dealt with all this on my own.' He put an arm round her shoulders and gave her a long, firm hug. Yes, he felt a lot more confident about being Amanda, no longer looking over his shoulder to check if someone in the bar recognized him. Looked like they should have come earlier to get seats, but he liked taking hours to get dressed, with Julie turning up to offer fun tips on which lipstick to use and wig to wear. The slow slow morph into Amanda in front of the wardrobe mirror had been a long personal journey going back several years. It still took an hour or two to make sure her posture was natural, that the timbre of her voice was right.

The heavies had intruded into his private, Amanda space when they left that stupid bollard on his bed. But in some way it had shredded his procrastination, too.

He felt sad at how drained and on edge Julie looked these days, even in the club's dimmed lights. There she went again, gripping that phone of hers, as if hoping for a text or call to change her life, to tell her what to do. Without her strength in the past few months, there was no way he'd be right here, wearing a dress again in this club. She wasn't the only reason why he'd changed his mind about Amanda and ended years of ambivalence, but he could never admit to her that Tom had also prodded him to a place where he was finally comfortable in Amanda's skin. The arrogant shit's utter self-belief in what he did and sod everyone else had woken up Nick. There's a time in everyone's life when they needed to be a bit like Tom. Turning his back on Amanda would have screwed him up for the rest of his life, and it was frightening to think how close that came to happening. He and Amanda were not separate people who could cleanly part ways after some cold calculation: they were two facets of the same person.

'Christ, look at what he's, I mean she's, wearing over there. A light blue dress with red hair? For fuck's sake,' Julie giggled to cut across his thoughts.

'You see what having a personal stylist saves me from,' he joked, raising his glass in toast.

'Cheers, Amanda. Like I said earlier, I think you're so

brave.'

He put his arm around her again and kissed her on the side of her head as she continued talking. 'I know Tom's only supposed to be moving out temporarily, or a breather as we're calling it, but I'm not putting any money on him coming back. Do you know I actually went to a cat cafe near you the other day just to get some unconditional love? But they wouldn't take a credit card!'

Not sure whether she was joking or briefly wallowing in self-pity, he took a gulp of wine, leaving a smear of lipstick on the rim of his glass. God, how that made him feel like a real woman.

'It's sad how things are turning out between you and Tom, but you must have been half-expecting it given what you've been telling me. I hope it doesn't get messy and drawn-out,' he said, surprised to see no sheen over her eyes, let alone a tear. Bet she's over him already, and glad to be moving on. 'Look, I wouldn't worry about what Tom's up to. Let's face it, you won't starve whatever happens, and there are plenty of guys out there who want to meet some-one like you.'

She shrugged. 'Do you think you could sit down with my lawyer to say what you've dug up on him, as I'm going to have to start negotiating a settlement soonish?'

Her switch to a businesslike tone shocked him and he briefly turned away to survey the room and get his breath back. No way would he do anything of the kind, he thought, instantly picturing Tom turning up on his doorstep with the two heavies in tow.

'I think it's best you keep me out of this. As in totally out of it!' he spluttered. More quietly and composed, he continued, 'I'm not going to do anything remotely like that. I'm not the fucking UN. This is totally between you and Tom. End of story. I'm sure you can understand where I'm coming from. I've got enough personal shit to deal with as it is.'

'OK, OK. Bad idea. I won't mention it again,' she said, stumbling over her words and squeezing his arm for forgiveness. 'Look, I need a pee and then I'm going outside for a quick ciggie, if that's all right with you. You'll be OK on your own for a bit, won't you?'

He nodded and stroked her arm.

After she'd gone, he thought about the email he'd read that morning. It was from the consultancy, asking if he could go to New York pronto for a few months to replace someone who was leaving at short notice before a project had finished? Usual strategising, resource efficiencies stuff, plus fab downtown pad, rent-free, of course. 'I know you luuurv Niew Yoik', the chatty Senior People and Talent Facilitator had signed off.

He usually replied to most offers beyond London's inner travel zone with a flat 'no thanks', but this one could be the perfect escape route, now that things were getting a little too intense with Julie, Tom and everything else round here. And let's face it, life over the pond would fly by and he didn't want to be around Shoreditch if that cocky reporter actually wrote something on the Posties. Yep, he could be away long enough to have a fling, even find a girlfriend. Hopefully someone a bit more accepting of Amanda this time. And when did a project ever finish on time? Clients always demanded extra ammo to trim more fat off the payroll while the consultants were at it, which meant more hours to expense. It would easily be long enough to reboot with old Yankee mates who had slipped off the Christmas circular email list, but not long enough to lose touch with everyone over here. Then again, where were his London friends these days? Complete bloody radio silence after being sucked into a procreating wormhole at warp speed, waiting to be spat out when the kids went to college, or divorce came knocking, or both.

Yep, they'd come up for air in a year or two, gagging for a few bevvies away from suburbia. In the meantime, a stretch of water between himself and siliconeasta land would be no bad thing. The speed of change round here was unsettling and about to smash his daily routine. Mavis had told him they were selling up, that Jimmy's Cafe would become a restaurant. Or was it an eatery? How much preaching about some obscure vegetable being underrated could someone take? No, Jimmy's would be relegated to just another hipster soup kitchen. He did laugh, though, when Mavis mentioned that what she called the homosexual fun and games parlour was going to be bulldozed to make way for another boutique hotel. Jeez, the sight of Gingernuts padding down a dark corridor with Tom in tow, clutching a big brown envelope, had been surreal. Should he share that with Julie one day?

'That was quick. Guess what, I've been offered an assignment in the Big Apple. Do you think I should go?' he asked as she walked up to him, holding two glasses of wine. Good, she remembered to buy white and not red this time. Didn't want teeth the same colour as lipstick on a night out. 'I bet the East Village has changed since I lived there.'

'I'm going to miss you, but I'll definitely visit, though

Tom – if he's still around – will suspect again that we are having it off. I've always told him you're a gay man in a straight body, but he can't get that into his head. It matters bugger all what he thinks now, I suppose.'

'And as I've always said, you're an alpha male in a woman's body,' he replied, and was rewarded with the first genuine smile in months.

They lapsed into an easy silence as he looked at the people around them, wondering what they did in their lives, outside the confines of this club. Probably nothing very different to himself, he was coming to realize. Leaving Julie to fiddle with her phone, he nipped to the ladies to send an email to the consultancy, telling them he'd take the job, subject to the usual terms and conditions, of course. He couldn't wait to buy a dress in Bergdorf Goodman. Amanda deserved a treat after what she'd been through.

17

'FOR THE LAST TIME, LIZZIE, who helped you bake the Chelsea buns?'

Frank articulated each word slowly, standing close enough for her to feel his warm, fetid breath on the side of her face.

'Want me to chisel it out of you?'

It was late evening in Hope Wharf, and his patience was wearing thin. Lizzie was on her back, pinned by rope to the workbench, her head resting awkwardly on a vice at one end while her stockinged feet dangled over the other. He was pleased that each time he spoke into her ear, she tried squirming away from his bristled chin which scraped against the side of her face, making the angular block of grey metal dig deeper into her nape. His frustration was rising and he began pacing round the bench, pausing every now and then to press his crotch into her feet or thrust his face into hers, his acrid breath jolting her like smelling salts. Getting nowhere, he slapped a wooden mallet into the palm of his hand as he stared down at her. Four chisels had already been hammered into the bench near her legs, shoulder and hip as if she were in a knife-throwing act at the circus.

He chuckled again at how easy it had been to overpower her in the washhouse, though only after narrowly missing being hit on the head by the tongs she'd somehow managed to grab. He should have finished her off there and then. Shoving her head into the tub of water would have done the trick, but curiosity had got the better of him. How could he pass up on the chance to settle things good and proper, to find out who helped her try to poison him? She couldn't have done it on her own, as he'd never seen her at Daddy Burtt's.

No, there had been an accomplice among the volunteers. Those stuck-up goody-goody scum had it in for him from the start. Elsie had to be a part of this, but that was no more than a hunch.

In the meantime, he would wear Lizzie down. The woman would fess up, and he had loads of time to kill anyway. There was no chance of getting rid of her that evening, he thought, glancing at the cart by the door, already stacked high with straw and rubbish. The foreman at the dust destructor had warned him that engineers from the Electricity Board would be making routine checks overnight, so best to stay away. Tomorrow was Saturday, a much better time in any case as there would only be a skeleton staff on duty. An extra day would also allow a decent smog to build up, if the weather forecast was anything to go by. No chance of another pea-souper, but it should be thick enough to keep nosy parkers off the streets, though for the sake of his nerves, he might check that PC Crisp was off duty before wheeling the contraption onto the street.

'Come on Lizzie, you can scream all you want, my little lovely. It's only ducks that'll hear you. Well, the ones you didn't poison with your Chelsea bleeding buns, that is.' This time she didn't try to face away but looked puzzled, her body still apart from her feet, which twitched violently every now and again. He paced round the workbench again, noticing how each time he came into sight, her eyes rested on the bulge under his kilt.

'Want a butchers, my lovely? Bet Ted didn't have ones like these. You wouldn't be the first tart round here to get her hands on them, I can tell you. One more time then: who's been helping little Lizzie at Daddy Burtt's?' He slammed the mallet down on the bench just inches from her right knee, making her legs jerk against the rope.

He noticed how the mention of Ted in the past tense deepened the fear in her eyes, and was finally making her say something, much to his relief, as time was ticking by.

'I don't know what you're talking about. Let me go. I won't say anything about this. Please,' she said faintly, turning her head to one side to stop welling tears from blocking her eyes. The droplets coursed down her cheek and soaked into the chipped surface of the bench.

'What, let you go? No chance of that, my little lovely,' he said. Couldn't afford any loose lips, let alone new loose ends. He grimaced. Everything would be done and dusted by tomorrow night. Nothing, absolutely nothing, would be left to chance this time.

'Let's start again, Lizzie. You're not trying very hard, are you? Who's been helping you? Was it Elsie? Has she been telling you what to do?' This time he was standing out of sight behind her head.

No response, apart from more twitches of the feet.

With a loud sigh, he picked up the mallet and began

circling her again, slamming it down on the workbench each time he finished a lap or wanted to emphasise a word as he repeated the same question, his voice getting louder each time.

'Shhhhheee... told me... ttttto... do... nothing,' she stuttered.

'That's not what I want to hear, Lizzie. That's not what I want to hear.'

Still getting nowhere, he decided it was time for a break, to rest his aching feet and back. Perhaps there was a better way of doing this, like cops in the cinema: maybe try a softer approach to break her down after she'd stewed a bit. He went to the side room, sat in the armchair and leant over to wind up the gramophone. With his little finger delicately cocked in the air, he lowered the needle onto the third Vera Lynn song and sat back, chuckling to himself at the thought that nobody would be meeting Lizzie again after tomorrow night. Eyes closed, he hummed to the tune until he felt calmer, while every now and then glancing into the main room. He could sees her legs straining against the rope, her skirt having worked itself to the top of her thigh as she tried wriggling free, but the knots were so tight it would take a knife to cut her free when the time came to bundle her into the cart. Shame he hadn't kept a Chelsea bun: he could have stuffed it down her throat, give her a taste of her own foul medicine.

With his eyes closed, he began thinking how things must change after tomorrow night, after all this mess had been finally cleared up. Those Posties didn't appreciate him. Oh, they made all the right noises about treating him like family, sending him food when he was sick, telling him to take time off and have a proper rest. It was all just words. It was about time they did more. They owed him after all he'd done for them. He knew everything about their sleazy deals, the forgery, the perversions. Not an honest day's work among that lily-livered lot. And as for the director? Who the hell did he think he was? No, it was time they took special care of Frank. Would they pay him off if he promised to keep his mouth shut? Perhaps a free place to live? After all, he'd helped them bag enough properties by now. Surely they could find a couple of spare rooms for him to call his own, and not have to pay rent again. Ah, owning his own home just like the Posties, now that would make people sit up and take notice. It would show his parents that he could make his own way in the world like a normal person, and also end the snide comments about him being no more than a stupid lackey, a misfit, a freak. Yes, he'd wipe the smiles off their faces in no time, once everything was done and dusted, once everything was back in order.

He woke up with a pounding heart as the final song was ending. Cold and stiff, he stretched out his arms and legs a few times to get rid of his pins and needles. He was starving, ready for a slap up meal. It would have to be fish and chips. No problem leaving her on her own for half an hour as she couldn't escape, though he'd stuff his hanky in her gob to keep her quiet.

'Well then, Lizzie Datchett. I reckon it's time for you to spill the beans. I'm not asking much, am I? Just tell me who helped you with the Chelsea buns.' He spoke with his mouth so close to her nose that she almost retched while staring at the ceiling, refusing to make eye contact, her defiant mood infuriating him even more.

He picked up the mallet and began walking round the workbench in a tight circle, stopping when he reached her feet, with the intention of slamming the tool down near her left knee.

'Leave her alone, Frank.'

With the mallet frozen mid-air, he swivelled round to where the voice was coming from. Due to the poor light in that part of the room, it took him a few seconds to make her out, but from the voice he already knew unmistakably that it was Elsie. There she was by the door, a key dangling from a metal ring in one hand, the other hand clenched. He should have taken back the spare key when Ted finished the cabinet.

'Well, well, well,' he sneered. 'The cavalry has arrived, and all dolled-up for a night on the tiles, I see. Who's the lucky man tonight, Elsie?' He lowered the mallet slowly, though did not put it down.

She edged forward to stand under the main light, not taking her eyes off his pale unshaven face. How deranged he looked with that filthy shirt glued by sweat to his chest, she thought. His kilt hadn't been washed for days, either. She could almost smell his madness as they stared at each other across a silent and still Lizzie. He'd forgotten to lift the needle from the record, the gramophone still emitting a dull, rhythmic scratching. Outside, the rattling engine noise of a barge became louder and then cut dead, as if the vessel was berthing. Who could that be? He wasn't expecting anyone.

'Put it down, Frank. You're surrounded. There's no point.' Elsie smiled, crossing her arms and leaning back on her heels like a teacher catching a misbehaving pupil in the act.

Her tone infuriated him but he smiled, thinking what a fine woman she was. If only he could twist his fingers through those big shiny curls and kiss her bright red lips again. The crossed arms made her breasts swell even more. The woman had never looked so good. She was also not afraid of him, and that would be her biggest mistake.

'Found a new feller, then? Suppose I wasn't good enough for you, was I?' he said, swinging the mallet in a high arc over his head and smashing it down within inches of Lizzie's knee, making her whole body convulse.

Elsie put the keys in her pocket and brought out a whistle, which she blew hard. Somehow the sight of red smudges round the metal mouthpiece brought back memories of that afternoon they spent together a week or two ago in the next room. His thoughts were cut short when the door of the warehouse slammed open and three people in heavy navy overalls entered along with wisps of smog, making it hard at first to see their faces.

As they too came into the light and began circling him, he realized they were only women.

'It's your choice, Frank. Do you really want to mess with us?' Elsie asked, flicking her head to one side to stop a limp curl from blocking her right eye.

'You think a bunch of shoplifters scare me?' he laughed loudly, twisting from side to side to keep an eye on all four of them as they edged slowly towards him, each one – apart from Elsie – gripping an iron bar.

He began swinging his mallet in all directions, making them stop in their tracks.

'Come any closer and I'll drown you out there like kittens in a sack,' he jeered at the two in front of him, but before he could turn to check on Elsie, he felt a cloth being clamped on his nose and mouth, and he slumped to the ground.

'Good work, girls,' Elsie said, throwing the rag away. 'Right. Daisy, cut Lizzie free while I tie him up. Maggie, grab the cart.'

18

THE HEAT WAVE WAS COAXING a steady stream of people onto the towpath, with many wearing sunglasses to shield their eyes from the heavy glare that bounced off the canal's smooth surface.

'Isn't this desperately sad? I'll miss this place so much,' the director said, looking down at the scene from the glass-walled penthouse on top of Hope Wharf.

He spotted carp weaving their way through weeds and plastic bags as his eye followed the stretch of water towards the west of the capital. Cyclists were carefully weaving their way past the people, trying to avoid a collision, just like him in his dealings with the Posties. What was there to show for his Herculean diplomatic efforts? Bugger all. He'd failed miserably to bring them round to his way of thinking, to prick their conscience about the need to preserve their heritage. And so here he was, the last director of Shoreditch. Then again, being last-in-line was not unfamiliar, having no kids himself.

'What are you going to do with that faux Chippendale monstrosity?' his short stubby companion asked as he sat like a Buddha on the parquet, using a big felt-tipped pen to write 'archives' on the side of a cardboard box for the removal men to fetch later in the day.

'No idea, to be honest. I'll store it in our lock-up garage for now,' the director said. 'By the way, did Fry confirm he'll be joining us for our farewell toast?'

'He certainly did. We Posties need our fixer-in-chief at historic times like these, don't we, Mr Director?' The companion beamed mischievously, then clambered onto his feet with a loud grunt.

'Quite. You know, the canal down there reminds me of the story I heard about a fixer we had in the 50s. I remember Daddy complaining that the chap became a little too devoted to his job and they tried curbing his enthusiasm permanently, as it were. It all went horribly wrong, of course. Daddy said it cost them a bomb to keep a lid on it – and a few weeks later he disappeared anyway. Well, apart from his kilt, of all things, which they found wrapped round the propeller of a barge moored just down there, near the pop-on cafe. I never did get to the bottom of it all.' The director's voice trailed off.

'One for the historians among us, Mr Director,' said his companion. 'Maybe we could sponsor a student to write a PhD on us? And yes, it is desperately sad because I'll have no reason to call you by your title for much longer! Director Emeritus doesn't quite have the same right ring to it. Back to work, then. All the Postie files are on this memory stick. I'll leave it to you to find a safe home for it. This is one piece of kit we don't want hacked.'

The director went to the other side of the room to check on the street below and was just in time to see Fry getting out of an open-top sports car. How wise a previous director had been to make Fry's aunt a Postie after unstinting service that Daddy had always refused to divulge. Shame she never made it to old age to enjoy her new found riches, though they say she had a good time while she was with us. And thank God her membership was passed on to Fry. He's certainly earned it of late, the director reflected, with a few nods. Yes, that man clearly had that same resourceful Pooter gene as she did. Though it has to be said he did have a tendency to be more earnest about the Postie cause than some of those born into it! The director smiled at the spring in Fry's gait: no doubt he was moving on in more ways than one after leaving that busybody wife of his. There's a lucky lady or two out there, waiting with open arms.

'Fry's here. I'll buzz him in. Can you get the bubbly from the fridge?' the director said to his friend. 'I hope it's a "reserve". After all, we can't toast farewell to the Old Nichol with plonk!'